THE

SADDLE CLUB

COLLECTION

B O N N I E   B R Y A N T

BANTAM BOOKS
TORONTO · NEW YORK · LONDON · SYDNEY · AUCKLAND

THE
SADDLE CLUB
COLLECTION

THE SADDLE CLUB COLLECTION
A BANTAM BOOK   0 553 40904 2

First publication in Great Britain

"The Saddle Club" is a trademark of Bonnie Bryant Hiller.
The Saddle Club design/logo, which consists of an inverted
U-shaped design, a riding crop, and a riding hat is a
trademark of Bantam Books.

This collection first published 1994

including

HOOF BEAT
Bantam edition published 1990
Copyright © 1990 by Bonnie Bryant Hiller

RIDING CAMP
Bantam edition published 1991
Copyright © 1990 by Bonnie Bryant Hiller

HORSE WISE
Bantam edition published 1991
Copyright © 1990 by Bonnie Bryant Hiller

Bantam Books are published by Transworld Publishers Ltd,
61–63 Uxbridge Road, Ealing, London W5 5SA,
in Australia by Transworld Publishers (Australia) Pty Ltd,
15–25 Helles Avenue, Moorebank, NSW 2170,
and in New Zealand by Transworld Publishers (NZ) Ltd,
3 William Pickering Drive, Albany, Auckland.

Printed and bound in Great Britain by
Cox & Wyman Ltd, Reading, Berkshire

THE SADDLE CLUB

HOOF
BEAT

BONNIE BRYANT

For Nancy Kaplan Mansbach, cofeature editor
and fellow LULLA winner

"Easy, boy," Carole Hanson said, patting the black foal's neck gently. Samson eyed Carole warily, then glanced at his mother, Delilah, who stood nearby.

Carole held a halter in her hand. She showed it to the foal. He looked at it curiously, but there was no fear in his eyes. This was the third day in a row that Carole had brought the halter to the fence by his paddock. She thought he was ready to try it on.

Although Carole was only twelve, she was an experienced rider. With Samson, she hoped to become an experienced trainer as well. Samson had been born at Pine Hollow Stables, just a few months before. Carole and her best friends, Stevie Lake and Lisa Atwood, had been present at the birth. It had been one of the most exciting experiences they'd ever had. It was hard to believe, even now, that the fine strong foal who stood next to Carole had once been the scrawny new-born, struggling to stand up and take his first sip of milk. He'd grown tremendously in the first months and could now run around the paddock he shared with his mother for long periods of time. Still, he was just a baby, Carole thought with a smile. Every time she stepped into the paddock, the little foal ran to hide behind his mother's tail.

Stevie and Lisa stood by the fence outside the paddock. Lisa held Delilah on a lead rope. The girls knew that if the mother stood still, the foal was more likely to stand still as well. Stevie and Lisa held their breaths while Carole put her arm over Samson's neck to place the halter on his head.

The three girls were accustomed to working together. They'd become best friends at Pine Hollow and had formed The Saddle Club. The club had only two rules. The first was that members had to be horse crazy. That was easy for them. The second rule was that they had to be willing to help one another. Since there was always plenty going on, they'd worked together a lot.

Carole was the most experienced rider. She'd been brought up on Marine Corps bases where, as a colonel's daughter, she had taken riding lessons all her life. She was determined to spend the rest of her life with horses, as well.

Stevie, the only girl in a family of four children, had started riding so she would have something to do that was different from anything her brothers did. She worked hard at her riding and she was very good—as long as she wasn't in trouble with Max, the owner of the stable. Stevie had a knack for practical jokes and getting into hot water and frequently seemed to lead her friends right into it with her!

Although Lisa, at thirteen, was the oldest of the trio, she was the newest to horseback riding. She had started only a few months before and had begun riding because her mother thought it was something every proper young lady should know *something* about. Mrs. Atwood hadn't been prepared for the fact that, after her first lessons, Lisa had wanted to learn *everything* about it. When Lisa discovered how much fun riding was, and when the three girls had formed The Saddle Club, Lisa had somehow found the courage to tell her mother she wanted to give up some of the other "proper young lady" activities her mother had insisted upon, like painting, ballet, violin, and needlework. Mrs. Atwood hoped this was a temporary situation, but Lisa knew better. Her mother was no more enthusiastic about Lisa's horseback riding than she was about her daughter's straight-A report cards. Mrs. Atwood didn't think proper young ladies *needed* straight A's.

"Okay, boy," Carole spoke softly, "here we go." She stood by the foal. Although she knew the foal could not understand her words, she wanted to keep him calm with her tone of voice. Samson stood still. She laid the nose strap of the halter across his muzzle.

3

He pulled back quickly. Carole stood her ground. She touched his muzzle with the leather once again. This time, Samson didn't pull back. She removed it. He stood still. She looked over toward the fence, wanting reassurance from her friends.

"You're doing fine," Lisa said. "He's ready. I can see it in his eyes."

Carole patted the foal once again. Then, while talking to him softly and confidently, she slipped the halter around his muzzle and drew the crown strap up behind his ears. She had it buckled before Samson knew what was happening.

The foal shook his head, trying to rid himself of the halter. It didn't budge. That made him shake all the more. He looked to his mother for help. She only glanced at him, then turned her attention to the sugar lump Lisa held for her.

"Good boy," Carole said. "That's it. That's all there is to it. Good boy," she repeated. She tried patting him, but he was shaking his head too vigorously to notice.

Carole thought that was enough for the first day. As quickly as she'd put it on, she removed the halter. Samson shook his head a final time, then discovering the odd feeling had gone, he turned his attention to his mother's udder. He was ready for some lunch.

Lisa released Delilah's lead rope. Carole climbed the fence quickly and the three of them watched the horses together.

"That was really neat," Lisa said. "Everybody should be able to see that kind of thing happen."

"If everybody came here to see it happen, it wouldn't be so special for us," Stevie said. "We wouldn't be able to get our front-row seats, would we?"

"No, I don't want everybody here," Lisa said thoughtfully, rolling up the lead rope as she spoke. "I just wish everybody could understand the experience—share in it, you know? Like, I think it would be great to be able to write about that kind of thing and let people know how it feels to be with horses."

"Well, maybe," Carole said dubiously. "Except that I'd never be able to describe it."

"Some people can," Lisa argued, following Carole into the stable. "There are a lot of great writers who would know just exactly what to say."

"But they weren't here," Stevie reminded her. "So, now, it's just us who know what it was like to watch Samson have a halter on for the first time."

Lisa slung the looped rope over her shoulder and led the way back to the locker area where they would change their clothes. She thought she could still feel her heart beating with the excitement of the scene—the first training of a foal. It *had* been exciting. Why *couldn't* that experience be shared?

"Ooh, pee-yew," Stevie groaned, entering the locker area. "I just hate the smell of paint, don't you?"

Carole wrinkled her nose. "Sure," she agreed, "but it's got to be done." Carole could be very matter-of-fact sometimes.

Stevie peered into the tack room where the paint smell originated. "What a disaster area!" The floor was scattered with saddles, bridles, halters, and spare parts. The walls were freshly white.

"Maybe we should offer to help put the stuff back," Carole suggested.

"You don't have time," Stevie reminded her. "You promised to sell tickets at the shopping center for the library raffle today and tomorrow, remember?"

Carole's jaw dropped. "Oh, no!" she said. "I'd forgotten all about it."

Stevie smiled at her friend. "You always forget everything, unless it has to do with horses, don't you? That's one of the reasons you keep me around—to remind you, right?" she kidded Carole.

Carole sat down on the bench and removed her boots. "I can't believe I forgot about that! The problem is—" She paused and crinkled her nose in concentration.

"I bet we can help," Lisa said brightly. "Whatever it is."

"Maybe you can," Carole conceded. "The problem is that I'm supposed to be there all day tomorrow so I won't be able to work with Samson. Today's lesson should be reinforced right away."

"That's no problem at all," Stevie said quickly. "Lisa and I can do that. All we need to do is to get the halter on for a few seconds, right?" Carole nodded.

Lisa slipped out of her riding clothes and into her

street clothes. Stevie and Carole chatted about the library raffle. The first prize was two weeks at Moose Hill, a sleepaway riding camp. All three of them had daydreamed about going, but it seemed unlikely that their parents would go for it. They'd already been on two trips this summer—to a dude ranch and to New York City! Stevie said she wanted to buy all the raffle tickets, then realized that she didn't have any money.

Normally, Lisa would have joined in the conversation, but just then, Lisa's mind was on something else. She couldn't stop thinking about Samson's first training lesson and how much she thought other people would enjoy learning about it. She smiled, remembering.

"Say, dreamface," Stevie said, noticing Lisa's faraway look. "What's on your mind? You planning to go to Moose Hill by yourself?"

"Oh, no. I was just thinking about Samson," Lisa said. "It was just so much fun to be a part of his first lesson. Everyone should be as lucky as we are! It's news that people should get to hear about."

"News, news," Stevie echoed, then her face lit up. "That reminds me. I've got some news! I can't believe I forgot!"

"Well?" Carole prodded, pulling on a pair of gold cotton shorts.

"What is it?" Lisa asked. Stevie sounded excited and Lisa had learned long ago that when Stevie was excited about something, it was usually something neat, even when it meant trouble.

7

"I'm going to have a sister!" Stevie announced.

"Your mother's—?" Lisa began, stunned. It wasn't so long ago that she'd thought her own mother was going to give her a baby sister or brother. She hadn't been excited at that prospect at all!

"Oh, no!" Stevie said, giggling. She pulled her T-shirt over her head and started to tuck it into her denim cutoffs, then changed her mind. She left the shirt untucked. "Not a baby. What I mean is that this girl, Trudy something, is going to stay with us for a couple of weeks. She'll be like my sister because she's just about our age, and finally I'll have an ally against all those brothers of mine!"

"Hey, now *that's* news," Lisa said enthusiastically. "Is she some kind of foreign exchange student or something?"

Stevie shoved her boots to the back of her cubby and crammed her riding clothes into a zipper bag. "If you call Washington a foreign place, then yes," Stevie said. "See, her mother works with my mother in D.C., and her parents won this trip to Hawaii, but it's only for two. Her mother was going to give it up because they couldn't take Trudy, but Mom invited Trudy to visit us. Her mother said she's never been to the country before. Can you imagine?"

"Sure I can imagine," Lisa said. "After all, except for the American Horse Show in New York City, it's not as if we've spent much time in the city, is it? I think it would be weird living in a city, and I bet Trudy will find it weird living with you."

"I just hope she isn't too weird," Stevie said. "After all, it's going to be my only chance to have a sister."

"I didn't mean that it would be *Trudy* that's weird," Lisa said, pursing her lips so Stevie wouldn't see her smile.

"You think *I'm* the weird one?" Stevie challenged.

Lisa couldn't hold her giggle. Stevie joined her. Stevie *was* a little weird, but it was a nice weird as far as her friends were concerned.

"Carole, your shirt's on backward," Stevie said, changing the subject as she watched her friend pull down the ends of her polo shirt.

Carole looked down, confused. "I could have sworn . . ."

"You know," Stevie teased, "maybe you ought to wear shirts with pictures of horses on them. Then you'd always put them on right."

"Ha, ha." Carole grinned, then shook her head. "The trouble is, you're right. I am a total flake. Who knows what I'll do next?" She jammed her hands into her jeans pocket. "Oh, no," she said, genuine distress in her voice.

"What's the matter?" Lisa asked.

"Where's the money?" Carole began. She reached to the bottom of her pockets and wiggled her fingers in vain. "My dad's birthday-present money . . ."

"You're getting him some tapes, aren't you?" Stevie asked.

Carole nodded. Her father was crazy about things from the fifties and sixties. She'd been saving for a while to get enough money to buy him some old record albums he particularly wanted.

"In your riding pants?" Lisa suggested.

Carole searched the pockets of her breeches, but the money wasn't there. "It's fifteen dollars! I can't lose it. His birthday's only a couple of weeks away. If I . . ."

"How about your wallet?" Stevie suggested. "Where is it?"

"Oh, that's in this pocket," Carole said, tapping her rear pocket. "But Dad's birthday money isn't there. See, if I kept it there, I'm afraid I'd forget that it's special money and I'd spend it."

"Your bag?" Lisa asked.

Carole tore the clothes out of her backpack, but there was no money there. She sat on the bench, put her elbows on her knees and her chin in the palms of her hands. She frowned, trying to think hard. "The last time I saw it, I had it in my hand. I remember that. I just don't remember what I did with it."

Lisa felt awful for Carole. There was nothing she could do. Carole just *was* forgetful and a little flaky. This wasn't the first time she'd forgotten something important. Lisa recalled the time Carole had almost left her clothes and sleeping bag behind when they'd gone on an overnight trip.

"I sometimes carry money in my shoes," Stevie suggested.

"That's it!" Carole said, brightening. "It's in my boots." While her friends watched, Carole reached into the toe of her right riding boot. "Got it!" she said, and pulled out two crumpled bills, a five and a ten.

"Carole!" Stevie said. "That's no way to treat money—especially big money like that."

"I know," Carole sighed. "But I just have to find a place to stash it until I can get to the mall to buy the records for Dad." She looked at Stevie. "You helped me find it," she said. "Will you help me keep it?"

"Of course," Stevie agreed. "If you really want me to."

"That would be great. Then you hold on to it for the next three weeks. I'm going to the mall the Saturday before his birthday. Give it to me then." Carole slapped the money into Stevie's hand. "Don't give it to me before then no matter how much I beg, okay?"

Stevie looked at the money and then looked at her friend. "Are you sure?" she asked. Carole nodded. Slowly, Stevie took out her own wallet, lifted the flap to a hideaway compartment behind the billfold portion of it, closed the flap back over the money, and tossed her wallet back into her backpack. "Don't worry that it's going to be mixed up and confused with my money," Stevie said. "All I've got is four cents and nobody's going to mix up your fifteen dollars with my four cents."

"I know that," Carole said. "I trust you. Besides, you only ever have four cents! I'd better run. Thanks. See you both!"

With that, Carole picked up her things and practically ran out the door.

"You know, there are a lot of exciting things happening," Lisa said to Stevie as she finished putting her things neatly into her cubby. "Between Samson's training and your new 'sister,' there's a lot of news at the stable."

"Sure, I can just see the headlines in tomorrow's paper," Stevie said sarcastically.

Lisa thought it was all in the way you looked at it, and the way *she* looked at it gave her an idea. A *great* idea, she thought, with a secret smile.

LISA CLUTCHED HER portfolio so tightly that she was sure she was crumpling the papers inside. She looked at the sign on the door. It read WILLOW CREEK GA-ZETTE. Her knees felt weak. She took a deep breath. It didn't do anything to make her knees feel better. She knocked on the door anyway.

"C'mon in!" a gruff voice responded from inside.

She opened the door and peered around it.

What she expected was something like *The Daily Planet* city room—a sea of desks, each with its own computer screen and keyboard, most being operated by frazzled and dedicated reporters, determined to tell the truth to the news-hungry people of Willow Creek.

What she *saw* was something different. There were three desks. Each looked as if it had been rescued from the junk pile. One did, actually, have a computer on it. One of the others had an old-fashioned desktop manual typewriter. The third may have had a type-writer on it, but Lisa couldn't be sure. It was piled too high with back issues of *The Gazette* to see anything else.

"Mr. Teller?" she asked timidly.

"That's me," the man said, pushing his glasses onto the top of his head. He was mostly bald, with a craggy face and very bushy eyebrows that made him look a little frightening. "And you must be the girl who called about the horses—Lisa, is it?" He smiled at her. He had one of the nicest smiles Lisa had ever seen. As soon as he smiled, she wasn't frightened any more.

"Lisa Atwood," she said, sighing with relief.

"Come sit down," Mr. Teller said. He glanced around. "There must be a chair here someplace. This office is famous for its walking piles of papers, you know. If I turn my back on a clear space, some pile of papers comes to fill it up!"

Lisa laughed. He stood up and moved some papers off a chair onto the floor. Lisa sat down quickly. She turned to the pile he'd just made on the floor. "Sit, and stay!" she commanded.

Mr. Teller laughed at her joke. "I think we're going to get along," he said. Lisa knew he was right. "Now, tell me again about this idea of yours."

"It's about horses," she began. "See, I ride at Pine Hollow. A lot of other girls and some boys in town do, too. It's a very busy place. There are lessons and classes, horses being born and trained. There are shows and events. Not everybody is interested, of course, but there's so much going on there that's *news* for the young riders in town that I think you should have a column about it in the paper."

"Interesting," Mr. Teller said, sitting back in his chair. "Any idea who might be able to cover the subject?"

Lisa knew he was teasing her a bit. He already knew that she wanted to write it because she'd told him on the telephone.

Lisa blushed. "Well, I have a lot of experience writing," she said. "I do well on my papers in school—I've brought you a few samples . . ." She reached for her portfolio.

"It's okay," Mr. Teller said. "I believe you get good grades, but how well you write classroom essays may not have anything to do with how well you write newspaper columns."

"I thought you might say that," Lisa told him. "That's why I also brought you some samples of the writing I did for the school newspaper last year." She handed him three of her favorite stories. One was about a new science teacher. The other two covered her class field trips.

"Good thinking," he said. He glanced quickly at the clippings. "Hmmm . . ." He looked up at her. "Okay, Lisa, you can write. What's the angle here?"

This was the moment Lisa had dreamed about all

last night—when she'd been sleeping. She'd actually spent most of the night awake, worrying about this interview. In her imagination, it had *never* gone as smoothly as this. "'Hoof Beat,'" she said, looking Mr. Teller straight in the eye. "The name of the column is Hoof Beat." Lisa thought that was pretty clever. Since the subject a reporter covered was called a beat, and since she'd be covering horses, Hoof Beat seemed the perfect choice.

Mr. Teller leaned back in his chair again. Lisa had the feeling he always did that when he was thinking. He looked to the left and to the right, though there was nothing in either direction for him to see but piles of papers. Finally, he looked at Lisa again.

"Deal," he said. "I want five hundred to seven hundred and fifty words a week. That's two to three typed pages. Copy is due Wednesday noon. It's your byline, I won't make changes in the stories, unless I have to correct English. You can come in Tuesday night and use the typewriter over there if you want."

Lisa looked dubiously at the ancient relic. "No thanks. We've got a computer at home. I'll use that. It's easier for me."

"Would be for me, too," Mr. Teller joked. "Anyway, I'll pay you fifteen dollars a column."

"You'll *pay* me?" Lisa couldn't believe she'd heard the words correctly. She was stunned. "Every week?"

"Of course I'll pay you," Mr. Teller said gruffly. "If I don't pay you, you may start thinking this isn't important. It *is* important. I'm going to be counting on two to three pages of copy from you every week. I'll hold space for it. If you let me down, I'll be in trouble. I don't want that. You don't want to not get paid. See?"

Lisa just nodded. She was too excited to speak.

"All right. This is Thursday. Think you can have your first column in by next Wednesday?"

For fifteen dollars, she'd have it in that afternoon! "Yes, sir, Chief!" she said, standing at attention. Her portfolio fell onto the floor and her A papers were scattered everywhere. She flushed with embarrassment.

"See what I mean about paper walking around this office?" Mr. Teller said, crouching to help her pick up the mess. Lisa smiled, knowing he was trying to make her feel better. "Oh, and one more thing . . ."

"Yes?"

"Don't call me Chief. 'Mr. Teller' will do nicely."

Lisa stuffed the last of the papers into her portfolio, shook her new boss's hand, called him Mr. Teller, not Chief, and left the office.

Lisa practically floated down the stairs, she was so excited. She was a reporter—with a beat of her own! This was the most exciting thing that had happened to her since she'd discovered horseback riding. She had a job. It was a real job, the start of a real career.

Sure, she told herself, *The Willow Creek Gazette* wasn't exactly *The Washington Post* or *The New York Times*, but it was a start. After all, she was only thirteen. If she got a running start at her age, she could land something bigger on the *Post* while she was in college. Maybe get bylines. Investigative reporting was what she'd aim for. She could go undercover, tracking mobsters and drug smugglers or maybe even uncover government scandals. She'd go to war zones and interview soldiers, talk to dictators and presidents. And spy stories—she could reveal double agents who were jeopardizing democracy. With that kind of reporting, she'd get a Pulitzer Prize—maybe two! And that would bring her to the attention of the Nobel Committee . . .

But first, she realized with a start, she had to write an article about training Samson.

STEVIE STILL COULDN'T believe how cute Samson was. She'd seen him being born and she'd watched him stand and nurse for the first time. Since then, she'd seen him almost every day—and each time she saw him it was as exciting as the first time.

He was a lot bigger, of course. He'd grown a tremendous amount in the first months of his life, but he was still little and he was still very cute.

Samson stayed near his mother most of the time, though now he would sometimes venture as far away as the other side of the paddock, a distance of perhaps twenty feet. But if somebody approached the paddock, Samson would usually trot quickly to his mother's side. Delilah was always there waiting for him. She'd nuzzle him and comfort him when he was frightened. Stevie thought she was a very good and attentive mother.

Stevie was alone with Samson and Delilah today. Carole, she knew, was at the shopping center, volunteering for the library. Lisa had promised to come help Stevie later. She'd called Stevie in the morning, saying something about an appointment. She had been awfully vague. Normally, this would have upset Stevie, partly because of her curiosity and partly because she had been counting on Lisa's help. However, she was excited about being the only person working with Samson. She'd watched Carole the day before and was sure she could do it. It would be a lot of fun, too.

"Hi, there," she said, greeting mother and son in their paddock. Delilah glanced at her with little interest. Samson snuggled up to his mother's side.

The first thing Stevie did was to put a halter on Delilah, then she fastened the lead rope to the fence of the paddock. Delilah cooperated the way she always did. There was no problem at all.

"Good girl," Stevie said, patting her firmly on the neck. She wanted to show Samson that she was friends with his mother. "See, boy, you can trust me. Your mom and I are old pals."

The foal ducked around his mother's rear.

"I mean it," Stevie said to him. "We've ridden together lots. She'll tell you. As a matter of fact, she even tried to throw me once, but I held on!"

That was a vivid memory to Stevie. The first year she'd been a rider, she'd ridden Delilah on a trail. She had been wearing sneakers and her foot had slipped out of the stirrup and the stirrup had started banging on Delilah's belly. Not surprisingly, the horse hadn't liked that at all and had started acting up. Stevie had held on to her mane for dear life, and most important, she'd gotten her footing again. It had been enough to make her want to wear cowboy-style boots with a high heel now when she rode.

"Good old pals," Stevie repeated. Then she climbed up over the fence and into the paddock. She walked along Delilah's side, approaching Samson slowly. She didn't want to frighten him. She held the halter in her left hand, behind her back. She showed him her empty right hand. He didn't seem very interested in it. He stepped back, away from her.

Stevie stepped toward him. He stepped back again. She tried again. He did it again.

"This is almost like dancing class!" she said.

She moved to the right. He moved to the left. She shifted. So did he. She giggled.

Stevie hopped a few inches off the ground. Samson fled, running all the way around the ring until he came to the far side of his mother. Then he snuggled up to her.

Stevie crept around Delilah's rear. Softly, she put her hand on Samson's flank. He moved away from her again.

She loved to watch him move. There was something about the colt's gaits that was different from an adult horse's gaits. Stevie realized that it must have to do with the proportions of the animal. The colt's legs were relatively longer than his mother's, and he almost seemed to bounce as he moved. Stevie could have watched him for hours.

Samson took cover next to his mother. Stevie peered under Delilah's belly at the colt.

"Peekaboo!" she said, startling the colt. He bolted, quickly circling the paddock. He returned to his mother, staying on the side away from Stevie. Once again, she peered under Delilah's belly. This time, Samson was waiting for her. He peered right back at her. "Peekaboo!" she said, and he circled the paddock.

"Smart boy!" Stevie said, genuinely impressed that the colt had learned the game so quickly. Playing with Samson was as much fun as playing with a puppy, and Stevie quickly found that he liked fun and games.

Stevie slung Samson's halter over the edge of the paddock fence and the lead rope with it. It was going to be easier playing games without being bothered by those things.

Stevie tried several varieties of peekaboo—sometimes meeting up with Samson under his mother, sometimes in front, and sometimes behind. Delilah stood obediently still, ignoring the shenanigans of her colt and Stevie. Stevie wasn't surprised that Delilah didn't participate in any way. She was a well-trained horse and knew that when she'd been haltered and tied someplace, it was her job to stand still and await further instructions.

When Stevie tired of peekaboo, she taught Samson how to play tag. Samson won hands down. Every time Stevie reached for him, he dodged her and ran in the opposite direction. He was good—really good. She tried faking him out, reaching first with her right hand, and then when he began moving away from her reach, she'd quickly extend her left hand and tap him with that. It only took Samson a bit to figure out that the surefire way to evade her was to back up and turn around. And when Stevie chased after him, he just ran faster.

Stevie was beginning to wonder if she could teach Samson to play follow-the-leader when Lisa arrived.

"Come on in and see what I've taught Samson!" Stevie said, inviting Lisa to join the fun.

"I think I'd rather watch," Lisa said. "Unless you need me, I mean."

"No, we're having a ball. I never knew a horse as smart as this! Wait'll you see."

Stevie demonstrated peekaboo and tag. Lisa could hardly believe what she was watching. She'd seen horses trained to do some very complicated things, but she'd never seen a horse having as much fun as this.

"You try," Stevie said. "I'm sure you'll be as good at it as I am. He makes it easy."

Lisa was tempted. It looked like an awful lot of fun. But she had a job to do. She had a column to write and she wanted to surprise her friends with it. Now she really had something to write about!

"I can't," Lisa said to Stevie. "There's something I have to do."

"But you just *got* here," Stevie reminded her.

"I know, but . . . well, I've got to do it."

Stevie could tell there was something Lisa was keeping from her, but right then she was having too much fun with Samson to care what Lisa was up to. She just told Lisa she'd talk to her later and returned to her games, barely noticing as Lisa left for home.

Follow-the-leader, it turned out, was a much harder game to play. She walked ahead of Samson and then skipped, sort of like a trot. He was following her all right, but she didn't think he was doing what she'd been doing. The only way she could tell was if she stopped and turned around. Every time she stopped and turned around, she found that Samson had stopped, too, and was looking straight at her. Then, if she tried to let *him* be the leader, all he did was to go over and stand by Delilah. The third time he did it, he also began nuzzling his mother for something to eat.

Stevie realized that she, too, was beginning to be hungry, and since she was also rather tired, Samson was probably tired as well. She glanced at her watch. It was nearly one o'clock. She'd been playing with Samson for more than two hours—and it seemed as if it had been just a few minutes. She'd only promised Carole to be with the colt for fifteen or twenty minutes, but that had turned out to be not nearly enough. Wouldn't Carole be pleased!

She didn't want to disturb the nursing colt. He seemed so peaceful, in sharp contrast to the lively little creature she'd just been playing with. Stevie climbed up on the paddock fence, loosened Delilah's lead rope, removed her halter, and then climbed down. She was halfway back to the tack room before she remembered the halter and lead rope she'd brought out for Samson, which she'd never had the chance to use. She returned to the paddock and found the contented little colt lying down on the cool earth in a shady spot of the paddock, sleeping very soundly. She grabbed the halter and lead and took them back into the stable.

She was greeted by the familiar and unpleasant smell of fresh paint. "Ick," she said, wrinkling her nose. There was nobody around to sympathize with her. Most of the girls who were usually in her class were on the trail with Red O'Malley. Stevie could have gone with them, but she'd had a lot more fun with Samson.

She was about to sit on the bench nearest her cubby when she realized the bench was sparkling white and obviously freshly painted. Her jeans certainly didn't need a white stripe across the seat!

Complaining out loud to nobody, she sat down on the floor and pulled her backpack out of her cubby. She'd wear her jeans home, but she wanted to switch into her sneakers first. Boots were great for riding, or working in the paddock, but not for walking.

It only took a few seconds to make the change. She

didn't even bother tying her laces. She rammed her boots back into her cubby, zipped up her backpack, and was ready to go when she realized that she hadn't seen her wallet—not that it mattered much. She'd spent three of her four cents on a chewy mint and that didn't leave much in the way of spending money. Still, she didn't want to lose the wallet. It had her library card in it.

She checked her backpack. It wasn't there, not even in the outside zipper compartment. Annoyed, she sat back down on the floor and pulled her boots out of her cubby, figuring that she must have shoved it into the back when she put her boots away. It wasn't there.

Stevie was annoyed with herself. She didn't like to lose things. She knew she hadn't taken it out of her backpack since she put it there the day before, but it looked as if it was gone. Not that it was a valuable wallet; nor that she had much money in it, certainly nothing to steal. It was just that . . . Then she remembered: Carole's money had been in the wallet. Carole had asked her to hold on to her fifteen dollars so she could buy her father a birthday present—and it looked a lot like it had been stolen!

Stevie suddenly had an awful empty feeling in the pit of her stomach. Fifteen dollars! How could this have happened?

The cubbies weren't locked, but everybody at the stable knew everybody, and it was hard to imagine who would steal something from a friend. Certainly Carole didn't take it. Lisa was out of the question, too.

Stevie's vivid imagination went to work. First, she tried to remember who had been there when Carole had given her the money, but it just didn't seem possible that one of the other young riders could have taken the wallet. One of the stableboys? she asked herself. She shook her head. Perhaps it was an outside job— maybe someone wandered in off the street, into the empty locker area, just looking for loose wallets. That at least seemed possible, but it was a little difficult to imagine thieves who would waste their time in the kids' locker area of a stable. Stevie realized she was about to daydream up an international plot, so she stopped herself. At that moment it didn't matter how the wallet had disappeared. It did matter that it *had* disappeared. She needed to talk to Max.

Stevie found Max in Barq's stall, examining a hoof. He angled the horse's hoof so that it was centered in the stream of sunlight slanting across the stall. He alternated cleaning out the hoof with a hoof-pick and gently prodding the hoof tissues with his fingers. Stevie waited. She wasn't feeling patient, but it would be useless to try to interrupt Max while he was caring for a horse.

"Got it!" he announced finally. He eased the hoof-pick between the horse's shoe and foot and manipulated it gently until a pebble dropped into the straw on the floor of the stall. Max released Barq's hoof. The horse put it back onto the ground and continued munching at his hay as if nothing had happened.

"What's up, Stevie?" Max asked as he stepped out of the stall and fastened the door behind him. "I saw you heading for Samson's paddock; everything okay there?"

"Oh, sure, Samson and I had a great workout," she said. "But I do have a problem." She told him about her wallet and Carole's money.

"Boy, that's tough," he said. He shook his head sadly, sympathetically.

"Sure is," she said, sensing that Max would find a way to solve the problem. "I knew you'd help me out."

"Oh, I'm not sure there's anything I can really do to help, Stevie," Max said. "But you've learned something."

This was definitely *not* what Stevie was hoping he would say. He was saying exactly what her parents would say.

"That's not fair, Max," Stevie wailed. "The money got stolen. In *your* stables. I couldn't help it."

"Stevie, this is a public place. There are no locks on the cubbies. They are there for the convenience of our riders—not for security. I'm sorry about Carole's money, but it was careless of you to stash that much money in an open area. Next time, just remember that I can lock valuables in my desk."

He walked toward his office. Stevie trailed after him. She just had to get him to help her.

"Next time? There won't be a next time, Max! Carole will never speak to me again! It's money for her dad's birthday! Do something!"

"Maybe I should," he said thoughtfully.

Stevie waited. The fact that it was Carole's money had swayed him, she was sure. Max scratched his head thoughtfully.

"I know," he continued. "As soon as we finish with the paint job, I'll put another sign up in the locker room about locking valuables in the office."

A lot of good that'll do me, Stevie thought. Angry and disgusted, she went home.

THAT EVENING, LISA sat on the comfortable chair in her room, her legs over one of the soft arms, her back against the other. She was thinking.

She'd already made a list of things she could write about in her first column. That was good. The problem was that there were more than fifteen items on the list and there was no way she could write about fifteen things in five hundred words. Mostly she wanted to write about Samson's training, but there was so much to describe about it that she hardly knew where to begin. She needed an angle. Then she got an idea.

The New Student, she wrote.

> *Pine Hollow Stables' newest student is also its youngest. His name is Samson. He's two months old.*

*He's about four feet tall, has short black hair, pointed
ears, and a cute tail. He is Delilah's colt.*

Lisa liked it. She thought it was a good idea to make
the point that it wasn't just the riders who learned at
the stable. The horses had to learn, too.

Lisa was about to describe the colt's first lessons when
her mother called upstairs to tell her the phone was for
her. She'd been so interested in what she was writing
that she hadn't even heard the phone ring. She
reached across to her bedside table and picked up the
receiver.

"Oh, Lisa, I'm so glad you're there!" Stevie said.
Lisa recognized the frantic tone in Stevie's voice im-
mediately. It didn't concern her too much, though.
Stevie often had a frantic tone.

"What's up?" Lisa asked, still gazing proudly at the
paragraph she'd written.

"It's Carole's money—it's gone!" Stevie said.

Then Lisa knew Stevie had a good reason for the
frantic tone.

Stevie told her what had happened. "It just wasn't
there when I came back from the training session. Did
you see anybody lurking near the cubbies when you
were there?"

Lisa thought for a minute. "The place stank so
much from the paint job that I just ran through," she
said. "I didn't see anybody, but that doesn't mean anything. They could have been there."

"I know they could. They *were*. And you know, I've been thinking. Remember the time Polly Giacomin couldn't find her riding crop?"

Lisa did remember. Polly had been so upset about it, she'd cried all through their class. "What a baby she was!" Lisa said.

"Maybe, but it never did show up. And remember when Meg couldn't find her keys?"

"Sure, but who would take her keys?"

"I don't know, but I'll bet you *anything* it was the same person who took my wallet."

"You think there's somebody stealing stuff from the cubbies?" Lisa asked, now very interested.

"Let's just say that I think it looks suspicious," Stevie said.

Suspicious was just the word. And when there was something suspicious going on, people needed to know about it. Lisa tore a piece of paper from her pad and picked up her pen again.

Suspicious Thefts at Pine Hollow! she wrote.

On the other end of the line, sitting in the Lakes' kitchen, telephone at her ear, Stevie waited for Lisa to offer to lend her money. But Lisa was quiet. "So, listen," Stevie said. "Can you help me out?"

"You bet I can!" Lisa said.

The words she'd been waiting to hear. "All fifteen dollars?" Stevie asked.

"Oh, no. Not that way," Lisa said. "Sorry. I'm broke now. But I'll help you another way."

"You sound just like Max," Stevie said grumpily.

"Huh?" Lisa responded.

"I suppose *you* think it's my fault, too," Stevie said.

Lisa didn't answer. Stevie thought she'd sounded kind of distracted. She was about to give her a piece of her mind when there was an interruption. Her mother entered the kitchen and with her was the most amazing girl Stevie had ever seen.

"Stevie, this is Trudy," Mrs. Lake said. "Trudy, this is my daughter, Stephanie."

"Lisa, I've got to go," Stevie said, hanging up the phone hastily, all thoughts of Carole's fifteen dollars fleeing from her mind.

She spun on the kitchen stool to face Trudy and then blinked her eyes to be sure it was for real. Trudy was a girl about her own age, and that was where the resemblance between them stopped, for Trudy was dressed in the most outlandish outfit Stevie had ever seen.

First of all, she was wearing an oversize Hawaiian-pattern shirt, over a black spandex skirt. She wore purple tights blotched with yellow splatters, with black bobby socks over the tights, and black gym shoes. On each wrist there were at least ten plastic hoop bracelets of bright colors to match her shirt. Her earrings were big yellow plastic hoops. She wore eye shadow that picked up a lot of the colors from her Hawaiian shirt and the bracelets. And then there was her hair. Her hair was bleached blond and cut straight. On her right side, it was cut above her ear. It got longer and longer as the hairstyle continued around her head, until on her left side it hung below her chin line. She wore a bow smack on top of her head, made of the same material as her Hawaiian shirt.

Stevie decided she looked wonderful. "Is it Halloween already?" Stevie asked with a grin.

"You like it?" Trudy responded.

"I've never seen anything like it," Stevie told her. "Even when we were in New York, where there were some pretty wild looks, nobody dressed like that!"

"I put the outfit together myself," Trudy said.

Stevie slid off the stool, picked up one of Trudy's suitcases, and said, "Come on, I'll show you to our room. We're sharing. Hope that's okay."

"Sure," Trudy said. She picked up the other bag and followed Stevie up the stairs.

Stevie dropped Trudy's suitcase in the corner of her room. Trudy piled the one she was carrying on top.

"That's your bed," Stevie said, pointing and sitting down on her own bed. Trudy sat on hers. "Does your mother actually *let* you dress like that?" Stevie asked enviously.

"Not really," Trudy said, smiling mischievously. "I mean, she wouldn't exactly choose these clothes for me, but see, I'm on a clothing allowance, so I get to buy what I want. And this is what I want."

"Cool," Stevie said. "But how do you do the eye makeup?"

Trudy offered to show her. Within ten minutes, the bathroom was littered with little plastic containers and foam-rubber applicators. The two girls stood side by side, stretching to be close to the mirror. Trudy demonstrated how to mix colors for the most interesting effect.

"I'm getting this funny feeling," Stevie said, admiring the pink and blue butterfly she'd just drawn over her right eye.

"What's that?" Trudy asked.

"I have a suspicion that our mothers thought that if you and I got together for a couple of weeks, I might be a good influence on you."

Trudy exploded into a fit of giggles. "We'll show them," she said.

"Yeah, but that's not even the funniest part," Stevie said. "The funniest part is that I think it's the first time in my life anybody's ever thought I would be a good influence on anybody! Hey, what do you think about a little silver lining on the lower wing of the butterfly?"

"I think gold would be better," Trudy told her. "It'll match the sparkles we're about to put on your cheeks!"

"*Outrageous!*"

LATER THAT NIGHT, Stevie lay back in bed, watching the patterns that car headlights made on the ceiling of her room. Trudy slept soundly in the bed next to hers. It had been such a busy day that she really needed some time to think about everything that had happened. At first, all she could think of were the wonderful things that had happened, training Samson and meeting Trudy. Then she recalled the bad news about Trudy. She didn't ride horses. She'd never ridden horses, and she wasn't especially enthusiastic about learning to ride horses. Stevie would change that, she was sure.

Then there was the matter of Carole's money. Nothing was going right on that. Max wouldn't make it up to her. Lisa wouldn't give it to her. She just had to get fifteen dollars for Carole. There was no way she could earn it in time. She was going to be much too busy having fun with Samson and Trudy to take on any old baby-sitting jobs. Besides, she'd tried to earn money in the past and hadn't been awfully successful at it. And she certainly couldn't *steal* it like the jerk who had taken Carole's money in the first place. That left only one possibility. She would have to borrow it. From whom?

Her mother? No way. Once her mother learned how it had gotten lost, she wouldn't lend her any money. She'd say exactly what Max had said. Her father? Ditto. Her brothers? Now there was a possibility. She knew that her twin brother, Alex, still had some of his birthday money left. He might lend it to her—but he would want interest. Maybe Michael, her little brother, could be talked into a loan. Her oldest brother, Chad, was out of the question. She didn't call him Scrooge for nothing! She decided to approach Alex and Michael first thing in the morning.

There was something else she had to do first thing in the morning. She had to begin working on Trudy to get her to ride. Trudy was a really neat person, but it would be hard for her to be a close friend unless she could ride. The image of Trudy on horseback made Stevie smile to herself in the dark of her room. She just hoped that horses were color-blind!

THERE WERE TIMES, Lisa thought, when Stevie was just too much. This was one of them.

It was the day after the disappearance of Stevie's wallet and the appearance of Trudy. Their riding class was over and The Saddle Club was about to give Samson his next lesson. Stevie was in the locker area of the stable where their classmates were changing out of their riding clothes. Stevie was telling absolutely everybody about the theft of Carole's money, asking them if they could lend her some, and telling them not to tell Carole. Lisa was quite certain that a secret shared by fifteen girls would not be a secret for long!

And to top it off, Stevie had talked Trudy into keeping Carole away.

"Don't let her out of your sight," Stevie had said. "Stick to her like a tattoo."

Lisa thought that it was an appropriate phrase. Trudy, after all, was dressed like a tattoo! In any event, Trudy and Carole were well out of earshot and Stevie was doing her sales pitch.

"It's money she's been saving for months for her father's birthday!" Stevie told Anna McWhirter, one of the girls. "It was stolen in broad daylight!"

"I don't have a penny to spare," Anna told Stevie. "I'm saving up to buy myself a new riding hat."

"What happened to the old one?" Stevie asked.

"It just disappeared one day. It was getting too small for me anyway. But until I buy a new one, I have to use the ones here and I'd rather have my own."

Just disappeared? That seemed very mysterious to Lisa, and strangely consistent with some other things she'd been observing recently.

"It seems like things are always disappearing around here," Veronica diAngelo said. "I've never found the riding gloves I used for the gymkhana. They were *very* expensive, too. I know somebody stole them."

Usually, Lisa instantly dismissed everything snooty Veronica said. In this case, she thought she might make an exception.

Stevie spun to look at Veronica. Lisa knew just what was on her mind. Veronica was very rich. She was the daughter of one of the wealthiest men in town. She was also an unbearable snob and The Saddle Club girls despised her. Nevertheless, in Stevie's current state of panic, all Stevie was going to be thinking of was how rich Veronica was. Lisa knew Stevie was going to ask Veronica to lend her the fifteen dollars. Lisa knew she wouldn't be able to watch Stevie with a straight face, so she left the locker area. Stevie gave her a dirty look.

Lisa headed through the stable and across to Samson's paddock.

Trudy stood next to the fence, outside the paddock. She watched Carole silently.

"Isn't he cute?" Lisa asked.

"Yeah," Trudy said. "Nice pony."

"He's actually not a pony," Lisa said. "A pony is a *small* horse, not a young horse. Samson is a foal or a colt. When he grows up, he'll be a horse." Lisa liked explaining horse facts to other people. It didn't seem like it was so long ago that she didn't know anything— when she would have made a mistake like that. She was proud of all she'd learned. It was going to be fun to have somebody new to teach about horses.

"Looks like a pony to me," Trudy said.

Lisa decided to hold off on the lessons for a bit. It was just possible that Trudy wasn't as eager a student as Lisa had been.

Carole finished putting the halter and lead rope on Delilah. She handed the lead to Lisa, who looped it around the cleat on the outside of the ring. Lisa knew that the cleat was on the outside for the horses' safety, and she was all ready to explain it to Trudy, but Trudy didn't seem very interested. Lisa just did the small chore and returned to Trudy's side.

Once again, Carole patted Delilah's neck to show Samson that they were friends. She held the colt's halter and lead in her other hand behind her back. Carole was aware that Samson was watching her alertly. As before, she approached him calmly, expecting him to stay by his mother's side where she could put the halter on him.

It didn't go that way. As soon as she rounded Delilah's rear, Samson took off. That was odd. He didn't seem frightened of her, he just seemed to want to run. Since she'd rarely seen him run before, except when his mother was also running, she was surprised. She stood still next to Delilah. Samson returned, taking shelter on Delilah's other side.

Carole peered around Delilah's rear. Samson peered around Delilah's rear. Carole spotted Samson. Samson spotted Carole and hid again quickly. Carole smiled to herself. It was just as if he were playing peekaboo. She squatted down to look at the colt from under his mother's belly. Samson lowered his head and looked through Delilah's legs at Carole. As soon as he could see her, he withdrew. Carole laughed again. He *was* playing peekaboo.

It was fun, but it wasn't training.

Carole stood up and walked calmly around Delilah's rear. She paused for just a second, but it was enough. Samson took off like a shot. He circled the paddock and then returned to his mother's other side. Carole tried again. So did Samson.

"What's going on with you?" she asked. His answer was to run away again.

It didn't seem as if he was frightened. He didn't run in fear. Instead, it was more as if he were playing a game—just the way he'd played peekaboo, only this time, it was tag and she was It.

When Samson went to circle the paddock yet another time, Carole decided to show him she wasn't playing the game. She left Delilah's side and walked over to Trudy and Lisa.

"What's going on with him?" Carole asked.

"I wonder if you could teach him to fetch," Trudy said. "I got my dog to do it very easily. That kind of game seems to come naturally to a lot of animals."

Carole ignored the suggestion. The purpose was not to teach Samson games, but to teach him to wear a halter.

"Was he doing this yesterday?" Carole asked Lisa.

"Oh, yes," Lisa said. "Stevie had a great time with him."

"Did she get the halter on him?" Carole asked.

"I don't know," Lisa answered. "I couldn't stay very long. But I know she spent a lot of time with him, so she must have." Lisa glanced at her watch. "Oops, I've got to get going now. See you!"

Carole noticed that there was something secretive about Lisa, and she seemed to be doing a lot of disappearing lately. Normally, Carole would have been very curious. Today, however, she was much more interested in what was going on with Samson.

"Okay, see you," she said. She returned her attention to Samson. "Come on, boy. It's time for you to learn some manners."

If Samson thought that the proper way to respond to somebody who was walking toward him was to run, then she'd just have to teach him to walk toward somebody who was standing still. He had to learn to come to a call.

She stood next to Delilah and whistled. Samson's ears perked up. He looked at her, interested. She whistled again. She continued that until, finally, the colt walked over to her. As soon as he was within an arm's length of her, she reached out to pat him—his reward. It was the signal he'd been waiting for, so he bolted, playing tag again.

Trudy laughed. Carole did not.

"It's so *funny!*" Trudy said.

"Not from where I'm standing," Carole said. She tried again. The same thing happened several times until, finally, the horse realized that Carole wasn't playing the same game he was. He stood still long enough for her to pat him, but it was nowhere near long enough for her to put the halter on him.

"It's as if we've never done this before," she said in total frustration. "Somehow, he's forgotten everything I taught him just two days ago. Poor Stevie must have had a terrible time yesterday. Did she say anything to you?"

"Not at all," Trudy said. "She just said she had a lot of fun."

"Well, this isn't fun. He must not have been doing this!"

Carole held out the halter for Samson to examine. He looked at it very tentatively, curiously. She remained still, not wanting to distract the excitable colt. He stepped toward her extended hand.

"I don't believe that girl!" Stevie huffed, storming out of the stable area. "Veronica diAngelo is just impossible. Impossible. She wouldn't give me the time of day, much less lend me money. I must have been crazy to ask her!"

Samson bolted.

Carole sighed. Nothing was going right today. Just when there seemed to be a chance that Samson might learn something, she was interrupted. There was no point in losing her temper at Stevie, though. That was just the way she was.

"What's the problem?" Carole asked resignedly.

"All I did was ask Veronica a simple question—"

"Nothing about Veronica is ever simple," Carole reminded her. "So what did you ask?"

"I've just got to get some money," Stevie said. "So I thought maybe she could lend me some. You wouldn't be able to lend me a few dollars, would you?"

"Stevie, you know I'm saving up every penny for my dad's birthday."

Carole could have sworn that Stevie blushed. "Oh, yeah, right," Stevie said. "Well, I'm not all that desperate, so forget I even mentioned it, will you?"

Stevie grabbed Trudy's arm and pulled her back toward the stable.

Carole reflected on her day so far and quickly concluded that *everybody* was acting strangely. Lisa was into a disappearing act; if Stevie was desperate enough to try to borrow money from Veronica, she was in trouble; Samson wasn't doing any of the things she'd worked so hard to train him to do the other day. And Trudy? Carole suspected that Trudy wasn't any more strange that day than she usually was, but that was strange enough!

It was time to quit for the day. Carole climbed up over the fence, took off Delilah's halter and lead rope, and returned the tack to the tack room.

Some days, nothing went right.

6

LISA COULDN'T HELP grinning. She opened the copy of *The Willow Creek Gazette* and read the words "Hoof Beat by Lisa Atwood."

It was like a dream come true. The article had come out to just six hundred words and Mr. Teller had seemed happy about that. Most of the article just listed the classes Max offered for young riders. Mr. Teller had said she had to include that even though it didn't really seem like news. The last part *was* news.

And there's bad news at Pine Hollow this week: Stevie Lake's wallet was stolen out of her cubby while she was working in the stable. The wallet had more than $15 cash in it.

There were apparently no other young riders at the stable at the time of the theft, but many of the riders knew that Stevie would be there at that time and that she had the cash in her wallet. Stevie was holding the money for her friend Carole Hanson, who had worked and saved the money to buy her father a birthday present. This reporter hopes that whoever took the money will come forward and return it. If it is returned right away, nothing will be said.

Lisa sighed happily. She was glad both that she had news to report and that she'd done it in such a good way. She'd told what had happened, but even more important, she'd given somebody the opportunity to correct the wrong that had been done. Maybe the thief thought she could get away with it. Or maybe, just maybe, the thief was beginning to feel bad, and with the encouragement from her article would have second thoughts about taking somebody else's property and return it.

Carefully, Lisa folded the newspaper and put it in her backpack to take to the stable. Most people in town did read the paper, and it was probable that they would have noticed *The Gazette*'s newest feature, but just in case, she wanted to have it with her.

It seemed to Lisa that the fifteen-minute walk to Pine Hollow had never gone faster. The whole way there, she thought about how pleased Stevie was going to be with what she'd done—how she'd asked the thief to return the money. And she also thought about how relieved Carole would be to have the story out in the open so that she had a real shot at getting her money back. Most of all, she thought about how jealous absolutely everybody was going to be. She, Lisa Atwood, had her own column in *The Gazette*.

She was still floating on air when she entered the locker area. The whole place was full of her classmates. They were all talking to one another in little groups. In one corner, Polly Giacomin was showing some friends a new pair of sandals. In another, Betsy Cavanaugh was talking furiously with two other girls. Anna McWhirter was talking with Lorraine Olson. Lisa was thrilled. Almost certainly, everybody was talking about her.

The first person who spotted her was Stevie. She and Trudy had been standing near the doorway, talking intensely.

"Did you see?" Lisa asked proudly, pulling the paper out of her backpack.

She was expecting Stevie to shriek with joy. Stevie shrieked all right, but it wasn't with joy.

"How could you do that to me!" she shrieked.

"What do you mean?"

"Writing about losing Carole's money—she's furious at me now! I'd already borrowed six dollars to give to her. I was going to get the rest in time, but you blew it. She may never speak to me again!"

Lisa was genuinely surprised to learn that Stevie hadn't even told Carole about it yet. Carole was her best friend. How could Lisa have known Stevie would keep something like that from Carole?

"But you'd *have* to tell her eventually," Lisa said. "I just saved you the trouble."

"Maybe I *would* have had to tell her eventually," Stevie said, "but *I* should have done it, not you." She spun on her heel and returned to the bench next to her cubby.

That sounded exactly right to Lisa. Stevie *should* have done it. Stevie was angry at her for doing something she should have done in the first place! It was just like Stevie to lose her temper without thinking over what she was saying, Lisa thought. She'd get over it. In the meantime, she wasn't going to let Stevie's little temper tantrum interfere with her pleasure over her first publication.

She ignored Stevie and found an empty cubby next to where Anna McWhirter was sitting. "Did you see?" Lisa asked, brandishing *The Gazette*.

"I saw," Anna said coldly. Lisa suspected she was jealous. She'd get over that in time. Jealousy would eventually turn to admiration, she was sure.

"Do you think it'll make the thief return the wallet?" Lisa asked.

"It wasn't me, so you can just forget about that!" Anna said. She gave her boot a final tug, stood up, and walked away.

That surprised Lisa. She hadn't expected that kind

of reaction at all. Then she remembered that Anna's hat had been stolen, too. Lisa decided that Anna was jealous all right. She was jealous that Lisa had mentioned the theft of the wallet, but not of Anna's hat. Well, she could do something about that in the next article she wrote, but it would be a week until that one came out.

Lisa busied herself getting ready for class, but her mind was on her next article. She didn't notice when Veronica diAngelo came and stood next to her.

"I suppose you brought a search warrant," Veronica said. "You can look all you want in my cubby for Stevie's wallet. You won't find it there."

Veronica spun around and walked away too fast for Lisa to respond—but she wouldn't have been able to say anything anyway. Lisa was more than a little surprised by Veronica's reaction. Veronica was always convinced that everything she did was better than anything anybody else ever did. She was the last person at the stable that Lisa would have expected to be jealous. It made Lisa feel good that Veronica was so obviously jealous of *her*. Maybe, like Anna, she was a little jealous of Carole, too, just because Lisa hadn't said anything about the theft of Veronica's riding gloves.

Lisa finished pulling on her boots, collected the tack for Pepper, the horse she usually rode in class, and was about to leave the locker area when she noticed a tight knot of girls in one corner. Betsy Cavanaugh was in the center, her face red with anger and streaked with tears. Lisa had always liked Betsy. She didn't like to see her so upset about something.

"What's the matter with Betsy?" she asked, walking over to the group.

"It's none of your business," Meg Durham spat out angrily.

"Oh, yes, it is," Betsy said, overriding Meg. Then she turned to Lisa. "Look," she said. "Just because I was here when Carole gave Stevie the money doesn't mean I took it."

"I never said you did," Lisa told her.

"Well, you said one of us took it and there weren't all that many of us there at the time. Two people have already asked me about it, but I'm telling you, I didn't take it! If you want to know who did, why don't you find out who just bought herself a new pair of sandals!"

Betsy glared at Lisa, ignoring the tears as they spilled out of her eyes and down her cheeks. Lisa was really sorry Betsy was so upset. Lisa doubted that Betsy had anything to do with the theft because she was such a nice girl. Sometimes the truth hurt, she realized. And sometimes the people who got hurt by the truth were innocent people, like Betsy.

Betsy wiped her tears with her bare hand, streaking her face even more. Lisa always carried tissues. It was one of the things her mother made her do. She pulled the little tissue pack out of her pocket and offered it to Betsy.

"No thank you," Betsy said. "I've gotten enough

from you already today." She sniffed and then turned her back on Lisa. Confused, Lisa shook her head and walked away. It was time to tack up Pepper.

Pepper, it seemed, was the only one who wasn't jealous or angry at her, she mused as she slipped his bridle over his head.

"Oh, you're here," Carole said, genuine surprise apparent in her voice.

Lisa looked up, startled; she hadn't heard anyone's footsteps. "Of course I'm here, where else did you think I would be ten minutes before class?" Lisa asked. An awful lot of people seemed to be behaving very strangely today. She had the sinking feeling Carole was going to be another one of them.

"Hiding out," Carole said. "But you're brave."

Lisa finished buckling the bridle and turned her attention to Pepper's saddle. "I heard you're not speaking to Stevie. Why? Because she lost your money?"

"No. Because she didn't tell me about it."

"I told her she should have," Lisa said, feeling vindicated.

"You told *everyone* she should have," Carole said.

Then Lisa knew for sure that this was going to be another strange conversation. "Just exactly what do you mean by that?" Lisa asked defensively.

"I mean that you told the whole world about some things that were just between friends. I asked Stevie to do me a favor and she tried, but she made a mistake. Now the whole world knows about it."

"It was *news*," Lisa reminded her.

"But it wasn't anybody else's business!"

"Stealing is *everybody* else's business," Lisa snapped. "It happened. I didn't write anything that didn't happen."

"What you wrote made it sound like one of the girls here stole Stevie's wallet with my money in it. That's not news. It's a wild accusation!"

Lisa could now feel herself getting angry. Carole obviously just didn't understand what journalism was all about. It was her job to tell the facts. As long as she stuck to the facts, she wasn't responsible for how other people interpreted them.

"I didn't say that any of those girls stole the wallet," Lisa reminded Carole. "I just said that they were there at the time Stevie got the money. Personally, I don't have any idea who stole the wallet, but I'll tell you one thing—if my article gets the thief to return the money, you'll be thanking me, and so will everybody else."

Carole shook her head. "I suppose," she said. "But it seems a high price to pay for fifteen dollars." And then she walked off to finish tacking up her own horse.

Lisa returned her attention to Pepper. She put the saddle pad on his back, then lifted the saddle up and placed it carefully on the pad. She slid the pad and saddle into place and reached under Pepper for the girth, pulling the strap tight and fastening the first buckle.

"They just don't understand," Lisa said to Pepper.

"Journalism is reporting facts. All I did was to report the facts. I didn't say *anything* that wasn't true. And besides that, Carole's just angry because she's found out that she doesn't have any money to buy her father a present."

Lisa gave the girth a final tug as if to emphasize her statement and the piece of leather snapped in her hand. This just wasn't her day. Now she'd have to go to Mrs. Reg and get another girth. Sure as anything this would make her late for class.

The hallway in the stable area was filled with her classmates and their horses on their way to the outdoor ring. She made her way carefully among them, noting that absolutely nobody spoke to her. How different it was from what she'd been expecting that day! She'd thought everybody was going to be happy for her and proud of her. She was expecting congratulations and hugs. All she was getting was cold shoulders. She was relieved to get to Mrs. Reg's office and the tack room.

"I need a new girth," she said. "Pepper's broke." She gave Mrs. Reg the broken strap.

Mrs. Reg examined it carefully. "I just wanted to make sure somebody didn't cut it," Mrs. Reg explained.

"Who would do something like that?" Lisa asked.

"Well, you never know in a hotbed of crime like this place . . ." Mrs. Reg left the thought dangling as she found a new girth and gave it to Lisa.

Lisa took the girth, thanked Mrs. Reg, and returned to Pepper's stall. Methodically, she began to replace the old girth with the new one. She could hear the class begin in the nearby outdoor ring.

Lisa sighed. Even Mrs. Reg was annoyed with her. And that just meant that even Mrs. Reg didn't understand the responsibility of the press. She'd read about reporters who had gone to jail to protect their own rights as journalists. This wasn't exactly the same thing, but it did seem to Lisa that, like some of the finest journalists in the world, she was suffering. But suffering to protect the right of freedom of the press seemed to her like a small price to pay.

She finished buckling one side of the new girth and was about to start the second when she heard her name, from the outdoor ring.

"Where's Lisa?" Max asked the class.

"I don't know, and I don't care," somebody answered.

The words were like a slap in the face. And they proved to her that she was right. They didn't understand. But they *would* understand. No matter how difficult it was, Lisa had to continue her work. She had to make the thief realize that she wasn't going to let up until the wallet was returned.

This was no time for class, Lisa decided. She was late already, and besides, there was more news for the world to know—more to report. Quickly, she removed the saddle and bridle from Pepper, returned the tack to the tack room, changed back into her street shoes, and began the walk home.

All the way home, she was writing her next article in her head. Her friends would see. She'd make them see.

7

"THESE ARE SUCH silly clothes!" Trudy exclaimed, looking at herself in the dingy mirror in Pine Hollow's locker area.

Stevie laughed out loud. Trudy was dressed to go riding. She wore an old pair of her jodhpurs, low boots, and a plain blue shirt. The outfit looked very normal to Carole, especially when compared with the outfit Trudy had worn walking into the stable!

"You think *those* are funny clothes?" Carole asked.

Trudy stepped back so she could see all of herself at once in the mirror. She squinted as she examined the total effect. "Yup," she said, nodding. "They're funny all right, but I don't mind. You guys are dressed funny, too, so I don't stand out."

Carole almost took Trudy seriously until she spotted the twinkle in her eye. The idea of Trudy's being afraid to stand out in a crowd was just plain crazy. All three girls started laughing at once.

Trudy was different from anybody Carole had ever met, and she liked her a lot. She was glad Trudy was visiting Stevie, and she was particularly glad that Stevie had finally convinced Trudy to try horseback riding.

"You're going to love this," Carole assured Trudy while she handed her the tack she would need for Patch. The girls had gotten Max's permission to take Trudy on a short trail ride through some neighboring fields and a wooded area. They were under strict orders not to go faster than a walk and not to show off.

Carole didn't have to be told these things. She knew that a new rider would be safe enough, especially on a calm horse like Patch. But a calm horse could become a dangerously frisky horse if the other riders on the trail were trying stunts.

"Is my horse really big?" Trudy asked, eyeing Patch's saddle warily.

"He's big enough," Carole answered evasively. "But don't worry, you're with us. We'll take care of you."

"Riding is great—just you wait," Stevie said. "It's the most fun thing we do. You're going to love it."

Stevie had expressed Carole's feelings exactly. Riding was the greatest thing in the world as far as she was concerned. The minute Trudy was in Patch's saddle, Carole was certain she was going to see how wonderful it was.

In fact, the only thing that came close to the fun of riding itself was sharing the experience with friends. And that was the only sour note of the day: Lisa wasn't with them.

Carole and Stevie had talked about it. They were both still a little annoyed with her for writing the article about Stevie's wallet and Carole's money, but they thought Lisa had had an awful time of it on Friday and must have learned her lesson, so they wanted to make up with her. Lisa had told Carole she was really much too busy to come riding on Monday, but said she'd be at class on Tuesday as usual. It wasn't like Lisa to pass up a chance to ride. Carole was about to try to convince her to change her mind when Lisa had told her she had to go. Before Carole could say another word, Lisa had hung up.

Carole didn't know whether she was more disappointed that Lisa hadn't wanted to listen to her or that Lisa was missing from their trail ride. She did know that she felt uncomfortable with the rift. The Saddle Club was used to being united. It just didn't feel right when something came between them.

Carole finished saddling Barq. She walked him to the stable exit, fastened his lead to a cleat by the door, and helped Stevie finish saddling Patch for Trudy.

Within a few minutes, Trudy was in the saddle. Her face now had an even more pained look than it had when she'd arrived at the stables.

"The horseshoe," Stevie said. "We have to show her that. It'll make her feel better."

Carole agreed. While Trudy clung to the English saddle's abbreviated pommel, her knuckles white with the effort, Carole led Patch to the stable's good-luck horseshoe. "Touch it," Carole said. "Just touch it with your right hand. It's one of our traditions. All riders touch that before they go for a ride. No rider at Pine Hollow has ever been seriously hurt."

"There's always a first time," Trudy said, reaching tentatively for the well-worn good-luck charm.

"But it won't be today," Carole said positively, smiling encouragement at Trudy.

"Don't make fun of me," Trudy said, returning her hand to clutch the saddle.

"I'm not and I won't," Carole assured her. "Stevie and I both rode for the first time once. We were scared, too." She handed Trudy the reins. Trudy grasped them so tightly that Patch thought she was signaling to step backward. Obediently, he did so, terrorizing Trudy even more.

Carole saw what was happening and got Trudy to ease up a bit. She realized as she was doing it that Trudy really had no idea at all what she was doing. Normally, a new rider would have some sense of how to hold the reins, how to balance, how to signal the horse to go and stop. Not Trudy. She seemed as uncomfortable riding a horse as Carole thought *she* would be living in a big city.

"I think he's ready to walk someplace," Trudy said, "so we'd better get going before he changes his mind."

Carole laughed to herself, but she wasn't laughing *at* Trudy. Carole had the feeling that what Trudy really meant was that they'd better get going before *Trudy* changed her mind. Considering how much Trudy was not enjoying her ride so far, Carole found herself really admiring Trudy. She was obviously scared, but she was still willing to go ahead, just because she'd said she would give it a try. Carole thought that showed a special kind of courage.

"Yes, let's go," Carole said. She mounted Barq and touched the good-luck horseshoe herself. Stevie, who had already mounted and touched the horseshoe, was in the lead.

Carole's job was to follow. The order on a trail ride was always carefully planned. An experienced rider led the pack. The newest riders were in the middle, and another experienced rider was at the back where she or he could most easily spot trouble with the new riders. Carole was comfortable with this role, and on several occasions she'd had a chance to help a rider who needed it. In spite of Trudy's fear, Carole was quite sure that the girl's basic common sense would keep her from getting into any trouble. Anybody who was as scared as Trudy was would do anything to stay safe!

The horses ambled across one of the fields behind the stable, aimed for the woods. All three horses knew the trail well. They walked easily. The steady pace seemed to put Trudy a little bit at ease. Carole kept her eyes on Trudy, but her thoughts wandered. She thought again about Lisa and concluded that there was nothing she could do until Lisa was ready to listen. She thought about the fifteen dollars and what she was going to do about her father's birthday. That was a more serious problem. Stevie had assured her dozens of times that she'd get the money for her. She seemed convinced that it was, in fact, her fault, and she wanted to make it up to Carole and to her father.

Carole wasn't sure about either of those things. She wasn't sure it was Stevie's fault, *and* she wasn't sure Stevie would be able to come up with the money in time for the birthday. That was troublesome, but she couldn't think of a solution.

A long time ago, Carole had learned that when there was no way to solve a problem, worrying about it wasn't going to help and might just hurt. As soon as she became aware that she was worrying pointlessly, she turned her mind from Lisa and the money.

It was a lovely day, though very hot as usual for a late-summer day in Virginia. The grass in the field was high and sweet-smelling, flecked with the blossoms of wildflowers here and there. Barq reached for a bite of juicy clover. Carole shortened the reins in time to keep him from all but the smallest taste of it. It wasn't a good idea to permit a horse to munch as you rode. Between-meal snacks weren't any better for horses than they were for people. She patted him on the neck as consolation for the tasty treat he'd just missed. In front of them, Patch swished his tail first to the right, then to the left, discouraging the hungry flies from biting him. Carole smiled contentedly. There wasn't anyplace in the world she would rather have been right then than on horseback, on a scenic trail, in the sunshine.

Trudy was doing fine. In fact, she was doing better than fine. Carole noticed that her arms and legs were now relaxed. She held the reins with one hand and gestured with the other as she talked to Stevie. They were discussing hairstyles, and considering Trudy's own hairstyle, it didn't surprise Carole that Trudy needed to use wild gestures to describe them!

"How do they make the spikes stand up?" Stevie asked Trudy.

Trudy was comfortable talking about punk hairstyles, and she eagerly explained the differences between gels and mousse. Being comfortable in her conversation made her comfortable on the horse. Carole didn't think that Stevie really cared about spiking her hair. But Stevie was smart. She was putting Trudy at ease to make her more comfortable on horseback.

As they chattered on about hairstyles and eye makeup, Stevie led them through the woods and into the creekbed that ran down the sloping hillside. On a hot day, it was refreshing for the horses to splash through the water. The riders could enjoy it, too.

"Let's stop for a minute," Carole suggested. "Flat Rock's right ahead."

"Oh, great idea," Stevie agreed. "You're going to love this, Trudy!"

There was a large rock by the side of the creek where they could sit, dangle their feet in the fresh water, and cool off before the ride back.

A few minutes later, they were all enjoying the rest.

"We've got a lot of things in the city," Trudy said. "But we don't have *any*thing like this!"

"You like it?" Stevie asked.

Trudy slapped a mosquito and brushed an ant off her arm. "Well, let's just say it's different."

Stevie and Carole laughed. So did Trudy.

"You can say that again!" Stevie said, recalling the trip The Saddle Club had made to New York recently. "When we were at the American Horse Show, we got to do a lot of neat things, but we never dangled our feet in a cool stream!"

Trudy smiled. "It's probably smart to avoid any water in New York that doesn't come out of a tap," she joked.

"I mean everything about this place is different," she continued. "In the city, we don't have grass in front of everybody's house. We don't even have houses—we have apartments. Nobody's got a pool and nobody rides horses, except on the merry-go-round. We don't hang out at malls like we did yesterday, and we don't go everywhere in cars like you guys do. We ride subways and buses, and we hang out at our friends' apartments. Like I said, it's *different.*"

"This is better, isn't it?" Stevie asked. She was excited to have a chance to show off Willow Creek and horseback riding to Trudy. She wanted Trudy to like them as much as she did.

"I'm having a good time, Stevie, I really am. But the city is home. I like the city. I even miss it a bit."

"Oh," Stevie said. She couldn't think of anything else to say. Trudy had surprised her. Stevie wouldn't have thought that anybody would prefer living in a city to living in the country and being able to ride.

"I think I know what you mean," Carole said. "As a Marine Corps brat, I've lived in a lot of different places. Each was different, but each was home, too. And home is nice, whatever it is. Right?"

"Something like that," Trudy agreed. "But I'll tell you one thing. Two weeks ago, I wouldn't have thought anybody could ever get me up on a horse. No way, nohow. Now that I've done it, I wonder why I was so scared. Horses are okay."

"Okay" wasn't the word either Stevie or Carole would have used, but considering where Trudy had started less than an hour ago, that sounded like a major endorsement of horseback riding. Carole and Stevie were satisfied with Trudy's progress.

"If we don't get you back on time, Max will send out a search party," Carole said, giving the cool water a final smack with her bare foot. Stevie glanced at her watch. It was definitely time to go. The three girls put their boots back on and had a nicely uneventful ride back to Pine Hollow.

As far as Stevie and Carole were concerned, the

only thing wrong with the whole ride was that Lisa hadn't been along to enjoy it with them.

WHILE HER FRIENDS were riding in the woods with Trudy, Lisa was very busy. She had a deadline to meet. As before, most of her article concerned the routine events at Pine Hollow. She wrote about the stable's newest horse, Topside, which Max had bought from one of his ex-students, champion Dorothy DeSoto, and about the class of youngest riders. They were working on mounting and dismounting by themselves from the mounting block. Then she got to the real news.

> *After last week's news about the theft at Pine Hollow was reported, many other incidents of apparent* theft have come to light to this reporter. At least one riding hat was stolen, as well as a pair of expensive riding gloves, a riding crop, and a set of keys. Since these thefts took place at different times, it is difficult to determine whether they were all done by the same thief or several. One thing is certain: Young riders at Pine Hollow must watch their personal property carefully!*

Lisa leaned back from her desk and reread the words she'd written. It was true. Every word of it. That was what journalists were supposed to do. They were supposed to write what was true.

She was a journalist.

8

STEVIE AND CAROLE talked to one another on the phone early on Friday—as soon as each of them had read Lisa's latest column.

"I can't believe it," Carole said. "It's worse than the last one!"

"She's going to be in *so* much trouble—and she's making trouble for everybody else. She makes Pine Hollow sound like a den of thieves!"

"We've got to talk some sense into her," said Carole.

"You can only talk to somebody who's listening," Stevie said. "And the last time I talked to her about her column, I can tell you, she wasn't listening."

"That must have been the time she said that you and I 'didn't understand the principles of journalism.'"

"Either then, or the time she was sure that anybody who criticized her was just jealous of her success."

67

Carole shook her head. "It's just not like Lisa to be so stubborn."

"You're right about that. There's just no talking to her at all."

"It doesn't mean we shouldn't try," Carole said.

Stevie agreed. It was clear that something had to be done, and it was going to be better if Lisa's friends did it. She and Carole discussed the best approach.

According to her mother's magazines, Stevie told Carole, this situation called for the careful use of *psychology*. Carole was ready to try it a few hours later when they all met at the stable.

LISA HOPED THAT her riding classmates would receive her second effort better than they had her first. She thought that by now they would be getting used to the idea that a reporter tried to right wrongs. And certainly riding clothes and wallets being stolen qualified as wrongs.

The first thing she saw when she approached Pine Hollow Friday morning was that Carole, Stevie, and Trudy were standing outside, apparently waiting for her. She smiled tentatively, hoping she'd find them glad to see her. They waved. Lisa breathed a sigh of relief.

"How did you like my new column?" she asked. She just couldn't wait to hear what they thought.

"Oh, it was just great!" Carole said.

"I loved the part about Topside," Stevie said.

Lisa had known Stevie would like that. Stevie loved Topside. She smiled, pleased with herself.

"And I liked reading about the youngest class here," Trudy said. "They already know more than I do!"

Lisa laughed. Then she realized that her friends weren't talking about the meaty part of her article. "And the things about the robberies?" she asked.

"Well," Carole began. "We think there's a little problem there—or at least *could* be."

Lisa didn't like the sound of this. "Just what does *that* mean?"

"It kind of sounds like you think there are a lot of things being stolen at Pine Hollow," Stevie said.

"But it's true!" Lisa defended herself.

"How do you know?" Trudy challenged her.

"Because people told me," Lisa said.

She was so disappointed. Here she was, talking with her very best friends—the ones she thought she could count on to be happy for her, to be proud of her—and all they wanted to do was to criticize her! They were just as jealous as all the other girls in the stable!

Stevie knew right away that they'd made a mistake. They'd agreed to tell Lisa what was good about her column before they tried to tell her what was wrong with it, but the wrong-with-it part wasn't going to sink in. All they'd managed to do was to hurt her feelings and make her defensive. The look on their friend's face told the whole story.

"Hey, Lisa," Stevie said, trying to change the subject smoothly. "Carole and I are going to work with Samson for a while before class. Want to help?"

"Right, I could use some help," Carole added.

"No thank you," Lisa said coolly. "I need to get ready for class, and besides, I've got to make some notes for my next column. I've got a deadline, you know."

The chill in her voice said everything her words didn't. Stevie knew that for then, at least, there was nothing else to say. She told Lisa they'd see her in class, and she and Carole and Trudy left to work with Samson. Stevie was eager to get out of Lisa's way. She didn't want to be on Lisa's mind when Lisa was working on her column!

As soon as they'd left, Lisa went to the locker area. She did want to make some notes, but she didn't want to do it with her friends butting in. She'd had enough advice for one day. Working in front of anybody else would just invite more.

She sat on the end of the bench in the locker area and reached down into the bottom of her backpack. She had brought something very special—a miniature tape recorder so she could just talk into it when she thought of something she wanted to include in her next column. She clicked the RECORD button and began talking.

"Trudy," she said. Then she clicked off the machine. She thought Trudy was interesting and she wanted to write about her. It was easy for people to make judgments about others based on how they looked. But it was clear there was more to Trudy than that. Just by saying her name onto the tape, Lisa was reminding herself to think about what she wanted to write.

At that moment, the subject of her thoughts returned to the locker area.

"Do you know where I can find a lead rope?" Trudy asked. "If Carole ever catches Samson," she explained with a grin, "she wants to try to lead him around. Personally, I think Samson is having too much fun playing tag to want to be led anywhere!"

"There's a hook on the wall over there," Lisa said, pointing into the tack room. "You can take any one of them. They're all the same."

"Thanks," Trudy said, and turned to follow Lisa's directions. She paused, then turned back to Lisa. "You working on another column?" she asked, obviously noticing the tape recorder.

"Yes, I am," Lisa said cautiously. "I use this to make notes to myself—reminders, really, of things I want to write about. It's the sort of thing we reporters do."

"I think what you're doing is very interesting," Trudy said.

"You do?" Lisa said, surprised. This was the first time anybody had expressed any interest in what she was doing. "Everybody else is just angry with me. Jealous, you know."

"No, I think it's interesting," Trudy said. "Nobody from my neighborhood could do that, you know."

"Really? You mean nobody there has the writing talent? I'm sure if they tried—maybe even you . . ."

Trudy shook her head, making her dangly white and purple earrings click and clatter. "That's not what I mean. I think it's a city-country thing."

That didn't sound right to Lisa and she told Trudy so. "But the greatest newspapers in the world are in big cities! Investigative reporting began in a big city. For me, this is just practice, until I get my shot at a *real* newspaper. How can you say this wouldn't happen in a city?"

"I guess I'm not saying this right," Trudy said. "You see, I don't think what you're doing could happen in my neighborhood. In the city, everybody lives very close to everybody else. Here, your neighbors are across a driveway and a garage, maybe a hedge or a flower patch or even a big lawn. Where I'm from, your neighbors are across the hall, maybe on the other side of a wall. You sneeze, they say 'Gesundheit.'"

Lisa grinned.

"We don't all like each other, but we get along by minding our own business most of the time. It's a way of adding space between people who are really crowded together. I get along with all my friends because if I see something somebody didn't want me to see, or if somebody tells me something, I *don't* tell. I guess because there's really no privacy, you've got to pretend by minding your own business. But out here, it seems, you've got the real space between you, and that makes it real different. You can go ahead and write about private things you only learned because you are somebody's friend. Things that they might not have said if they'd known you were going to write about it. I guess it's just different."

"Oh," Lisa said, disappointed to learn that Trudy apparently wanted to criticize her, too. She'd thought she was going to get genuine admiration from Trudy, but what she'd gotten was just another lecture from somebody else who didn't understand what real journalism was all about: to report the truth.

"Trudy! Did you get lost?" Stevie walked into the locker area.

"Oh, no," Trudy said. "I was just talking with Lisa. Sorry." Quickly, Trudy walked over to the hook where the lead ropes hung, selected one, and followed Stevie out the door toward the paddock. "See you, Lisa," Trudy said.

Lisa listened to the footsteps receding down the stable's hallway and sighed. They hadn't even invited her to join them. It seemed to be her fate to be misunderstood.

A horse was led past the door to the locker area. That reminded Lisa that before her own class started, Max was giving a private lesson to a beginner. He'd told her she could observe the class for her column. She liked the idea; it would be good for her readers to be able to compare the beginners' group class she'd written about this week with a beginner's private lesson. Quickly, she shoved her things back into her cubby, taking only a pad and pen with her. She would distract Max and the rider if she whispered into the recorder during the lesson.

Lisa thought it was a great idea to be getting back to work. It seemed that the longer she sat in the locker area, the greater risk she had of getting another lecture about how to write a column for the newspaper. Besides, the smell of paint was giving her a headache.

9

"Now the secret to looking cool is being able to coordinate really different things," Trudy explained to Stevie and Carole, boldly leading the way through the accessories department of My Way, a clothing store at the local mall.

Trudy picked up one oversize scarf after another, examined each quickly, and tossed each back into the bin. "Not right, maybe—ugh! No way . . ." she said.

Stevie held a blouse Trudy had already chosen. It was hot pink, buttoned down the back, and was sleeveless with a mock turtleneck. Stevie thought it was very stylish as it was. The scarf Trudy held had some of the same hot pink in it—in blotches. There were also blotches of about forty other colors.

"This is really too go-with-everything," Trudy said, dropping the latest candidate. "See, what I have in

75

mind is to wear this blouse with my camouflage pants. The scarf I buy will have to bring the two pieces together."

"About the only thing that can bring this blouse together with a pair of camouflage pants is a can of paint," Stevie said, thinking out loud.

Trudy's eyes flashed with amusement. "Just you wait and see," she said. "You'll love it."

"You're not going to make me wear this outfit when you put it together, are you?" Stevie asked.

"I won't have to make you wear it," Trudy said. "You'll beg me to borrow it!"

"For the Mardi Gras costume party?" Carole teased.

Trudy laughed. "You'll see," she repeated, then went back to her furious search.

Stevie watched, fascinated. She couldn't remember when she'd had more fun at the mall or looking for clothes than she and Carole were having that afternoon with Trudy. She and Carole and Lisa had visited the mall many times, but it seemed that they always visited the same stores and looked at the same things—or at least the same kinds of things. Going to the mall with Trudy meant seeing things she'd never seen before. It would never have occurred to her to buy a pair of camouflage pants. She hadn't even known where they were sold. She did now. She'd also learned where she could buy sandals with straps that wrapped all the way up her legs to above her knees.

She hadn't bought any of these things, of course, but Trudy had. And Trudy just loved them.

There was a more serious side to Trudy, too, though. As soon as she'd seen the card table at the mall entrance where the library's raffle tickets were being sold, she'd insisted on buying a whole book of them. She didn't care about the prizes; she just wanted to be helpful. Carole and Stevie were both happy she wanted to give money to their town library.

Stevie glanced over to where Trudy was dancing around the scarf bin, humming to herself, and grinned. Sometimes it could be boring going shopping with somebody and not buying anything for herself, but being with Trudy was such an experience that Stevie didn't mind at all. Being with Trudy meant shopping for things she'd never buy—but it was fun! It was obvious that Carole felt exactly the same way she did. She, too, was watching Trudy's quest with rapt fascination.

"I think I like having a sister," Stevie confided to Carole. "Trudy's a lot more fun than all three of my brothers put together."

"That's not much of a contest," Carole remarked. "I don't think I remember you ever saying a thing about your brothers being any fun at all."

"They aren't."

Trudy pulled a scarf out of the box. It was actually olive green and hot pink.

"Yeah!" she announced to everybody within ear-shot. "Now I've just got to try it on!" Stevie was carry-ing the bag with the camouflage pants in it. Trudy grabbed it from her hand, took the pink blouse as well, and ran off to find a dressing room.

"You know, she reminds me of Samson," Stevie re-marked, watching Trudy wind through the shop in search of a dressing room.

"Sort of like a kid, you mean?" Carole asked.

"Yeah, I guess," Stevie said. "You know—if you let Samson do what he wants, he's just so funny! Trudy's the same way. She's always up to something."

"Yeah, I know exactly what you mean. Samson's just crazy . . . Hey, wait a minute!" Carole said, regarding Stevie carefully. "What did you mean when you said the thing about letting Samson do what he wants?"

Stevie shrugged. "Every time he does something, it's like another game. He really loves them. I started to teach him things like peekaboo and tag, but it was like he already knew them. He's a riot—just like Trudy." Stevie looked at Carole and saw the very odd look on her face. "Well, not exactly like Trudy," she said. "But you know, fun loving."

"You mean, you *taught* him those games?" Carole asked, suddenly beginning to understand what might have been going on.

"I hardly had to teach him," Stevie said. "He's a natural. I was going to put the halter on him, see, and we just got to playing . . ."

"But Stevie, you couldn't do that!" Carole exclaimed.

"Sure I could. It was *easy!*" Stevie said.

"Of course it was easy," Carole said, taking a deep breath to calm herself. "You wanted to play, he wanted to play. The trouble is that you went in there with a halter and instead of working with him, you let him play. Now every time somebody goes in with a halter, all he wants to do is to play."

"And he's so cute!" Stevie said.

Carole realized that Stevie still didn't understand what had happened.

"Sure he's cute, but he's got a job to do. When you're teaching a horse something, you have to stick to the work or else he'll get the idea that playing is okay. Horses forget what they learn very quickly unless you keep reminding them, just like little kids."

"You mean I shouldn't have played with him?"

"Not with a halter in your hand—especially not with one that he hadn't already put on. It's like you rewarded him for misbehaving. It's not that he's ruined for life or anything, but it means we have to begin at the beginning again and make him unlearn all the games just like he unlearned his manners."

"Aw, come on, Carole. Are you trying to tell me that I can't play games with Samson?" Stevie put her hands on her hips and glared at Carole. "He's not just your horse, you know."

Carole returned the glare. "Games should be a reward for work *well* done, not a reward for work *un-done!*"

"You're making a federal case out of this," Stevie said.

Carole could tell Stevie was getting angry. She didn't care. *She* was angry with Stevie for being so thoughtless about working with the foal. "I'm not making a federal case," Carole retorted. "I'm just telling you the facts. You didn't want to work with Samson at all. You just wanted to play with him."

"Yeah, and you're just jealous of all the fun I had. *That's* what's going on!"

"Jealous? Who's jealous?" Trudy asked, walking up to where Carole and Stevie were standing facing one another angrily. "Are you talking about Lisa? Because although I don't know her really well, I think she's okay and something's going to make her see that what she's doing isn't cool."

"We're not talking about Lisa," Stevie said, still looking straight at Carole. "We're talking about Carole. See, she's telling me that what I did, playing games with Samson, was bad to do, and I think she's just jealous because I had so much fun! What do *you* think?"

Both Carole and Stevie looked at Trudy and for the first time, noticed that she was wearing her new outfit.

"*I* think this scarf was exactly what I needed," Trudy said, pirouetting so they could admire the effect.

Both were surprised. Trudy was wearing the camouflage pants and the hot-pink blouse. She also had the scarf on, but was wearing it as a belt. The outfit was as flamboyant as anything either had ever seen, but on Trudy, it worked. "Now . . . if I can get some hair color to highlight the hot pink. Then . . . ooh, I think I remember seeing some earrings made of empty shell casings. I think they're in the shop we passed when we first came into the mall. What do you think for shoes?"

"Flats," Stevie suggested.

Trudy nodded. "Either that or combat boots."

Carole couldn't control it anymore. She started laughing. So did Stevie. Trudy laughed, too. When they'd all recovered, Trudy returned to the dressing room and changed back into her own clothes. Then Carole led the way to the check-out counter so Trudy could pay for her new outfit.

"I don't know how you do it," Stevie said as they waited in line, aware of the stares of other shoppers who noticed Trudy—what she was wearing and what she was buying to wear. "That's the weirdest outfit I ever saw, but on you, it's almost cute. How did you learn to dress like that?"

"My mother taught me," Trudy said.

"I can't believe that," said Stevie. "I've met your mother, remember? I saw her at my mother's office last year. Your mother is the most normal dresser I ever saw. I think she was wearing a pinstripe suit when I saw her. And maybe one of those little bow-tie things."

Trudy plunked her clothes on the counter and fished her wallet out of the mini–duffel bag that served as her pocketbook. "That's what I mean. See, my mother would *like* me to dress just like Lisa—everything matched and tailored. But one day, while she was picking out some plaid skirts and pastel blouses, I went into the Surplus Shop and found this really neat coverall outfit. I spent my money on that instead of the skirt and blouse she was choosing for me. One taste of punk and I knew I'd found my style. If my mother hadn't let me buy my own clothes, I might never have known."

The salesclerk began adding up Trudy's purchases. Stevie turned to Carole. "I think there's a lesson there," she said, grinning.

Carole cocked her head. "What do you mean?"

Stevie continued her thought. "Well, if I let Samson choose what he wants to do instead of making him do what I know he has to do . . ."

Carole nodded, hoping her point had finally gotten through to Stevie.

". . . Samson will end up dying his mane olive and hot pink, and wearing a camouflage saddle."

"Right, and all the other horses will be jealous," Carole added before bursting into laughter.

Trudy took her change and picked up her bag. "Come on," she said. "I remember where I saw the shell-casing earrings. While we walk over there, you tell me what's so funny."

"Only if you'll tell us how to make spikes in a horse's mane," Stevie said, following her happily.

Carole walked between the two of them, slinging her arms across her friends' shoulders. "What about horseshoe earrings for Samson?" she asked.

THIS TIME, LISA was sure everybody would be happy. There was a special spring in her step as she walked toward the stable the next Friday. She hadn't said a word in her column about anything's being taken from anybody. She hadn't said anything that could possibly point a finger at anybody in the stable. She'd included the usual things Mr. Teller made her include about who had learned proper reining techniques in the beginner class and who had jumped for the first time. And then she'd gotten to the good stuff.

She'd devoted all the rest of her column to Trudy. Trudy, she thought, was a very interesting person, and she wanted everybody else to know it, too. She'd written about how she dressed in such a unique manner, of course, but there was more than that to Trudy, and she'd covered that in her column. She'd written about how great it was to have Trudy visit Willow Creek and how much fun the riders were having with her there. She'd written about how Trudy was adjusting to the country and how different it was, just the way Trudy had told her when they'd been in the locker area. In spite of the fact that Trudy had sort of butted her nose in, Lisa liked Trudy, and this column was her way of introducing Trudy to everybody who might not have a chance to meet her during her short stay in Willow Creek.

This time, Lisa was sure, everybody was going to be happy with what she'd written. She was already planning her next column, too. She had the idea of writing an article comparing adult classes with her group's classes, and she needed to ask Mrs. Reg about it. So, instead of going right into the locker area, she veered off at Mrs. Reg's office first.

Mrs. Reg's office had two doors—one from the stable's hallway and one that opened into the tack room. The far end of the tack room was the locker area. Usually, Mrs. Reg could be found in her office or the tack room, but there was no sign of her right then. Lisa only had about fifteen minutes until class started so she couldn't go on a big hunt for Mrs. Reg. Hurriedly, she scribbled a note, asking Mrs. Reg when she could observe one of Max's adult classes, then headed for the locker area.

Something stopped her, however, before she left Mrs. Reg's office. That something was the sound of her own name on Veronica diAngelo's lips.

"Lisa's done it again, you guys—only this time, I think she's right on target!"

"Oh, shut up, Veronica!" came the familiar sound of Stevie's voice.

"Listen to this," Veronica said. From where Lisa stood in the shadows inside Mrs. Reg's office, Lisa could see Veronica. She'd just climbed up onto one of the freshly painted narrow benches in front of the cubbies. She held a piece of paper in her hand. Lisa recognized it as a newspaper clipping, and from the ad on the back, she realized it was a copy of her article. Veronica diAngelo was going to read Hoof Beat out loud.

Something was wrong. Of all the people who would want to meet Trudy, the last in the world was Veronica. Veronica was a snob and she didn't want to meet anybody who wasn't in her own class—social class, that was. Trudy was neat, but Veronica would never consider her good enough. Could it be that Lisa had descibed her so well that Veronica was interested? It didn't seem likely.

"'There's a new face at the stable these days—a *very* different face!'" Veronica read Lisa's words. The girls in Veronica's group laughed. The way Veronica said it made it sound like an insult. That wasn't what Lisa had written; at least it wasn't what she'd meant to write. "'By chance and good fortune, Trudy Sanders has come to visit. She is staying with the Lake family.'" Veronica looked up from the paper to her listeners. "Whose good fortune?" she asked. The girls laughed again.

"Veronica, stop it!" Stevie said. "You're making fun of Trudy."

"I am not," Veronica said. "I'm just reading a newspaper article, straight out of *The Willow Creek Gazette*. Finally Lisa is writing something I can believe in!"

"Don't be such a jerk," Stevie said, standing up. "Trudy's in Topside's stall, right across the hall, currying him until she can come watch our class." Lisa realized then that Trudy was so close she had to be able to hear every word. It made Lisa feel awful.

"But she's your friend, isn't she?" Veronica taunted. "Some friend."

Stevie was one of the most loyal people Lisa knew. Of course she would stand up for Trudy, no matter how bad Veronica made her sound.

"Yes, Lisa is my friend," Stevie said. "And she's a great friend, too. She's trying hard to do something important, and even though she's making some mistakes . . ."

Stevie went on, but Lisa didn't hear her words because her meaning was sinking in. Stevie wasn't defending *Trudy*. Veronica had been mocking her, *Lisa*.

Even after Stevie had finished and stormed out to tack up Comanche for class, Lisa was still frozen in place, hiding in the shadows of Mrs. Reg's office. She heard the rest of Veronica's presentation, too. Veronica continued to read Lisa's article, but now the words didn't sound like hers and the message certainly wasn't the one she wanted to convey. Instead of describing the Trudy she knew and really liked, she listened to words that seemed to insult Trudy, as if she weren't really as good as the girls of Willow Creek. Some of it was the way Veronica read, but a lot of the problem came directly from the words Lisa had written.

"'For Trudy, this visit to Willow Creek is an escape from the dingy city, where neighbors crowd upon one another . . .'"

Lisa realized with a start that that made it sound as if Trudy lived in a rat-infested slum, but that wasn't the case at all. Lisa felt a blush of shame rise. Could she really have written those words?

"'And of course, the most noteworthy aspect of Trudy Sanders is her unique wardrobe! Bright colors mix freely—even within her unusual hairdos! And when she matches her orange hair with some orange eyeshadow—look out!'"

Veronica and her friends laughed hysterically. Lisa didn't know whether they were laughing harder at her or at Trudy, and she didn't care. She'd made Trudy seem like a freak, not like the nice girl she was. How could she have done that to Trudy—and how could she have done that to herself? She felt she deserved all the mocking laughter Veronica and her pals could hand out, but it wasn't fair for them to laugh at Trudy for what Lisa had done.

"Isn't it wonderful?" Veronica asked her friends when she'd finished reading the column. "I'm so glad Lisa is writing this column now. At first, I wasn't sure, but this—*this*"—she started laughing and waved the column in the air—"makes all the trouble of the last few weeks worthwhile. Maybe next week she'll do a job on one of her other friends—if she has any left!"

Lisa could tell Veronica was just warming up to her subject and had lots more to say when she was interrupted by the public address system. Max announced that class would begin in five minutes. The girls hurried to collect their tack and go saddle their horses.

Lisa remained in Mrs. Reg's office, hiding in the shadows, unable to move. Thoughts raced through her mind, the words that Veronica had read echoing again and again. Everything that had sounded so cute and funny when she'd written it had come out sounding cruel and heartless as Veronica read it. True, Veronica could make a Valentine sound like a death threat, but the words were Lisa's. She'd written everything Veronica had read, and although she hadn't meant to at all, she'd made Trudy sound awful. Poor Trudy.

"Lisa, is that you?" Mrs. Reg's soft voice broke into her thoughts. "Are you crying, dear?"

Lisa brushed her cheek with her hand and was surprised to find it streaked with tears. She hadn't realized. She knew that they were tears of anger, tears of humiliation, tears of sadness, but mostly, they were tears for Trudy. She must have hurt Trudy very much and that was exactly the opposite of what she'd meant to do.

Then she could see what Trudy had been telling her. Friends don't treat one another the way she'd been treating her friends. They don't take things said in private and make them public the way she'd done with Trudy; they don't use others' personal problems for their own personal use, the way she'd done with the loss of Stevie's wallet. That wasn't what friendship was about; it also wasn't what journalism was about. She wasn't being a journalist, she was just being a gossip.

Mrs. Reg slipped her arm across Lisa's shoulder to comfort her. Lisa had the feeling Mrs. Reg knew exactly what had happened. Mrs. Reg always seemed to know.

"Oh," Lisa said, turning to the older woman, "Mrs. Reg, I've done the most awful thing!"

Mrs. Reg hugged her and then Lisa's tears came pouring out. On top of everything else, she didn't feel as if she deserved Mrs. Reg's comfort. That made her cry even harder.

"I've hurt so many people's feelings," she said. "I hurt Stevie and Carole and Anna, Betsy, and Polly—even Veronica—and now worst of all, I hurt Trudy's. I didn't mean to do it, but I did it. Everything I wrote was worse than the last thing I'd done. I'm just so awful!" She wanted to say more, but she was crying too hard.

Mrs. Reg reached for a tissue from the top of her desk and gave it to Lisa. Then a second and a third. She waited, quietly, until finally the last tear had dropped.

"Done?" Mrs. Reg asked.

Lisa nodded. "Definitely! I'm done writing, I'm done with my friends, I guess I'm even done riding."

"Hold on now," Mrs. Reg said. "Just because you've made a whole bunch of mistakes doesn't mean it's time to make a whole bunch more." Mrs. Reg led Lisa to the tack room bench where they both sat down. "I remember a rider we had here once," she began.

Mrs. Reg was famous for her memory of past horses and riders. It seemed to The Saddle Club that whenever there was a problem, Mrs. Reg had a story to tell. Lisa and her friends had learned long ago that her stories were usually worth listening to.

"This rider started riding here when she was about your age, but she'd already been riding for years. Max knew right away that she had talent, but she also had problems. Lots of them. See, not only had she been riding for years, but she'd been riding wrong for years. She wanted to be a championship rider and Max thought she could be among the best. That was the only place they agreed. See, she'd gotten the idea that her job, as a rider, was to control the horse. From the minute she'd get into the saddle until she got out, she held that poor animal in check, tugging on the reins, squeezing him with her legs, hitting him with the whip. He'd usually do what she wanted because he knew she was the boss."

"Isn't the rider supposed to be the boss?" Lisa asked.

"Yes and no," Mrs. Reg said. "The rider certainly needs to establish who's in charge, but once that's clear, the object should be to work together. If the rider spends all the time controlling, then there's no time to cooperate. It works and there's no question that you can ride that way, but it's no way to be a champion."

"I bet Max didn't like her being so mean to his horses," Lisa said. "Did he refuse to let her ride here?"

"Oh, no," Mrs. Reg said. "He knew she was going to be a good rider and he wanted to work with her, so he started her from the beginning. First, he had her work with all the horses on a lead rope, then a lunge line. That gave them more freedom and let her learn what they could do without her legs and whip. Also, he had her give them carrots every time they did something right for her."

"Was that sort of an apology to the horses?" Lisa asked.

"Exactly," Mrs. Reg said. "When she'd made friends with the horses, she actually began liking them and trusting them. So he started her in a beginner's class and taught her from scratch."

"Oh, she must have been so bored!" Lisa said.

"Not at all," Mrs. Reg said. "See, you're only bored when you're studying things you already know. She *was* a beginner. Almost nothing she'd done before was going to be of any use to her. She had to work very hard."

Mrs. Reg stood up as if to dismiss Lisa. As usual, her story was ending before her listener was ready for the end. Lisa stood up, too.

"So what happened then?"

Mrs. Reg looked at her as if she were a little surprised that Lisa didn't already know the answer. "Why, she became a champion, of course. Now, if you see Red, tell him I need him. He's just got to get on with the painting. Can you believe the smell? I can't stand it. I'm sure the horses can't either. And I also have to call the grain and feed man . . ." Mrs. Reg strode into her office and picked up the phone. Lisa was left alone with her thoughts.

Since Mrs. Reg's stories were usually lessons in disguise, Lisa's next step was to figure out just what the lesson was. Obviously, she had to learn something about journalism from the very beginning. She was a long way from being ready for a job as an investigative reporter. But first, what did the lead rope and the lunge line and the carrots have to do with journalism?

Then she understood. Just as the championship rider had to apologize to the horses she'd hurt before she could begin again, she, Lisa, had to apologize to the people she'd hurt before she could learn anything about writing. She had hurt a lot of people, she knew, but the one she'd hurt most had been Trudy. That was the place to start.

It was too late for her to join the class now, and besides, Lisa didn't want to face any of her classmates just yet. The most important thing was to find Trudy and talk to her.

Lisa shoved her things into her cubby and headed for the outdoor ring where the class was taking place. Trudy liked to sit on the fence and observe, but Lisa could see from inside the stable that Trudy wasn't there. She checked Samson and Delilah's paddock. No sign of her. She looked in the feed room, Max's office, the stalls, and the tack room. Trudy was nowhere to be found.

"Trudy?" Red said when Lisa asked. "I think she's having a private lesson. She asked me to show her how to tack up Topside."

"Trudy?" one of the painters said when Lisa stopped him. "The one with the colored hair? I saw her riding by herself out toward the trails."

By herself? Trudy didn't have anywhere near enough experience to ride by herself. What could she have been thinking of? Lisa wondered.

Then Lisa knew: Trudy was running away, the only way she could think of—on horseback.

Lisa guessed that Trudy had waited until the class was in progress before taking Topside out of the stable. Everybody would be too busy then to notice.

Lisa knew that Trudy could be in real danger out there by herself. An inexperienced rider had no business on the trails alone. Even on a gentle horse Trudy could be in real trouble. Topside wasn't a gentle horse. He was a champion show horse—spirited and determined. Trudy Sanders was no match for him.

Lisa knew that she could ask Max for help, or Mrs. Reg or Red or any other rider. She also knew that she was the reason Trudy was gone, and she would be the reason Trudy would come back.

LISA HAD NEVER saddled her horse faster than she did that day. Pepper seemed to understand that this was no day to play games. He stood completely still and even lowered his head so she could put the bridle on. She patted him in thanks, remembering Mrs. Reg's story.

Lisa led her horse to the stable exit out of sight of the outdoor ring and mounted him. She didn't want her classmates or Max to see that she was going out by herself. Obviously Trudy must have done the same thing. That meant that she had at least started out on one of the trails that began at the back of the stable. Lisa began to consider the options before she realized she had forgotten something very important. She had forgotten the good-luck horseshoe.

She turned Pepper back toward the stable, walked

him up to the doorway, and brushed the horseshoe with her hand. Then she was ready to begin her quest.

But which trail? Sitting tall on Pepper's back, she surveyed the possibilities. All of the Pine Hollow students knew the trails because they'd ridden them time and time again. There were four starting at the back of the stable that Trudy might have taken. First was Lisa's favorite, the mountain trail, which led into the woods and up the mountain. Then, the forest trail. It headed straight for the mountain and wound through the woods. The creek trail started out on a hill and followed the creek that gave Willow Creek its name. Finally, there was the field trail. It snaked through nearby fields, running into the woods parallel to the river that Willow Creek became. Beyond it was the highway. Until it got into the woods, it wasn't a very pretty trail—certainly Lisa's least favorite.

Lisa decided on the mountain trail and signaled Pepper to head to the left when something occurred to her. Trudy was a city girl. She *liked* concrete, especially the kind that could be found on the highway. If she was actually running away, she'd know that the highway could lead her home.

There were two problems with that. The first was that the river was deep, wide, and dangerous at the point where the trail reached it. The other was that it was right next to the highway where trucks honked, cars backfired, and sirens sometimes wailed. Topside was a champion, but he was also skittish. Highway noises could frighten Topside and Trudy wasn't experienced enough to control him. Lisa realized she didn't have a minute to spare.

She turned Pepper toward the field trail. "Come on, boy," she said. "We've got a job to do!"

Pepper seemed to understand her. His ears perked up alertly. He tensed, ready for her next instruction. She nudged him in the belly and shifted her weight forward in the saddle. Pepper broke into a fast walk, and when he was warmed up, Lisa got him to trot and then canter. It was the best chance for Lisa to catch up with Trudy before she got into trouble. Unless Topside got out of control, Trudy was too inexperienced to do more than walk him.

The grass in the fields had been cut for the harvest so Lisa could see clearly around her. She kept a sharp eye for anything suspicious in the grass and was relieved when there was nothing to see.

If she'd been able to travel straight to the creek, it would have been only about a mile, about a ten-minute ride. But the hilly fields made it impossible to go straight and she had to follow the trail. It took her more than forty-five minutes to reach the final hillock. When she crested it, she found Trudy.

Her first instinct was to laugh at the sight, a hundred yards away down the hill on the edge of the river. There stood the city girl, sopping wet and hopping mad. Her usually stand-up hairdo hung limply on her neck. The pinkish dye she'd sprayed on that morning had seeped onto her yellow shirt. But the funny part of the scene was the fact that Trudy was standing almost toe-to-toe with Topside, hands on her hips, and her chin jutted out in the most determinedly stubborn look Lisa had ever seen as she concentrated on her battle of wits with the horse. Topside wasn't budging. He returned her glare with a bored stare. As Lisa watched, Trudy made what looked like an attempt at delivering the last word and walked around to the horse's left side, picking up the reins. She was ready to mount. She was following all the instructions Carole and Stevie had apparently given her because she was making a good start. But as soon as she lifted her left foot to put it in the stirrup, Topside took two steps to the right, leaving Trudy unbalanced with her foot in the air. She fell down.

Lisa giggled. Then she realized it wasn't really a funny scene, certainly not to Trudy, who had experienced enough unhappiness for one day. Trudy must have attempted to cross the river and Topside had thrown her. The horse understood that the minute Trudy got back on him, she was going to try again. He didn't want to cross the river. The easiest way for him was to not let her mount.

There was no telling how long the standoff could have gone on. Lisa noticed that the whole time, Topside's ears were twitching alertly, aware of the noises of the highway. One honk and he'd take off. The risks were too great that he'd hurt Trudy when he did it.

Lisa gave Pepper a signal to continue. The hill was steep and he had to go slowly, step by step. The delay worried Lisa. She had the feeling that Trudy needed her help a lot more than Trudy realized.

As Lisa watched with concern, Trudy once more took the reins. This time, however, instead of moving slowly toward the championship horse, she dashed up to the horse's left side and sprang upward, clinging to his saddle for all she was worth. Topside took off at a trot. Trudy held on, somehow managing to get into the saddle. She even got one foot into his stirrups.

"Hold on!" Lisa cried, now close enough to be heard. "You're doing great!"

Trudy glanced at her. Her surprise was apparent, but her fear—and anger—was even more obvious.

"Leave me alone!" Trudy yelled back at her. "You've done enough harm already! Go away!"

In her agitation, Trudy yanked at Topside's reins. The motion was sudden and firm and gave a clear message to the horse. Topside halted immediately.

Lisa sighed with relief.

A passing eighteen-wheel truck blasted its horn and Topside took off at full speed.

Trudy was jostled so badly that the one foot that was in a stirrup slipped through it. Now she had lost any chance to use her feet for balance, and Lisa knew that she was at a very definite risk of being thrown by Topside. If that happened when her foot was sticking all the way through the stirrup, she could be dragged along by the horse.

There wasn't a second to lose! Once again, Pepper understood her urgency.

"Grab his mane, hold on!" Lisa cried, knowing that if she held the mane tight, Trudy had a chance of keeping her balance. Topside swerved to the right, Trudy lurched to the left, her left foot dangling treacherously through the stirrup.

Pepper galloped along the hillside, parallel to the runaway horse, but well above him. There was no way Pepper could gallop *down* the hill. It was an extremely dangerous thing for a horse to do. Lisa just had to stay as close as possible until the hill flattened out in another hundred yards.

"I can't control him!" Trudy yelled.

"Don't worry, I'll be there as fast as I can. Just hold on!" Lisa yelled.

She tried to sound confident. She didn't feel it at all. She just hoped that Trudy didn't realize what a dangerous situation she was in. The last thing Trudy needed was to get more panicky than she was.

Lisa felt as if it were almost a dream, as if she were watching the action from very far away. She was aware of the horses, racing along the riverbank. She felt the power of the horse beneath her, she heard the thunderous clamor of hoofbeats, but the only thing she saw, really saw, was Trudy's foot dangling through Topside's stirrup. It drove her as she had never known she could be driven. Slowly, achingly slowly, she got Pepper to move downhill, closer to Topside, closer to the dangling foot. "Hold on," she whispered in her horse's ear. "Hold on. Don't let go of the mane. Don't fall. I'll get there. Please be okay . . ."

Pepper didn't understand the words, but certainly he knew the urgency in Lisa's commands. He lengthened his stride and moved farther down the hill, nearing the runaway champion.

Even as Lisa and Pepper caught up to the horse and pulled in front of it, even as Lisa reached for the reins, which flapped wildly around the horse's neck, the only thing Lisa could see in her mind's eye was Trudy's foot dangling dangerously through the stirrup.

Lisa reached down and grabbed Topside's reins with her right hand, holding her own in her left. As soon as Topside felt the first pressure from his reins, he slowed.

"Whoa there, boy," Lisa said in a low voice. His ears flicked toward her. "Ho up, there now," she told him. He came to an abrupt halt.

The stop was so abrupt that Trudy lost whatever semblance of balance she still had and nearly fell out of the saddle. Her grip on the horse's mane saved her.

"Is it over?" she asked in a shaky voice.

"It's over," Lisa told her. She took a deep breath, trying to be matter-of-fact. "Now get your feet in the stirrups, hold on to the reins, and let's get back to the stable."

"Do I have to ride?" Trudy asked. "Can I walk?"

"Did you ever hear the one about getting right back on the horse?" Lisa responded.

"Sure, but I never fell off." Trudy grinned impishly. "And besides that, I don't have to prove anything to myself. I know already that riding's not for me."

Lisa smiled. "You did fine, Trudy, you really did. An awful lot of riders wouldn't have handled that anywhere near as well as you did."

"I did?"

"Yeah, you did. Now let's go back. We can talk as we ride. I have some things to say to you."

Trudy took the horse's reins, adjusted her feet in the stirrups, and gave Topside a little nudge to get him going. He looked around at her, then obediently he followed her instructions.

"He's a little ashamed of himself," Lisa explained. "He knows he was naughty. He probably even knows he put you in danger. He'll be good now. He's trying to say he's sorry." She paused. "I wish I could do it as easily because I owe you as much of an apology as Topside does."

Trudy didn't say anything then and Lisa was glad. She had a lot to say, and although she wasn't sure exactly how to proceed, she knew the words would come to her. She just hoped she'd be able to say what she wanted better than she'd been able to write it.

"I think I owe you at least two apologies. First of all, when you said all those things to me about neighbors and friends, I didn't understand what you were really saying. Now that I've hurt you by making my second mistake, I do understand it. Gossip isn't news. Just because somebody *says* something doesn't mean somebody should print it. I made a lot of people unhappy with those articles about the thefts. I really messed up, I know. I had no right to use my friends just to get a good angle for a newspaper story."

Trudy still didn't say anything, but she was listening and that was all Lisa could really ask for.

"That's the first part of the apology. The second is more complicated. I know you heard Veronica reading the stupid story I wrote about you. I couldn't believe how insulting it sounded when I heard her read it. I didn't mean it that way! I really didn't. What I wanted people to know is that you're a neat person. You're not like anybody I've ever known before—and that's okay, but I guess that wasn't what I wrote because when Veronica read it out loud, it sounded awful. I'm sorry. I'm really sorry. I don't know what I can do to make it up to you."

"There's only one thing," Trudy said. "Only one way you can make it up to me."

"Yeah, what is it? I'll do it," Lisa promised.

"You did it already. You saved my life."

Trudy put her hand up for a high five. Lisa gratefully clapped her hand against Trudy's.

"Friends?" Lisa asked.

"Sure," Trudy agreed. "Unless being your friend means I have to ride horses."

Obviously, her recent experience had not made Trudy horse crazy.

"I think being friends means letting each other be themselves. I won't try to make you into a preppy country girl who rides if you won't make me into a funky punky city slicker."

"No way," Trudy said. "Day-Glo orange isn't your color!"

Lisa laughed. It was the first time she'd laughed in a while. It felt very good.

12

"DO MY EYES deceive me?" Stevie asked Carole. The two of them were standing in Samson's paddock. They were trying not to move because they didn't want to encourage the colt to run.

"Stay still," Carole said.

"I can't," said Stevie. "If you'll turn very slowly, you'll see Trudy and Lisa riding in from the field trail together. It looks a lot like they're laughing together, like they're having fun together."

"You mean, like they're speaking to one another?" Carole asked.

"See for yourself."

Carole turned slowly. It was just as Stevie had said. "I don't believe it!"

Samson stepped toward Carole. She stood motionless except to open her hand enough for Samson to spot the sweet baby carrot she held in her hand. He sniffed tentatively and stepped closer, much more interested in the carrot than in the halter and lead rope that hung across her wrist. She patted him with her other hand. He stood still, waiting. She offered him the halter. He sniffed that curiously. She broke the carrot in two and gave him half. As he munched, she put the halter on him. He barely seemed to notice. This was his first carrot, and to Samson, that was much more interesting than the halter. Carole gave him the second half of the carrot. He lipped it up eagerly.

Samson was so busy with his newest experience that he simply forgot to notice the halter. He swallowed the final taste and looked at Carole for some more. She patted him.

"More carrot?" Stevie asked.

"No," Carole said. "This is a one-carrot lesson. See, we want him to learn about the halter more than about the carrots. Give the other carrot to Delilah."

Stevie offered it to the mare, who chomped on it noisily. Samson stayed near Carole. She suspected that his motive had more to do with carrots than trust, but she knew that trust would come in time.

Samson then realized he had a halter on. He shook his head. It didn't budge. He shook again.

"I'm going to leave it on a little longer this time," Carole said to Stevie. "I'd like it to stay on long enough for him to know for sure that it won't come off and it doesn't hurt. If we take it off too fast, he may conclude that it comes off when he shakes his head."

Carole slowly stepped over to the fence where Delilah's lead was fastened and where Stevie sat. She climbed up on the slatted boards and sat atop the fence next to Stevie. They watched the foal.

Samson continued shaking his head. He didn't seem angry or frightened, just curious and perhaps a little annoyed. When the halter didn't come off with shaking, he tried trotting around the paddock. That didn't work either. He nodded his head vigorously. Then he pranced around some more and came to the fence near Carole. There, he tried scraping it off his head by rubbing against the fence. Of course, that didn't work either.

Stevie smiled, watching him. "He's very funny, you know," she whispered to her friend.

"Yeah, I know," Carole whispered back, smiling at his antics. They didn't want to make loud sounds and startle the colt. "And I think I'm in love."

"I think he may be a little too young for you, Carole," Stevie quipped.

Samson was now staring at Carole, as if he realized for the first time that she was the one who had placed this mysterious thing on him. And that she was the one who could take it off. Carole didn't move.

"Isn't it time?" Stevie asked.

"Give it a minute more," Carole said, relaxing on the fence top. "I have a hunch it's time for lunch."

Delilah shifted her weight. The movement caught Samson's attention. He looked at his mother, then he looked at her udder. He hesitated a second, shaking his head one more time, but hunger overcame annoyance. He stepped forward, lowered his head, and began to nurse.

"Wonderful!" Carole said. "See, he's already comfortable enough to nurse with the halter on."

"Or else he's so hungry, he doesn't care."

"It doesn't matter which. The fact is he's doing it."

Lisa and Trudy joined them at the fence.

"He's so cute," Trudy observed.

"I thought you hated horses," Lisa teased.

"I do. But, he's not a horse. He's a foal or a colt—*not* a pony. He'll be a horse when he grows up, but for now, he's just a baby and that means he's cute."

"Nice work," Lisa said, pleased that Trudy actually remembered the things she'd said to her so long ago about Samson.

"Where have you guys been?" Stevie asked. "We missed you at class."

Lisa and Trudy exchanged glances. "We were on a little trail ride," Lisa explained. "Trudy wanted to try a few new things."

This sounded very hopeful to Stevie, who had encouraged Trudy to try a faster gait than a walk on horseback. "Oh, did you try trotting?" she asked.

Trudy looked to Lisa for the answer. She didn't know one gait from another. "Did I trot?" she asked.

Lisa grinned at her. "Nope, you skipped that one," she said. "You went straight to the gallop."

Stevie and Carole stared at them wide-eyed. "Gallop?" Carole asked.

Lisa and Trudy nodded.

"I think you've got some explaining to do," Stevie said to Lisa.

"Okay," Lisa agreed. "We'll tell you the story at your pool later this afternoon."

It was going to be a tough afternoon for Lisa. Not only would she and Trudy have to tell their tale of Trudy's nightmarish ride on Topside, but Lisa would have the opportunity to apologize to both of her best friends. She hoped she wouldn't have to save their lives, too!

For the next few minutes, the girls turned their attention to Samson, who finished his snack and then began rubbing his halter up against the fence again.

"Enough," Carole announced, dropping down into the paddock softly. "Here, boy," she said, holding her hands low. Samson stepped over to her and stood still while she removed the halter. "Good boy," she said, patting him. Grateful for his freedom, he once again pranced around the paddock. Carole climbed the fence while Stevie released Delilah's lead rope.

"Now can we play games with him?" Stevie asked hopefully.

"Not yet," Carole said. "I think we can begin doing

it next week, though. The first game we'll teach him will be follow-the-leader—on a lead rope."

"Okay, all right," Stevie conceded. "You were right, and I'm sorry I caused so much trouble."

"That's okay," Carole said. "After all, that's what friends are for!"

All four girls started laughing, and they were still laughing together as they headed for the locker area.

When they had all finished changing shoes, Lisa realized that she'd never spoken to Mrs. Reg about observing the adult class. Mrs. Reg was in her office. Lisa didn't want to miss the chance.

"You all go on ahead," she said. "I'll follow in a few minutes. There's something I have to speak to Mrs. Reg about. And I'll also have to talk to Max. Save some water for me, okay?"

It was a hot, humid day—too hot to stand on ceremony about getting to a swimming pool. Stevie, Carole, and Trudy agreed to proceed.

THIS WASN'T AN easy day for Lisa. She'd be glad when it was over, but until it was over, there was a lot of work to do. Not only did she have to talk to Mrs. Reg about the adult class, but she also had to thank her for helping her, and apologize for all the things she'd written about Pine Hollow. In fact, it seemed to Lisa that the list of people she had to apologize to was very long. It included Max and everybody in her riding classes—

even Veronica diAngelo. She took a deep breath. It was time.

Max was in Mrs. Reg's office when she knocked on the doorjamb, and both mother and son invited her in.

"I owe you both gigantic apologies," Lisa began in a rush. "I was trying to do something good for me that would be good for you, too, but I just didn't think about what I was doing. I made it sound as if nothing and nobody was safe here. I'm sorry and I won't do it again." Lisa looked down at the floor. She couldn't bring herself to meet Max's gaze.

"We knew you were just trying to help," Max said.

"But it didn't work at all," Lisa said. "It didn't help Stevie or Carole and it didn't help you. It didn't even help me!" She smiled, in spite of herself. "The first thing that did help me was your story today, Mrs. Reg. I knew you were telling me I had to make amends. I'm doing that now. I'm also planning a story for my next column, comparing young riders' classes with the adults'. Can I do that, Max? Will you let me observe?"

"Sure," he said, smiling wryly. "As long as you don't write about individuals in the classes."

"You mean you don't think I should include any unkind descriptions of particularly bad riders and tell the whole world who they are?"

"Something like that," Max said, now genuinely laughing.

"I think I've learned my lesson," Lisa assured the Regnerys.

Mrs. Reg checked the calendar and class schedule. There was a class the next day that would do well for both of them.

"Uh, thanks," Lisa said before she left. "Thanks a lot."

"I think we owe you some thanks," Max said. "Somehow Trudy Sanders convinced Red she had an okay to ride by herself. I'm grateful to you for going out and fetching her back. She wasn't in any trouble, was she?"

Lisa thought for an instant before she answered. If she told Max what had really happened, she'd get Red in trouble, plus Stevie probably because Trudy was her guest, and definitely Trudy. Everything had worked out all right in the end, so what difference did it make?

"No, everything was fine," Lisa said. "I caught her before she made a wrong turn and got lost or she might have been in trouble."

"Well, thanks," Max said.

Lisa had the feeling she'd just exercised some of her newfound knowledge about journalism as well as friendship. You had to sort through facts before you reported them. Not all facts are news. She felt good about herself, really good, for the first time all day.

Rummaging around in her purse, Lisa couldn't find her pad and paper to make a note of the adult class she'd visit tomorrow. She had to make a note to herself or she'd forget it for sure. If she couldn't write it, she could record it. She felt in the bottom of her backpack for the dictating machine, but it wasn't there either. Lisa felt an empty feeling in her stomach. That was a valuable machine that her father had loaned her. He'd be furious if she'd lost it, and she'd be paying for it with her allowance until she had gray hair!

Hurriedly, she dumped out everything in her backpack. She found some old pencils and a stale pack of chewing gum, but there was no sign of the dictating machine.

When had she used it last? she asked herself. She recalled sitting on the bench in the locker area, right before Trudy had come in, dictating Trudy's name to herself so she would remember to write the ill-fated column that had appeared in today's paper. She hadn't seen it since then, she was sure. She'd put it away in her cubby that day, but where was it now?

For a few nightmarish moments, Lisa considered the possibility that there *was* a crime wave at Pine Hollow. The same person who had stolen Stevie's wallet had come back for her dictating machine—or maybe the theft of the machine was purely for revenge!

Now frantic, Lisa got down on the floor to reexamine the inside of her cubby on the bottom row. The deep cubby appeared to be completely empty. She reached in as far as she could. All she could feel was bare wood and then the wall at the back. She scrunched down lower and extended her arm farther. Then she felt something. She felt the edge of a small metal case. It took all the stretching and reaching she could manage to grab hold of it. With a sigh of relief she pulled out the dictating machine. Somehow, it had gotten so far back in the cubby that it had gone off the back end of it and was wedged between the bottom shelf and the wall.

Grateful to have solved the problem, she dropped the machine into her backpack and headed for Stevie's. She'd had enough problems for one day!

13

"YOU DON'T HAVE to say anything," Carole told the weary Lisa when she arrived at Stevie's. "Trudy has told us the whole story. And don't worry, nobody's mad at you. You did a fabulous job rescuing Trudy, and anyway, we knew you'd eventually see what was happening with Hoof Beat. After all, you're our friend so you've got to be pretty terrific, right?"

Lisa smiled gratefully. "Thanks. It's a good thing I've got friends like you because when you mess up the way I have, you really need them!"

Stevie tossed a half-inflated beach ball at Lisa. "Come *on*! Go put on your bathing suit. We've been waiting for you so we could have chicken fights!"

"I'll be right back," Lisa promised, grinning over at Carole and Trudy. She headed for Stevie's room where she could change.

Stevie, who had been lying on her stomach on her towel, abruptly sat up. Although she was relieved to see the end of Lisa's weird behavior, she realized that all her troubles were not solved. She put her elbows on her knees and cupped her chin in her hands with a sigh.

"There's still one really big problem left," she said to Carole, "and that's your dad's birthday money."

"Something will work out," Carole said.

"Nothing's going to work. I've tried everything!" Stevie said.

"You're such a pessimist," Carole teased.

"Since when are you such an optimist!" Stevie retorted.

"I'm a realist," Trudy interrupted. "A realist knows that if you work smart instead of hard, problems get solved."

Carole and Stevie looked at her and burst out laughing. "Okay, smarty, what's our next step?" Stevie asked.

"I don't know," Trudy told her. "I always know what to say. I don't have to know what to do." She rolled over to sun her other side and put on her lime-green and black mirrored sunglasses to indicate she was done with her pronouncements.

"Okay, so we'll let the realist sleep," Stevie said to Carole. "Here comes our resourceful journalist. Let's see if she has any ideas."

It was such a hot, sticky day that Lisa didn't even

pause to greet her friends before she walked straight into the pool. She felt the cool water refresh her, almost cleansing the difficult day from her. She ducked into the clear water and swam the entire length of the pool.

She emerged, shook her head to clear the water from her eyes and ears, blinked twice, and said, "That feels wonderful!" She pulled herself up out of the pool, wrung the excess water out of her hair, spread her towel out by her friends, and lay down, content to do nothing. Stevie, however, wasn't going to let her do nothing.

"Okay then, beg, borrow, or steal?" she asked.

"Huh?" Lisa mumbled, already feeling sleepy in the fierce sun.

"The fifteen dollars Carole needs for her dad's birthday present," Stevie explained.

"Hmmm," Lisa said, reaching for the suntan lotion. "You know, I might have a solution for this. Let me think a minute." She began thinking about the work she'd been doing for the paper. She had certainly hurt enough people with her thoughtlessness. It seemed only right that she reverse the process. After all, Mr. Teller was going to pay her fifteen dollars a week. The least she could do would be to give Carole one week's worth.

"Hey, I could—wait a minute," Lisa said. Suddenly, Lisa's mind did a hop, skip, and jump. "I might even have two solutions to this problem." She sat up and looked at her friends excitedly. "Because I think I smell a—" She paused, thinking.

"A rat?" Stevie supplied. Lisa shook her head.

"A skunk?" Carole suggested. Lisa shook her head again.

"Well, *what?*" Trudy demanded, peering at them over the top of her sunglasses.

"I smell fresh paint!" Lisa announced.

"Of course you do," Stevie said. "That's all any of us has smelled at the stable for the last few weeks. The place stinks all the time!"

"That's it!" Lisa said excitedly. "*The* answer."

"It's not an answer, it's a problem," Stevie said. "I can't wait until they're done. It's taking forever because they just keep working on little pieces every day. It took them nearly a week just to finish up the locker area."

"And that's exactly what I mean," Lisa said. "See, whenever you paint, you have to move furniture around. Then when you're done painting, you move it back. Mostly, people would never really notice that the stuff had been moved, unless, of course, something didn't get back where it belonged."

"I think I see what you're getting at!" Stevie said excitedly.

Carole and Trudy just looked confused. Stevie explained, "What Lisa's saying is that the stableboys have been painting the locker area for weeks, and every time they do it, they move things—like the cubbies. Stuff that may have been way back in the cubby might, just might, be jostled out the back and get stuck someplace where somebody might not find it!"

"Oh!" Carole said. "Wouldn't that be something!"

"It sure would, and I'm not about to wait until Tuesday to find out if it's true. Let's go right now!"

Stevie didn't have to say it twice. The pool would be waiting for them when they got back. The girls pulled on shorts and tees over their bathing suits in record time and headed for Pine Hollow.

The stable was a short walk from Stevie's house, and they covered the distance quickly, barely talking at all. They were each too excited about the possibility of getting Carole's money back.

"Back again so soon?" Max asked, watching the girls parade past his office door.

"We're here on a hunch," Stevie said mysteriously. He shook his head and picked up his copy of *Horse Show.*

The locker area was empty when they got there. The wall of cubbies looked the way it always did, pushed up against the freshly painted wall.

"Lisa, you and Trudy get that end. Carole and I will take this one. We should only need to move the cubbies about six inches to see if your theory is correct," Stevie commanded, taking charge.

Everybody followed instructions. The block of cubbies was about ten feet long and almost five feet high. It was also two feet deep.

"One, two, three . . ."

They tried to pick up the shelves. They didn't budge.

"This thing weighs a ton!" Carole said, speaking for all of them.

"It doesn't matter what it weighs," Stevie said. "I know we can move it."

"Ah, the pessimist turns optimist!" Trudy teased.

"Save your breath for lifting," Stevie suggested.

"Four, five, six . . ." Lisa said. No more success.

"Why don't we try moving one end out from the wall at a time," Carole proposed. "That way, we can get extra muscle working together."

It worked. Quickly, they shifted to the other end and repeated the process. They did it again and again until Lisa, the smallest and skinniest of the crew, could squeeze behind the cubbies. Her friends stood on the other side and waited.

"One riding glove," she announced, tossing a brown kid glove over to them.

"Won't Veronica's daddy be happy?" Stevie said with a smirk.

"Three riding crops." They flew over the top, too. Carole wiped the dust off them and put them in the bucket where the crops were kept.

"A set of keys."

"Meg's, of course," Stevie said.

"Some underwear—red with white stars on them!"

"I wondered what had happened to these!" Stevie

said, grabbing them quickly and stuffing them back into her own cubby. Carole and Trudy laughed at her.

"Anything else?" Carole asked.

"Just this," Lisa said, her voice muffled.

"What?" Stevie asked, watching the top of the cubbies expectantly for the next item.

"Oh, just this old red wallet with fifteen dollars in it!" Lisa peered around the cubbies, a light gleaming in her eyes.

"All *right*!" Stevie yelled.

"I can't believe it!" Carole said.

"It's true. Believe it," Lisa told her, giving the wallet to Stevie. "And wait a minute, there's some other stuff here, too. I mean like money," she said, once again disappearing behind the wall of cubbies. "Here's a dime and three quarters, two pennies, and a—get this, it's a silver dollar."

"It must be interest," Trudy joked.

Lisa emerged from behind the cubbies and handed the change to Stevie. "If it's interest, it's yours since it was your wallet." Stevie put the change in her wallet, along with her own penny and Carole's fifteen dollars.

"Okay, let's move the cubbies back and get out of here. Our pool party's still waiting to happen," Stevie said. "And now we really have something to celebrate!"

Together, the girls shoved the cubbies back against the wall. They all felt so good about Carole's money that moving the shelf back was a lot easier than it had been moving it out. They stowed the recovered objects into each owner's cubby.

"Well, that's that," Carole said, slapping the dust off her denim cutoffs. "The entire mystery is solved and everything's been found."

"Not everything," Stevie said. "We found the gloves, the keys, and the riding crops, but what about Anna's hat?"

Lisa recalled that Anna had mentioned the disappearance of her hat. She had a feeling about that, too. "I wonder if one of the painters found her hat and didn't know what to do with it," she said, thinking out loud.

On the wall facing the cubbies hung dozens of nearly identical black velvet riding hats. Since hats were required, any rider who didn't own a hat could select one from the stable's collection.

"The easiest place to lose a black velvet hat is in the middle of a bunch of black velvet hats, don't you think? If we start on one end and work toward the other, I think we'll find that one of these hats has Anna's name in it."

It took only a few seconds. Anna's hat had carefully been stored on a very high hook, usually reserved for adult-size hats. Anna's hat was put in her cubby, and the girls were ready to return to the swimming pool.

"Last one in is a rotten egg," Stevie said.

"Nope," Lisa corrected her. "Today, there are no rotten eggs. We're all perfect!"

"Right," Stevie said. "And if you believe that one . . ." Laughing, the four girls threw their arms around each other and headed out the stable door.

14

"You know, I love the city, but malls are great!" Trudy announced when Mrs. Atwood dropped all four girls off the following morning to buy Colonel Hanson's birthday present.

"You mean you don't have malls in the city?" Lisa asked.

"Nope," Trudy said. "We've got lots of really cool stores in the downtown shopping area of Washington, but it's really not the same. It's neat to have so many different stores all in one building!"

"So, if we can't get her to like the country because of horses, malls will do it!" Stevie said. "I can't believe you have to leave tomorrow—I'm going to miss you. It's been fun pretending I have a sister. Will you come out here next weekend and go to the mall with us?"

"You bet," Trudy said. "Anytime. Malls are great!"

She glanced over at a group of boys dressed in colorful surfer shorts and tees who were hanging out in front of a burger place. The girls giggled.

"Okay, gang, enough sight-seeing—we've got work to do!" Lisa said, leading the group in the direction of the vintage-record store.

On the way, they passed the earring store where Trudy had gotten her shell-casing earrings. They also stopped at the department store and Happy Feet, the junior shoe store.

At the Preppy Puppy store, the girls couldn't decide which puppy was cutest—a cocker spaniel, a husky, or a spotted dalmatian—but they had fun cuddling them all!

Carole laughed as an overeager Yorkshire terrier covered her face with wet licks. "He's definitely cute," Carole said as she handed him back to the saleslady. "But not nearly as cute as Samson," Carole added to Stevie.

The Saddle Club practically had to drag Trudy out of the store. "Your apartment probably doesn't allow pets," Lisa reminded Trudy sympathetically.

After stopping for a soda, they went to the Scent Shop, where they sprayed themselves with a wild variety of perfumes.

"I think we smell worse than fresh paint," Stevie remarked, waving her hands in the air as they left the Scent Shop.

"I'm beginning to think the smell of paint is wonderful," Carole said. "After all, that was what gave Lisa the clue about where your wallet was."

"Okay, I love it, too. What's next?" Stevie glanced around the mall, looking for inspiration. "Look, over there!" She pointed to a makeup counter where they were offering free samples. "Trudy can show you how to do outrageous makeup on your eyes, right, Trudy?"

"Sure," she agreed. "But I don't know if they'll learn the butterflies as quickly as you did."

Lisa would never have imagined herself with eye shadow shaped like a butterfly, but when Trudy was done, she rather liked the effect. It was certainly different! "The new me?" she asked her friends, batting her eyelashes at them. They laughed and she did, too. "Well, anyway, I think I like my butterflies at least as much as Carole's rainbows!"

Lisa glanced at Carole and grinned. "Uh-oh, what's Stevie up to now?"

Stevie was intently staring into the countertop mirror as she drew a heart on her cheek with a red lip pencil. "Ta da!" she announced, spinning around from the counter.

"Cool," Trudy said with approval.

"I knew you'd like it. So, what's next?" Stevie asked. "I think that's my favorite question today."

"Well, you've done a good job of answering it," Lisa said. "I don't think I've ever had more fun without spending any money at the mall."

"So then it's time to spend. Here's the oldies record store," Carole said, leading her friends inside.

It always took Carole a long time to choose. Lisa and Stevie knew better than to help. This was too important to rush or to interfere with. Carole really wanted to be left alone on this job.

Stevie was eager to have more adventures, and Lisa and Trudy were willing to explore. They decided to leave Carole alone and come back to pick her up a half hour later. Carole was so intent on her mission that she barely acknowledged Stevie's suggestion.

"You know what I want to do?" Stevie said. "Remember the silver dollar you found?"

"Yeah," Lisa said, still feeling a little sheepish over their discovery of the Pine Hollow "thief."

"I want to find the place where they're selling raffle tickets for that library fund-raiser and I want to buy a raffle ticket. That's how I want to spend that dollar. I just have the feeling it's a lucky one."

"Okay," Lisa and Trudy agreed. The tickets were being sold at the small branch library in the mall. The girls had to pass seventeen tempting shops to get there. Since they only had a half hour, they didn't stop at any of them. Stevie felt very proud of that.

"Just one chocolate-covered pretzel?" Trudy begged as they passed Sweet Nothings.

"Maybe on the way back," Stevie graciously conceded. "We've got a mission to accomplish."

Lisa elbowed Trudy and grinned. "When Stevie's got a mission, that's when you've got to watch out!"

Stevie just stuck out her tongue and led the way up the escalator.

But when they got to the library branch, the usual card table for raffle ticket sales was gone.

"It must be over," Lisa said.

"No way—not until they have my silver dollar," Stevie said. "I'm going inside to ask."

Lisa and Trudy followed her inside.

Stevie loved the library. It was cool inside with subdued lights, nothing glaring or distracting. The whole place smelled of paper and bindings. It was filled with books that told wonderful stories and adventures of faraway places. Normally, she headed right for the animal-story section when she walked into the library, but not today. Today, she had another mission. The librarian was at the check-out desk.

"The raffle," Stevie said. "Is it too late?"

"Oh, I'm afraid so," the woman said. "We had the drawing last week. We're still trying to notify the prize winners. We'll take donations anytime, of course, but there aren't any more tickets."

Stevie pulled out her silver dollar. A silver dollar was a little special. Some people kept them as good-luck charms, she knew, but money in any form wasn't something Stevie could keep around for very long! Since a silver dollar *was* special, it needed to be used for something special. Even though she couldn't buy a raffle ticket, she had wanted the library to have the money. She decided to give it to them.

"Here, then," Stevie said. "You can have this."

"Why, thank you!" the librarian said, surprised and pleased. "And then next year, you come earlier and you can get some raffle tickets. Maybe you'll be as lucky as our grand prize winner."

"Who's that?" Stevie asked. "Someone from Willow Creek?"

"No, she doesn't live around here. I think she was just visiting. Somebody by the name of Trudy Sanders. We haven't been able to get ahold of her yet, but—"

"Did you say Trudy Sanders?" Stevie asked.

The librarian checked on a piece of paper on her desk. "Trudy Sanders, that's right," she said.

Stevie could feel the excitement rising in her. "And what did she win?" she asked.

"Oh, the grand prize is two weeks at Moose Hill Riding Camp. We need to find her soon. The camp starts in a week!"

"You've found her!" Stevie announced.

Excitedly, she signaled Lisa and Trudy to come to the counter and learn the good news. Stevie was too excited to speak.

Stevie and Lisa couldn't believe what incredible good luck Trudy had. They all shrieked with joy and hugged each other, jumping up and down. Usually, the librarians would make them leave for making such a ruckus, but since Trudy was the library's grand prize winner, they watched the girls with pleased smiles.

As soon as they'd gotten all the paperwork and the

certificate for the camp, the girls dashed out of the library and ran all the way to the record store. They found Carole just finishing up at the check-out counter.

It took only a few minutes to share Trudy's good news with Carole, but it took longer to convince her that it was true.

"This calls for a Saddle Club meeting to celebrate!" Lisa announced. "And I've gotten enough money from *The Gazette* to buy everybody a sundae!"

The four girls found an ice-cream shop that had exotic enough flavors to suit Stevie's weird taste. They found an empty booth and sat down.

"Hey, now that you're going to riding camp, you can be in The Saddle Club," Stevie said to Trudy while the waiter took their orders.

Trudy fiddled with her yellow parrot earrings. Then when the waiter had left to get them water, she said, "Look, I'd love to be in your club, but . . ." She paused, then looked across at Stevie. "I know you guys love horses. I'm sure they're great and they sure are pretty to look at, but they're just not my thing. Riding on the trail was okay. But riding along the river with Topside freaking out wasn't exactly a dream come true."

"But you were great. Lisa said so," Carole reminded her. "You just had an unusually bad experience. If you put your mind to it, you'll be a good rider."

"That's just the thing," Trudy explained. "I don't

want to put my mind to it. I really like you guys. And I'm glad we got to be friends. I'd like to visit again and I want you to come see me when you're in the city. But horseback riding? I'd rather wear plaid pants and turtlenecks!"

Stevie grinned. "You're going to have an awful time at Moose Hill then," she said.

"Oh, I would, if I were going, that's for sure," Trudy said. "But I'm not going."

"You're not?" all three Saddle Club girls said in a single voice.

"Of course not. Get real." The three friends laughed. "I want you to go in my place, Stevie. It's just a little thank-you for a really great visit with you."

All three girls turned to Stevie, who couldn't speak because her jaw had dropped.

When she could finally move and talk once again, Stevie did three things. First, she shrieked. Second, she hugged Trudy. And third, she had a proposal for Lisa.

"When we finish our sundaes, if you have any money left over, let's go back to the library and trade your dollar for the lucky silver dollar I gave them. I have the funny feeling we're going to need it to find a way for you and Carole to come to Moose Hill, too. I just can't see myself riding for two weeks without you two!"

Lisa and Carole agreed. The more The Saddle Club

stuck together, the more impossible it seemed that they could ever be apart.

"Here's to The Saddle Club at Moose Hill," Trudy announced, lifting her water glass in a toast.

The Saddle Club raised their glasses, too. "And here's a toast to our one nonriding, nonhorse-crazy, but definitely very cool member," Carole said, welcoming Trudy into their group.

Trudy grinned happily at her three new friends. She was as happy to be a part of their club as they were to have her.

"There's just one requirement," Trudy said to Stevie.

"Anything!" Stevie shouted.

"You've got to send me a postcard from camp. I want to hear about *everything!*"

THE SADDLE CLUB

RIDING CAMP

BONNIE BRYANT

For Penelope B. Carey

"WATCH HOW SHE does this," Carole Hanson said to Lisa Atwood. The two girls were standing in the passageway outside a stall at Pine Hollow Stables. Stevie Lake was inside the stall preparing Topside for a trip.

Carole, Lisa, and Stevie were best friends. They'd gotten to know each other at Pine Hollow and had formed a group called The Saddle Club. The club had only two rules, and they were easy ones: All the members had to be horse crazy, and they had to be willing to help one another. So far the three girls were the only active members of the club, although there were a few out-of-state friends who were honorary members.

Stevie finished fastening the final protective leg wrap on the big bay gelding horse, patted Topside reassuringly, and stood up. She clipped a lead rope onto Topside's halter and looked him square in the eye.

"Pine Hollow's Flight One to Moose Hill Riding Camp is now ready for boarding," she announced. "All passengers holding first-class tickets may proceed to the gate. And that means you."

Outside the stable, a horse van was waiting to take Topside to Moose Hill, the riding camp Stevie would be attending for the next two weeks. Stevie had been lucky. A friend of hers had won the camp session in a raffle, but since she didn't like riding very much, she'd offered it to Stevie. Horse-crazy Stevie didn't understand her friend at all, but under the circumstances, she decided it was just fine that her friend didn't like riding.

"I'm almost too excited to watch," Lisa told Carole. "I can't believe it. Two solid weeks of horses, horses, and horses. Nothing but horses!"

Carole nodded, her eyes wide with excitement.

"I can't believe how lucky we all are!" Stevie said.

"I still don't understand how you managed to convince Max to pay our way. How did you get him to sponsor us?"

There was a sparkle in Stevie's eye. Convincing people, especially Max Regnery, the owner of Pine Hollow Stables, to do things they might not actually *want* to do was one of her specialties. "It was easy," she said airily, dismissing Carole's admiration. "A mere sleight of hand."

"More like sleight of mouth, if I know you," Carole added.

"Yeah, more like that," Stevie agreed, returning to her normal self. "Now let's see if I can do a sleight of hoof and get Topside onto the van."

She turned her attention to the horse. Topside was an experienced traveler. He was a championship show horse and had performed all over the world. Max had recently bought him when the horse's owner, Dorothy DeSoto, had been forced to give up competitive riding because of an accident. Now Topside was going to riding camp with The Saddle Club to get a new kind of show experience. The two-week session at Moose Hill would end with a horse show for the campers. It would be completely different from what Topside had known before, and Max had felt it would be good for both Stevie and Topside to try it together.

Carole and Lisa would be riding horses assigned to them from the camp's own stable. They loved the horses they usually rode at Pine Hollow, but Max couldn't spare two more horses for the session. Both girls also knew that it would be a good opportunity for them to try training on different horses.

"Come on, boy," Stevie said. She clucked her tongue and led Topside toward the stall door. Carole slid the door back to let them out. Stevie held the lead rope with one hand and a pail containing Topside's grooming gear with the other. She looked over her shoulder at the horse. He seemed to sense that something was up and twitched his tail excitedly. Stevie grinned over her shoulder at him, still leading him straight out of the stall.

"Stevie, watch your head!" Carole warned. It was too late, though. With a thunk, Stevie's head connected with the fire extinguisher on the wall of the stable opposite Topside's stall.

Stevie made a face and rubbed her head where she'd hit it. Then she crossed her eyes. Lisa giggled. Stevie had the ability to make almost anything funny. It was one of the things Lisa liked the best—and that sometimes annoyed her the most—about Stevie.

"Are you okay?" Lisa asked.

"Never mind her—what about the fire extinguisher?" Carole said, adjusting the big red metal canister. Stevie glared at Carole briefly.

Lisa laughed. She knew Carole was concerned about Stevie's bump, but it was just like her to be equally concerned with the safety of the horses. Just as Stevie could always see the funny side of a situation, Carole could always see the serious side—when it came to horses. It was Lisa's feeling that Stevie and Carole balanced each other. Sometimes that was a problem, since it meant Lisa was right smack in the middle. But most of the time it was a lot of fun.

"Come on, you guys," Lisa said. "The sooner we get Topside on the van the sooner we can leave for camp."

Carole began clucking at Topside, encouraging him to follow Stevie toward the van.

"I guess that means my job is to bring the tack, huh?" Lisa asked.

"Thanks." Stevie grinned.

Lisa walked toward the stable's tack room. It was one of her favorite places in Pine Hollow. At first glance, it was a mess. The room was covered with snaking leather straps hanging every which way and an endless row of saddles that required constant soaping and cleaning. That was the way it had first looked to Lisa when she'd started riding at Pine Hollow. After a few days, however, she'd learned that there was a strict order to everything. Each saddle was in a place that corresponded to its horse's stall. A matching bridle hung above each saddle. Spare leathers, carefully sorted by size, hung along another wall. There were buckets for metal parts, bits, chains, buckles, hooks, and rings, which were all meticulously grouped.

In fact, the whole room was organized very carefully. It just didn't look that way. Lisa wondered, as she looked at it now, how she could ever have thought it was messy. She quickly located Topside's tack and picked it up to carry it to the van.

It was exciting, and a little frightening, to think that she was about to become familiar with a new stable, a new horse, and new riders. Lisa, unlike Carole and Stevie, had begun riding just a few months ago. She didn't have as much experience as her friends did. She was sure she would enjoy Moose Hill, but she still felt a little uneasy. There was only one thing to do about that. Lisa hefted the saddle, adjusting its weight, and left the tack room.

There was nobody inside the stable. Everyone was watching Stevie load Topside. There was one last thing Lisa wanted to do before she left. Pine Hollow Stables had been around for a long time and had developed a lot of traditions. One of those was its good-luck horseshoe. By tradition, every rider at Pine Hollow touched it before going for a ride. Nobody was sure when the tradition had begun, or why, but everybody knew that no rider at Pine Hollow had ever been seriously hurt in a riding accident. Lisa glanced around. She felt a little silly, but she still wanted to do it. The horseshoe was nailed up by the door to the indoor ring. When she reached the doorway to the ring, she set Topside's tack on the ledge of an empty stall, stood on tiptoe, and reached up high, brushing the horseshoe with her fingers. The feeling of the smooth, worn iron comforted her.

She picked up the tack again and carried it through the stable to where the van and the station wagon and her friends were waiting for her.

Stevie had loaded Topside into the trailer by the time Lisa joined her friends and the crowd gathered in the driveway. Red O'Malley, Pine Hollow's most trusted stablehand, was driving Topside to Moose Hill. It seemed to Lisa that she and her friends were just being allowed to hitch a ride with the horse!

"Have we got all our stuff in the back of the car?" Carole asked, peering through the station wagon's dusty windows.

"I think we've got it all," Red said dryly. "Including the kitchen sink."

Carole was famous for forgetting important things, like clothes, when she went on trips, but the gigantic pile of luggage in the car indicated that she hadn't forgotten anything this time, since everything in the world was probably already crammed in the bags.

Finally it was time to go. The girls climbed into the station wagon and rolled down their windows so they could wave to their parents, their fellow students, Max, and his mother, Mrs. Reg. Before they were out of the driveway, Max was shooing the other riders back

7

inside. It was almost time for class to begin, and as far as Max was concerned, there were no good excuses for class to begin late.

"I don't think anything would keep Max from starting class on time," Lisa remarked.

"Oh, maybe a tornado," Stevie said.

"Not unless it leveled the barn," Carole added.

Lisa giggled. She was glad that Max was so serious about riding instruction. She hoped her teacher at camp would be as good.

"I'm a little nervous," she confessed to her friends. "I mean, you guys have been riding for years. You're used to other horses and other instructors. Pine Hollow is practically the only place I've ever ridden. Is it going to be okay?"

"You bet it is," Carole assured her. "Not only is it going to be okay, it's going to be great. It's important to have different experiences. And besides, you *have* ridden other places. Remember the Devines' dude ranch? And New York? Now those were *really* different. Moose Hill's going to be much more like Pine Hollow than those were."

"Not exactly," Stevie said. "Did you read the brochure carefully? I mean, did you read the part about one stablehand for every five riders? That's not quite like Pine Hollow, where there are only two stablehands for the whole stable and all the work is done by

8

the poor overworked riders, who have to muck out the stalls and clean the tack and groom the horses while the stablehands hardly ever lift a finger. Right, Red?"

Red snorted in response. It was true that the riders did a lot of work around Pine Hollow. It was one way the stable kept expenses down and made riding something more people could do. However, horses were a lot of work, and no matter how much the riders pitched in, there was plenty for Red and his co-workers to do. The girls knew that as well as he did.

"Go on," Red said. ' Have yourselves a real vacation at this camp, but don't come back to us too good to groom your own horses, okay? One of those is enough at the stable, thank you very much."

Red didn't have to name names. He was talking about Veronica diAngelo, the stable's spoiled little rich girl.

"Don't worry, Red," Lisa assured him. "Nothing, short of about ten million dollars, would make us as obnoxious as she is."

"Twenty," he said, and then turned all his attention to his driving. Lisa wasn't certain if Red had meant it would take twenty million dollars to make *her* obnoxious or if he thought twenty million was what Veronica had. She watched the hilly Virginia countryside slide by and thought about what she'd do with twenty million dollars. She'd build a stable for herself and buy a

9

horse. Two horses. No, one for every member of The Saddle Club. She'd hire loads of stablehands and she'd ride with her friends all day, every day. They'd enter all kinds of competitions and they'd win them all, because when the three of them were teamed together, they couldn't lose. She'd have a swimming pool—two actually: one indoor, one outdoor. She'd have a thick pile carpet in her room and her very own maid to pick up any of the expensive clothes she happened to drop on the floor. But, she told herself, she'd still take care of her own horse, and she'd never be as obnoxious as Veronica.

"Did you see her face?!" Stevie shrieked, abruptly bringing Lisa out of her daydream. Carole was laughing.

Lisa had no idea what they were talking about. "Who?" she asked.

"Veronica," Carole said. "You know, when she sat on the moldy hay. Didn't you see that?"

"Oh, yeah, I did. She kept swiping at the seat of her *designer* breeches. It was very funny and the harder she swiped, the angrier Max got." Lisa smiled, remembering the scene.

"Well, Max had left the hay bale out so that the salesman could see what he'd delivered, and Veronica just assumed it was a new throne for the princess."

"Got what she deserved," Lisa said. "A moldy

throne. Well, better her breeches than a horse's manger!"

"Absolutely!" Carole said seriously. "Horses have very delicate stomachs and moldy hay can cause colic, and that's no joke. To a horse, colic can be fatal! So if all that happened with that bale was that Veronica's pants had to go to the dry cleaner, well, we were just plain lucky."

"It's not so much luck as it is caution, you know," Red said. "Moldy hay will happen. You just have to test for it with every shipment and every bale."

"How do you do that?" Lisa asked.

"You feel it and see if there's any moisture, then you sniff at it for a funny odor."

"You can feel it for warmth, too," Carole said.

"Well, if it's warm, you're in real trouble," Red said. "That means that there's so much decay going on inside that it's heating up to burn. You want to get it far away from the barn as soon as possible. Those things can just about explode."

"You know one of the things I love about horses?" Lisa asked, thinking out loud. "I love the fact that there's so much to find out about them that you can learn about them no matter where you are or what you're doing, like in a car driving over the hills of Virginia. You can learn just as much out of the saddle as you can in it."

"It's just that it's more fun if you're in it," Stevie said, and the girls agreed.

"I have the feeling we'll be there any minute now," Carole said.

"Yep," Red agreed, turning the car and its trailer off the main road where the sign pointed to Moose Hill.

The road was narrow and shaded by tall maples, which made it suddenly cool in the hot August afternoon. Gradually the surrounding forest became pine and the road turned into a dirt trail. Red slowed down so the van wouldn't bounce in the ruts. After a half-mile, they saw a horse gate. Stevie jumped out of the car to open and close it for them. She clasped the latch carefully behind the trailer and rejoined her friends. Red drove them up a long hill on the winding road and then, as if it grew from the forest, there stood before them the stately red barn of Moose Hill Riding Camp.

"I THINK HE said our cabin was this one—the second one on the right." Lisa pointed to a small wooden bunkhouse. "Yeah, here it is, Number Three." She paused to readjust the weight of the three heavy bags she was carrying. Carole did the same.

"I hope Stevie knows what a wonderful thing we're doing for her, lugging her stuff while she checks Topside into his suite at the Hilton on the Hill." Lisa and Carole had agreed to carry Stevie's things for her while she got Topside settled in. They were both beginning to think Stevie had gotten the best of the deal. When they heard Stevie shout gaily from behind them, they were sure of it.

"Here I come!" Stevie announced her arrival. "And, hey, thanks for all the help. Boy, you won't believe the

13

barn! It's really wild. It's a big old farmer's barn with a few stalls—most of the time the horses are in the paddock—and this gigantic hayloft. It'll be a blast to mess around in."

"If we can move at all after carrying all this weight," Carole said pointedly.

Stevie got the hint. She took her bags from Carole and Lisa and followed them into the cabin.

The screen door slammed behind them. The girls found themselves standing inside a very plain rectangular room with a bathroom off to the side. There were six cots in the room, each with a cubby area with shelves for clothes and personal belongings. Lisa looked dubiously at her two large duffel bags while her eyes adjusted to the dim light cast by the single overhead bulb. She was sure she'd never fit all her belongings into the modest cubby.

"That one's my bed," an unfamiliar voice said to her. There was nothing friendly or warm about the greeting.

"Oh," Lisa said, startled. She turned to see a girl about her own age emerging from the bathroom. "I wasn't going to take your bed. I was just looking at how small the cubbies are. I was thinking about . . ." She was going to explain about how her mother always packed too much for her when she realized that the girl who had spoken wasn't listening. She'd picked up her riding hat and was striding out of the cabin.

"Hello to you, too!" Stevie said. The only response she got was the clatter of the girl's boots going down the steps of the cabin.

"Whew!" Carole remarked.

"Don't mind Debbie," another voice spoke. A girl they hadn't noticed before was sitting in a corner of the room, saddle-soaping her boots. "She just found out that Elsa, who won just about all the blue ribbons in the show last year, not only came back this year, but is in this cabin. My name's Nora."

For a second, The Saddle Club girls were too stunned to speak, or to return the introduction. It would never have occurred to any of them to be upset about bunking with a blue-ribbon winner. In fact, Carole was really excited about the idea of being able to spend extra time with somebody who knew more than she did and could teach her.

Then the girls composed themselves and made introductions. Nora showed them which beds were theirs and even helped Lisa figure out how to stuff all her things into the small cubby.

"Where's the blue-ribbon winner?" Carole asked Nora as the two of them put the sheets and blankets on her cot. Elsa's cot was next to Carole's and her duffel bags were there, but none of her gear was stowed and her bed wasn't made.

"Well, if I know Elsa," Nora began, "she's found a

private area in the field, out of sight of the barn and the main house, and she's working with her horse."

"You mean campers are allowed to ride without any supervision and no riding partner?" Carole asked, surprised. There was no way Max would let a young rider out alone. Even the best of them had to have a friend along, just in case.

"Campers aren't supposed to do that, but Elsa does it anyway," Nora answered.

"But it's so much more fun to be with friends," Stevie said.

"There are two things wrong with that," Nora said. "In the first place, nobody is Elsa's friend, and secondly, she wouldn't want to ride with somebody who might learn something from her. She's made it crystal clear that she intends to take home all the blue ribbons again this year."

"Oh, yuck." Stevie made a face.

"You know, that reminds me of what Kate Devine said about all the really good riders she used to compete with," Carole said. Kate was a junior championship rider who had quit competition because of people like Debbie and Elsa.

"You know Kate Devine?" Nora asked, her jaw dropping.

"Sure, she's an old friend of ours," Carole said. "Her dad and mine are Marine Corps buddies. In fact, just a while back, the three of us visited her on her parents' dude ranch. She's learned to ride Western and she loves it." Carole tucked in the final sheet, smoothed the blanket with her hand, and dropped a quarter on the bed to see if it would bounce the way it was supposed to in the Marine Corps. It didn't. She didn't care. She pocketed the quarter. "Let's go see the rest of the camp," she said to her friends.

"Want the grand tour?" Nora asked. "Listen, lunch starts in a half an hour. I can show you everything by then if you want."

That sounded pretty good to Carole. She'd only gotten a glimpse of the camp on the way in. "That'd be great," Carole said, speaking for Stevie and Lisa too. "We're almost done here—"

"I have an errand up at the barn," Nora said quickly. "Meet me up there, okay? You know where that is?"

"Yeah, the big red building with all the hay and the horses?" Stevie asked innocently.

"Don't mind her," Lisa said to Nora. "She jokes about everything. We'll see you up at the barn in five minutes."

Nora nodded and left The Saddle Club alone in the cabin.

"What a place," Stevie remarked, stuffing her belongings into the tiny cubby by her cot. "It's got all the ingredients to be the most wonderful place in the world—horses and kids who love horses—and we end up in a cabin with a riding whiz who keeps the secret of her success and a would-be whiz who won't talk to anybody!" She crammed her toothbrush in the last available space and stood up, looking at her friends for sympathy.

"I think the way to handle people like Debbie and Elsa is to ignore them. And since they seem willing to ignore us, it won't be hard to do," Lisa said.

"Yeah, and Nora seems nice enough," Carole reminded Stevie.

"Just watch out that she doesn't try to learn *our* riding secrets!" Stevie joked.

"As far as I'm concerned, she can have all my riding secrets," Carole said. "The only real secret to riding is that it's fun. I have a feeling that there are a few people around here who haven't learned that yet."

There were many ways in which the three members of The Saddle Club were very different, but that was one thing they agreed on completely. Lisa smiled to herself, thinking about all the fun riding she had ahead of her.

"I hate to change the subject from horses, guys," Carole continued, "but did the two of you happen to notice what I noticed down the hill?"

"More cabins?" Lisa asked. She'd seen a second cluster of cabins like the one they were in.

"Not just *more* cabins," Carole said. "*Boys'* cabins. The camp's coed, remember?"

"Yeah, right, big deal," Stevie said, sitting on her freshly made bed. "Pine Hollow's coed, too. The trouble is that if nine out of ten guys are cute, the tenth one rides at Pine Hollow. I have absolutely no interest in any boy who rides horses. I've never met one who wasn't a complete creep."

Lisa was a little surprised by the conviction in Stevie's voice. It was true that the guys who rode at Pine Hollow weren't exactly cute, but there was always a chance you'd find the right one, wasn't there? "Oh, come on, Stevie," she said. "Maybe Moose Hill is different."

"Fat chance," Stevie said. "You should have seen the guy who came in when I was putting Topside in the barn. He ordered everybody around like he was a male version of Veronica diAngelo!"

"So, maybe he's rich?" Lisa suggested. "I could learn to love a rich man."

Stevie gave her a withering look. "Not this one," she said. "Unless you really go for short, fat, and ugly as well. In that case, we've found Mr. Right for you."

"Well, what about the tall guy who held Topside's saddle for you?" Carole asked.

"That drip?" Stevie scoffed. "Oh, I admit that when I first saw him I thought he was kind of cute, but I asked him what his name was and he couldn't seem to remember. I'm telling you, the boys here are no better than the girls. Stick to the horses!" She grinned and stood up. All three girls had finished with their unpacking and were ready to meet Nora at the barn.

"Did you at least have a chance to meet some of the horses?" Lisa asked. "After all, I guess that's what we're here for."

"The horses are something else," Stevie said, leading the way out of the cabin. "There's a chestnut gelding who's a real beauty. He's got this incredible arch to his neck—I think there's some Arabian there—and he holds his tail high, like he's so proud of himself. He came over to me first thing and sort of hugged me. But then this paint mare got jealous and started prancing around the paddock so I'd notice her. Meanwhile two bays were pawing at the ground, like they'd seen the mare's act before and they were bored with it. And all this time Topside is watching, taking it all in."

All the way to the top of the hill, Stevie continued telling her friends about the horses. Lisa was so excited to be at Moose Hill she could barely contain herself. She decided Stevie was right. The girls didn't seem very nice and the boys were probably losers. It was a good thing the horses were so terrific!

WHEN NORA GAVE the girls their grand tour of the grounds, they found that the camp was basically laid out in an oval. The massive barn stood at one end of the grounds. The barn had paddocks on two sides, one at the upper level, one below. The lower one was connected to a stable area. There was a drive-in entrance on the third side of the barn, and an outdoor riding ring on the fourth. Beyond the riding ring was a huge grassy area about the size of a football field, where the riders could play mounted games like shadow tag. The mess hall stood on one side of the field; the rec hall was directly across from it. A regular sports field next to the rec hall provided space for unmounted games like softball or Frisbee.

The cabins were down the hill from the barn. The

boys' and girls' cabins lay on opposite shores of the swimming pond, separated from it by a small sandy beach. A short dirt road led from the barn to the cabin area. Other foot trails led through the woods directly to the pond and the mess hall.

The main area of the camp was an open space, with just a few trees around the edges of the paddocks and riding arenas. There was a shaded area behind the mess hall with picnic tables, where most meals were served in good weather. The cabins were in the woods, cooled by tall trees.

"The camp has about thirty riders at a time," Nora explained. "Usually, there are about twenty girls and ten boys. I think that's how many Barry said there were now."

Barry, they had learned, was the camp director. The girls had met him up at the stable, where he'd been overseeing the arrival of several horses. He'd been so busy telling the stablehands what to do that he'd barely acknowledged their presence. Carole had been very surprised that one of the stablehands needed so much supervision. His name was Fred and he didn't seem to know much at all. Carole made a mental note not to let Fred near her horse.

"Well, that's about it," Nora said to The Saddle Club girls. "Unless you want to tour the grain-storage area on the other side of the upper paddock, we're done."

"Thanks a lot for showing us around," Lisa said. "It seemed so confusing at first, but I think I can find my way around now."

"Oh, no problem," Nora told them. "It was fun. Listen, I'm supposed to help set the tables today, so I'm going over to the mess hall. You should come too, when the bell rings, okay? I'll see you there."

The girls agreed to meet Nora at the mess hall. Lisa and Carole wanted to wash up before lunch, but Stevie thought she ought to check on Topside one more time. They decided to regroup at lunchtime.

Stevie wasn't sure if the pond or the barn was her favorite part of the camp. There was something really wonderful about the barn. The thing about it was that it *was* a barn, not really a stable. The horses spent most of their time turned out into the paddocks or the field beyond them. The stabling area in the lower level was more like a resting place for sick or injured horses. It had a separate entrance for the horses from the lower paddock. The farrier—the blacksmith who put shoes on the horses—worked there as well, and horses in need of shoes were kept overnight in the stable area.

The upper level of the building, like most barns, had a sort of drive-through, convenient for delivery and pickup of feed and equipment. Large storage rooms stood on both sides of the drive-through.

Once Stevie had assured herself that Topside was doing just fine, she checked out the storage rooms. One, of course, was a tack room. Like Pine Hollow's tack room, at first glance it looked like a disaster area. But Stevie was pretty sure that there was an underlying order there, just the same as there was at Pine Hollow.

She looked to see where Topside's tack had been stowed by the stablehand. She didn't see it at first, but when she did finally find it, she wasn't so sure about the room's underlying order. Topside's tack had been dumped in a corner of the room—on the floor! Stevie was furious. She picked up the saddle and put it on the nearest saddle rack. Then she untangled Topside's bridle and laid it across the seat of the saddle, since the tack hook above the saddle rack was broken. She moved aside the stack of leathers that had been carelessly cast on the floor beneath the saddle rack and neatly stacked Topside's personal grooming gear there.

When she finished, Stevie grimly studied the rest of the tack room with a new skepticism. She now had the feeling that, unlike Pine Hollow's tack room, this one not only looked like a mess, but *was* a mess. So much for the highly touted stablehands of Moose Hill. And so much for her vacation from grooming! She'd take care of her own horse and gear, and she'd tell her friends to do the same.

When Stevie emerged from the tack room, she realized that there were no campers or staff members around. That could only mean one thing—and the grumbling in her stomach confirmed it. The lunch bell must have rung and she hadn't heard it. She found a cold-water spigot at the back of the barn and quickly washed her hands, wiping them dry on her jeans.

"Mess hall, mess hall," Stevie said to herself. "It's one of the buildings on either side of the riding field. But which one?" She guessed left. She was wrong. It took her almost ten minutes to figure out where the mess hall was. She felt totally stupid walking up to the picnic tables. Here she was, ready to start eating, and all the campers were working on their desserts.

She felt even more stupid when she realized that there wasn't a seat for her at the table where Carole, Lisa, and Nora were eating.

"I'm sorry. We tried to save you a seat, but someone took it," Carole said pointedly. She nodded toward Elsa, who was sitting next to Lisa and eating in sullen silence.

"It happens." Stevie shrugged. She almost felt sorry for her friends. She knew she wouldn't like eating with such a sourpuss. She looked around for another seat.

There was only one left, and just looking at it made Stevie's face redden. The sole remaining seat in the entire picnic area was at a table that was filled with boys. If she hadn't been starving, she might have skipped lunch altogether. But, she reminded herself, she'd spent her life eating with boys—even if they were only her brothers. Resigned, she walked over to the table.

"This seat taken?" she asked.

Seven boys looked up at her, apparently too surprised to answer. It annoyed Stevie to have to ask twice. "*¿Esta el seato es libro?*" she asked in totally fractured Spanish, responding to their rudeness with her own.

Six boys stared at her as if she'd just sprouted another head. The seventh burst into laughter.

"*Muy libro,*" he answered in equally bad Spanish. "Sit down." Stevie did.

It turned out that she was sitting across the table from the boy who had answered her question. She was inclined to like people who laughed when she was funny, so she took a minute to look at this one. Then it was her turn to be surprised. This guy, who had already proved that he was smart by laughing at her joke, was also unmistakably cute. He had short, light brown hair and intense green eyes. He was tall, with broad shoulders and a deep summer tan. What she noticed

26

most, though, was his smile. It was welcoming and friendly. And best of all, it was directed at her.

"Hi, I'm Phil Marston," he said. He smiled again.

"I'm Stevie Lake," she said, stumbling over her own name. What was the matter with her?

"You from around here?" Phil asked, and the conversation began. It turned out that he came from a town about ten miles from Willow Creek, where Stevie lived. She had heard of the stable where he rode. He was a year older than she was. He hadn't been riding quite as long, but he had more show experience. It turned out that they had a lot in common. They both liked riding and jumping. They were both interested in dressage. They both hated math. Phil thought he had too many sisters. Stevie said she had too many brothers. They had each brought a horse to camp. But while Stevie's belonged to Pine Hollow, Phil had his own horse, a bay gelding named Teddy, after Theodore Roosevelt because, Phil explained, when he had first gotten him, the horse was a rough rider.

Stevie laughed at Phil's jokes. Phil laughed at Stevie's. Neither noticed when the other boys at the table finished their lunch and left. They didn't even notice when Carole and Lisa arrived, until Carole announced their presence by clearing her throat several times.

"Ahem!" Carole grunted, sitting down next to Stevie. Lisa sat next to Carole.

"Oh, hi!" Stevie welcomed her friends. She introduced them to Phil. He smiled and nodded at them, but, Stevie noticed, he smiled even more at her. She liked that. She smiled back.

"I think we have a class to go to," Carole said.

"We do?" Stevie said. It seemed impossible that lunch could be over so fast. After all, she'd just sat down at the table a few minutes ago, hadn't she? She looked at her watch. It had been almost forty-five minutes.

"Do you have the same class we do now?" Stevie asked Phil, not even knowing what her class was.

It turned out that Phil had a jump class. The girls were having a flat class, so they might not see each other again for a long time—at least not until dinner, which was five hours away.

"Come *on!*" Carole commanded, tugging at Stevie's sleeve. "We have to change into our riding clothes, go to the stable, tack up our horses, and who knows what all else, all in about fifteen minutes."

"Carole's right," Lisa said. "And Phil has to do the same thing for his class, too. We've all got to get rolling."

"Okay," Phil agreed. He stood up. "I hope there'll be a *seato libro* next to you at supper tonight," he told Stevie. "And, uh, you too," he added politely to

are a very promising student. He expects great things of you. You may not have any ribbons yet, but it won't be long." Lisa turned bright red.

Some students continued to stare at her, but now Lisa felt better about it. Maybe she didn't have as much experience as most of the others, but she had potential. She just wished she could hang it in a cabinet on the wall.

Carole introduced herself and her horse, Basil. She'd been riding long enough that the other students respected her without support from Barry.

Then it was Stevie's turn. One look at Stevie and Lisa knew she would be in trouble. Stevie obviously hadn't heard a word anybody had said. She had a dreamy, faraway look in her eyes that could mean only one thing: Love.

"Hey, you!" Barry said, waving his arms to catch Stevie's attention. It didn't work. Carole reached her hand over to pinch her. Stevie absently brushed Carole's hand away.

"Stevie!" Carole hissed. "It's your turn! Time to introduce yourself and Topside."

Suddenly, Stevie looked panicked. She'd missed everything that was going on and had no idea what to say.

"Cough," Carole whispered, reaching over as if to help her friend. "Cough hard."

31

Obediently, Stevie began hacking. She was so convincing, she looked as if she were choking.

Carole thumped her gently on the back, trying to look as if she were helping her friend through a difficult coughing fit. "This is my friend Stevie Lake," she said. "Like Lisa and me, Stevie rides at Pine Hollow. She's been riding since she was eight. She's been in a lot of local shows and has a cabinet full of ribbons. There's one trophy there, but I think it's pretty dusty, so it might have been Best Beginner when she was eight and she doesn't take it very seriously. She's riding Topside, who used to belong to Dorothy DeSoto. Pine Hollow bought him from her when she retired from competitive riding. Are you okay now, Stevie?" Carole asked sweetly, now that Stevie's "fit" had stopped.

"I'm just fine, thank you, Carole. Just fine."

"Fully recovered?" Carole asked significantly.

"Mmm-hmm," Stevie said. "Thanks for the help."

Whatever else was going on in Stevie's mind, and Lisa suspected that a lot was going on in there, Lisa knew two things for sure: Stevie had learned her lesson about daydreaming in class, and Carole was a true friend—and a fast thinker!

AFTER CLASS, LISA dismounted and led Major to the barn, where he could be cross-tied and untacked. Some horses were likely to move when you were trying to work on them, so it always made sense to hook a rope on either side of the horse's halter to keep the movement to a minimum. So far, Lisa and Major were getting along pretty well. He was cooperative, and she was glad of it.

There were a couple of stablehands who could have untacked Major, but Lisa wanted the opportunity to work with him and get to know him. And there was no better way to learn about a horse than to take care of him.

Debbie was untacking her horse next to her. Lisa thought it was a good chance to be friendly.

"Barry's really a good teacher, isn't he?" she remarked while she removed Major's bridle.

"He's tough, if that's what you mean," Debbie said. "Sometimes I think he's too tough. You can only remember so much at one time—"

"That's not what Max thinks," Lisa said, encouraged by the girl's response. "Our instructor at home thinks you should be able to remember everything. After all, *he* does. Once, he told me eight things I was doing wrong at once!"

Debbie looked at her strangely. Probably Debbie thought that if Lisa could make so many mistakes all at once, she really wasn't worthy of riding with Debbie. Lisa decided on the spot that if that was the way Debbie felt, she really didn't want to have anything to do with her. She turned one hundred percent of her attention to Major, who needed a good brushing.

Brushing, Lisa found, was the perfect activity to do when you were angry. You grabbed the brush and scraped at the horse's coat. The angrier you were, the more vigorously you brushed, and the more your horse liked it. She could tell Major was enjoying himself.

By the time Lisa was finished, Major's coat was smooth and clean. He was ready for a drink.

Lisa led the horse to the trough at the paddock end of the barn. Fred, the stablehand, was there, holding on to three horses at once and paying attention to

34

none of them. It was a warm day and the horses were still hot. They were guzzling water, which was dangerous. Overheated, overwatered horses could get bad stomachaches.

Lisa wasn't sure what to do. She knew what Fred was doing was wrong, but how could she tell him? "Haven't they had enough?" she suggested.

"I don't think so," Fred said. "They're still drinking."

Of course they were, but that wasn't the point. Lisa didn't want to get into an argument with Fred, but she would if it meant keeping the horses from illness. Luckily Betty, the head stablehand, arrived and spoke for her.

"Fred, those horses have had enough water for now! Put them in the paddock and bring down a fresh bale of hay." Fred yanked the horses back from the trough and took them to the paddock. Lisa didn't like his yanking, either, but at least it wasn't dangerous to the animals.

Betty shook her head. "He's new," she confided to Lisa. "He's the son of some friend of Barry's and he's supposed to be this horse genius, but he isn't. He's more work than he is help."

Still muttering to herself, Betty left to help a camper who was having trouble loosening his horse's girth.

35

One thing was certain: Stevie had been absolutely right about the stablehands—or at least one of them. The best way to make sure their horses were well taken care of was to do it themselves.

She patted Major's neck and led him to the paddock, where he would stay until she could give him some fresh hay.

In a few minutes, Fred reappeared, carrying a bale of hay on a wheelbarrow. He dumped it onto the barn floor, snapped the wire that held it, and began breaking off flakes, which were chunks of the hay, for each horse.

Lisa took a flake to feed to Major. As far as she was concerned, fresh hay had about the nicest smell in the world. She sniffed deeply.

Something was wrong. It didn't smell right. It didn't smell rotten, but it just didn't smell like fresh hay. It had an odd odor.

Carole was just entering the paddock with her horse. "What's up?" she asked, noticing the funny look on Lisa's face.

"I don't know," Lisa said. "But the hay smells funny." She held it out to Carole.

Carole felt the hay, rubbing it between her fingers. She sniffed a few strands of it and then the whole bunch of it together.

"It's moldy," Carole said. "I sure hope none of the horses have had any of this."

"Fred just brought it down from the loft. He's over—"

Lisa didn't get to finish. When horses' well-being was at stake, Carole never wasted a minute.

"Betty!" Carole called out. She ran over to Betty and showed her the hay.

Within a few minutes, Betty gathered up all the hay from the bale that Fred had brought and put it in a pile outside, well away from the barn. Moldy hay could not only make horses sick, but it could also start fires. Betty didn't want to take any chances.

She had Fred bring another bale down, and together they tested it. It was just fine. Fred cut it open and each of The Saddle Club girls took a flake for her horse. The girls had to hurry a little. There was an unmounted riding class in five minutes, followed by an instructional film before dinner. Moose Hill might have a problem with at least one stablehand, but it was serious about teaching riding skills, and the girls wouldn't have any free time until after dinner.

They jogged across the field to the rec hall, where their unmounted class was taking place.

"Saddle Club Meeting after dinner," Carole said. "We've got a lot to talk about!"

Lisa and Stevie certainly agreed with that.

"Where shall we meet?" Lisa asked.

"How about by the pond?" Stevie suggested. "There's a clearing on the shore near our cabin."

The girls agreed that it would be a nice place to be in the evening. The water, stars, and moonlight would make the perfect setting for a Saddle Club Meeting.

"OUCH!" *SLAP!* "I got it," Stevie said. "One more wretched mosquito has met his maker. And here comes another to take its place." *Slap!*

The lakeside in the evening *was* a pretty spot, and unfortunately one million mosquitoes seemed to agree.

Carole ignored Stevie's tirade against the entire insect population of western Virginia. "I can't believe these girls," she began. "I've never seen such a snotty attitude—like they're too good to ride with anybody else!"

Lisa told them about Debbie's reaction to her casual remark about Max giving her eight instructions at once. "And the boys are just as bad," she added.

"Not all of them," Stevie said. They didn't have to ask her whom she had in mind.

"Not all of the girls are awful, either," Lisa admitted. "After all, Nora is pretty nice. And that girl Lily something, who was riding the gray, seemed friendly."

"Sure, some of them are fine. I guess *most* of them are fine," Carole conceded. "But the snotty ones are unbelievable. They are so convinced they're going to win all the ribbons at the show next week just because they won them before. And that they deserve them! Ugh, I *hate* that kind of snobbishness."

"So do I," Lisa said. "So does almost everybody. But what can we do?" She slapped a mosquito. "I mean it's not as if we can change them."

"Why not?" Carole asked. "I mean why not try to change them?"

"Oooooh, look," Stevie interrupted, pointing. On the far side of the pond, the sun was setting. Above the trees, the sky was streaked with a breathtaking array of oranges, yellows, and pinks. The scene was perfectly reflected on the glasslike surface of the pond.

"Very beautiful," Lisa agreed.

"Yeah, so romantic," Stevie said dreamily.

Dreamy was not Stevie's usual state. Carole didn't think Stevie had ever noticed a sunset before in her life, but she decided to keep that observation to herself. She tossed a small pebble into the water. It made circles, rippling the sunset's reflection.

A frog croaked.

"Oh, cute!" Stevie said.

It was too much for Carole. "Cute? What's so cute about a frog?" she asked grumpily. She was getting tired of this new nature-loving phase. Stevie had the good sense not to answer.

"So how are we going to change everything?" Lisa asked, resuming their discussion.

"Oh, yes," Carole said, brightening. "The obvious way. These girls think they're going to win all the ribbons, right?"

Lisa and Stevie nodded.

"So, we don't let them. *We* win them all instead. That'll show them!"

Her friends grinned wickedly. Carole continued, "The trick is going to be letting Elsa and Debbie get overconfident—not that they're not already. Anyway, what we've got to do is to *look* like we're bumbling beginners. You know, we'll make dumb mistakes so they can feel superior. Then, when the time comes— whammo! We'll take all the blues!"

"What a fabulous idea!" Lisa laughed. "Only it's mostly going to be you two, you know—partly because you know so much and partly because Stevie will be riding Topside. I think I feel a Saddle Club project coming on. We just have to work like crazy, right? And knock their boots off!"

"Yes!" Stevie said enthusiastically, suddenly drawn into the conversation. "We can do it. I know we can!" She slapped another mosquito. "Now can we please go inside?"

"Not quite," Lisa said. "There's another problem, in case you didn't know, and his name is Fred. I heard

Betty complaining. It seems he's new and he thinks he knows a lot, but he doesn't. If you care about your horses, you'll do all the work yourself."

Carole stood up and stretched. "He's trouble all right. I guess we were all thinking we could have a vacation from hard stable work here, but it's no vacation when your horse is in danger."

"Yeah, yeah," Stevie said, obviously anxious to conclude the conversation. She slapped another mosquito vigorously. "I think I'm being eaten alive!"

"Okay, I've killed enough mosquitoes for the night too. Your wish is granted, Stevie—we can go inside," Carole said, pronouncing the meeting over.

"Not a minute too soon," Stevie said. She and Lisa stood up to go. The sun had completely set and it took them a minute to get used to the darkness of the woods. "I think it's this way." She squinted.

Then the girls heard the sound of someone rustling through the leaves. They paused, unsure of what to do.

"Hello?" a boy's voice called. "Stevie, is that you?" It was Phil.

"Oh, yes, I'm here with Carole and Lisa," she said. Lisa could hear the excitement rise in Stevie's voice.

Phil came close enough so they could all see him. "It's such a nice clear night out, I thought maybe you'd like to go for a walk?" he suggested. He was looking at all three of them, but Lisa knew he was really speaking only to Stevie.

Carole didn't seem to realize it, though. "Oh, the mosquitoes are just terrible. We're heading back to our cabin. Some other time, okay?"

"What mosquitoes?" Stevie asked.

Before Lisa and Carole knew what was happening, Stevie and Phil were off for a walk around the pond.

"Is that what love is like?" Carole asked Lisa as they returned to the cabin. "You have absolutely no sense left?"

"I don't know," Lisa said. She scratched her arm. "But I'm glad I'm not in love. Stevie's going to be awfully itchy tomorrow!"

IF, TWENTY-FOUR hours earlier, someone had told Stevie Lake that she would be stumbling over bushes and roots in a mosquito-infested forest on a dark night without a flashlight, she never would have believed him. Now, she was doing all those things and she wasn't even questioning her sanity. She was having too much fun.

"Here's a place we can sit," Phil said, motioning to a grassy hill that overlooked the darkened pond. They sat down facing the water and continued talking.

Stevie had never had such an easy time talking to a boy. Phil seemed to understand everything she said and it made her talk even more.

She told him about The Saddle Club and some of the things they'd done together. He loved hearing about their trip to Kate Devine's dude ranch, The Bar None. He'd been to a dude ranch once, too, and had had a great time.

"Some people who ride English are really snobby about Western riding," Stevie said. "Not me. I like riding, period. Any kind of riding. I do English riding because that's what we have in Virginia, but I'll ride any way I can because I love horses."

"Yeah, me too," Phil agreed. "But I do really enjoy the competitions in English riding, don't you?"

"I haven't been in too many shows, so maybe I'm not the best person to judge—but if the competitive mood around here is anything to go by, I don't *want* to be in a lot of shows."

Phil looked at her in surprise. "What are you talking about?"

"Oh, how about Elsa and Debbie, for starters?" she said. "You were here last year, right? From what I heard from Nora and a couple of other people, we're talking killer competition. No nice stuff about doing the best you can and learning from others. Elsa won't talk to anybody in the cabin because she's afraid we're all part of some spy ring to learn her secrets for success and Debbie is just convinced that she's better than we are—you know, like we're not good enough to share the air in her cabin?"

Phil laughed. "It doesn't take you long to figure people out, does it?" he asked. "I mean you got those two right away."

"They don't exactly keep their obnoxious personalities hidden," Stevie said. "I wonder why Barry put them in the same cabin with one another—and with *us*. I mean things are not looking good for the next two weeks."

"You aren't thinking of leaving, are you?" Phil asked quickly. "I mean, I'd hate—"

Stevie had a nice warm tingly feeling when she realized that Phil was really worried that she might go away. "No, I'm not leaving," Stevie assured him. "And neither are my friends. We've got something else in mind."

"Oh yeah?" he asked, obviously curious. "What's that?"

For a moment Stevie faltered. The Saddle Club had never talked about secrecy. Still, she wasn't sure if she should tell Phil about something the club was doing. She could definitely trust him, but would it be right to tell him without consulting her friends?

"It's sort of a Saddle Club project," she began uncertainly. "We're working on a way to give Elsa and Debbie—and anyone like them—a taste of their own medicine. It's still in the planning stages."

"Oh," Phil said. Stevie thought he sounded a little hurt not to be in on the plan.

"It's really too bad you've got those two in your cabin," Phil continued. "It gives you the wrong impression of this place. Nobody else is like that—at least not that bad. Moose Hill is a wonderful place and Barry is a great camp director and instructor. I had a neat time here last year, and I'm beginning to get the feeling that I'm going to have an even better time this year."

Stevie knew better than to ask him what he meant by that. "Tell me about Teddy," she said, changing the subject.

Phil had owned Teddy for three years. He'd had a pony before that and Teddy was his first horse. Teddy boarded at the stable where Phil rode. The Marstons didn't have room for a horse at their house.

"I offered to share my bedroom with Teddy, but Mom pointed out that the stairs could be kind of tricky."

"Boy, I'd do anything to have a horse of my own," Stevie told him. "I'd even trade one of my brothers."

"What a sacrifice!" Phil grinned. "I thought you said you'd trade one of them for a pack of bubble gum!"

"That too," Stevie agreed. "Any day. And I don't like bubble gum."

"So if Topside isn't your horse, whose is he?" Phil asked.

Stevie explained how Max had bought him from Dorothy DeSoto when she'd injured her back and had to give up competitive riding.

"That's Dorothy DeSoto's horse? You mean *the* Dorothy DeSoto?" Stevie nodded. "I'm impressed," Phil said. "With a horse like that under you, you'll probably take *all* the ribbons in the show."

"You mean you don't think I have the skill to do it by myself? I have to have a championship horse?" Stevie was a little annoyed at his tone. It made her wonder just how right he was when he'd said that Elsa and Debbie were the only two obnoxious competitors in camp.

"That's not what I meant at all," Phil reassured her. "I just meant that a rider as good as you on a horse as experienced at Topside . . . well, you may be unbeatable."

"That's the idea," Stevie said. He smiled at her.

There was a long silence then. All Stevie heard was the gentle lapping of the pond water on the shore and the occasional hum of hungry mosquitoes. She bent her legs and wrapped her arms around them, hugging them close.

"You cold?" Phil asked. "You could have my sweater."

"I'm okay."

"Well, you *look* cold," Phil remarked, removing his sweater. He put it across her shoulders and left his own arm there as well—for extra warmth, of course.

"Thanks," she said. "I guess I *was* a little chilly. I just didn't know it."

"You're welcome," he said. Then he took his other hand and reached for Stevie's chin, turning her face toward his.

Stevie couldn't believe this was happening to her. Her mind was a jumble of confused thoughts and her heart was galloping like mad. *Phil was about to kiss her!* And she'd never been kissed by a boy before in her life! She didn't know what to do. Should she close her eyes? Open them? Look away? Look up? Or just plain run?

In the faint evening light, she could see Phil smiling at her. Was he as confused as she was? He didn't seem to be. Maybe he could read all of her thoughts and was laughing at her. What an awful idea.

"It's going to be fun riding with you," Phil said, breaking the silence. "I think I'll even enjoy beating you in the horse show!" he teased.

Then he hesitated. Stevie gulped . . . and in that moment's hesitation, there came a sound. It was the sound of taps on the camp PA system. That meant they were already supposed to be in their cabins—with the lights out.

"Boy, we've got to go!" Phil said, standing up suddenly. "Barry can be pretty strict about lights out. We'll have to run."

Stevie stood up, and Phil took her hand to lead her through the woods as they hurried back to the cabin area. He seemed to know his way very well, in spite of the darkness. Within a few minutes, he'd brought her to her front door.

"See you in the morning," he whispered, waving to her.

"Yeah," she whispered back and waved.

As soon as Stevie turned to the cabin, she saw Lisa and Carole waiting for her by the screen door.

"Get in here fast!" Lisa hissed. "Nora says there's going to be a bed check in about two minutes!"

Stevie dashed up the stairs. As fast as she could, she took off her sneakers. There wasn't time to change into her pajamas before the bed check. She just climbed into the bed and pulled the sheets and blanket up high to hide her clothes.

A moment later, the cabin door opened and Betty stepped in. Stevie peeked through one squinted eye. Betty glanced around the cabin and, assured there was a camper in each of the beds, turned to leave.

"Good night, girls. Sweet dreams," Betty said.

Sweet dreams? Stevie thought. *You bet!* She was still wearing Phil's warm sweater, and she pulled it around her shoulders and snuggled down in the bed. She touched her chin where Phil had touched it. *Sweet dreams, indeed!*

THE HARDEST TIME of the day at camp was in the first class after lunch. It was the only class The Saddle Club had with both Debbie and Elsa. It was the class in which they had to give Debbie and Elsa the impression that they were complete idiots.

"Stevie, what's the matter with you?" Barry said in an irritated tone. "You know your diagonals as well as you know your own name!"

"Oh, but could you review it for me one more time?" Stevie whined convincingly.

Debbie and Elsa smirked.

Lisa and Carole smirked, too, but for a different reason. Stevie was doing a wonderful job convincing Debbie and Elsa that she was a dolt.

The whole class listened patiently while Barry ex-

plained diagonals to Stevie. Diagonals are related to a
horse's trot. At the trot, the horse's diagonal front and
back feet move together, making a two-beat gait. The
rider is supposed to post, or rise and sit, with the two
beats. When the horse changes directions—or reins,
as it is called—the rider changes diagonals. That
means that the rider sits for two beats and then begins
posting again. New riders always found it a little complicated. Experienced riders did it properly, without
thinking. Stevie was an experienced rider, but she was
acting like the newest rider there ever was.

Elsa and Debbie gloated. The Saddle Club girls
knew that the more inexperienced they appeared, the
more certain Elsa and Debbie would be of victory in
the horse show. Their plan was working.

Mornings were easier on them than afternoons. The
girls had two classes every morning, and both were
without Elsa and Debbie, so they could be as good as
they wanted to be.

The first real class of the day was a jump class.
Stevie and Carole had been jumping for a while and
were quite good at it. Lisa had never jumped a horse
intentionally. One she'd had to make a very speedy
getaway from a bull in a pasture and had taken her
horse over a four-foot fence. Max would have blown his
stack at all three girls for being *in* the pasture with the
bull in the first place and would have totally lost it if

he'd learned how they'd gotten *out*, so they'd never told him about it and had sworn one another to secrecy. Also, having stayed on her horse on one jump didn't make Lisa an expert—just lucky.

While Stevie and Carole worked on perfecting style over jumps at all levels, Lisa worked with cavalettis.

Cavalettis, Lisa learned, were really just poles laid on the ground at intervals that would allow her and Major to get used to obstacles and to keep his strides even. Lisa strongly suspected that Major had a lot more experience in jumping over obstacles than she did. That was okay. Lisa was learning so quickly that she was sure she'd be jumping soon.

By the third day of working with cavalettis, Lisa found that the most important thing she had to do was to control Major's strides and to learn how long his strides were at various gaits.

"I can't believe how much fun I'm having beginning my jumping work," Lisa told her friends while they cleaned tack in between classes.

"Just wait until you really jump over something," Carole said. "There's nothing like it. When you do it, it will mean that you have a whole new kind of control over your horse and a whole new skill in your riding. Don't you agree, Stevie?"

"Oh, yes," Stevie said. "Phil and I both *love* jumping!"

Lisa and Carole exchanged glances. They were getting used to Stevie referring to herself as "Phil and I." It seemed that now that Stevie had a boyfriend, she was no longer one person, but part of a pair. It was always "Phil and I" or "Phil said" or some variation on the theme. Carole and Lisa both liked Phil, but Stevie was really carrying the "we" bit a little too far.

"Are you and Phil finished soaping the saddle?" Carole asked innocently.

The joke was lost on Stevie. "Phil? Is he here?" She turned, looking around for him.

"No, he's not actually here," Lisa said. "But you talk about him so much that he could be."

"Oh," Stevie said, blushing. Lisa would have thought that Stevie would be the last person in the world to blush, but she was doing an incredible amount of it these days.

"Do you think this is incurable?" Lisa asked Carole after Stevie had left to put Topside's clean tack away. Since they'd spotted Phil headed in the general direction of the tack room, the girls didn't think they'd see either of them until lunchtime, when they'd be flooded with new sentences beginning with "Phil and I" and "Stevie and I." It was strange to see an independent girl like Stevie become so immersed in another person.

"I don't know," Carole answered. "But it's hard to

imagine good old Stevie going through the rest of her life in a haze."

"That makes sense," Lisa said as she buffed the last square inch of Major's saddle. "Good old Stevie is still there, under all those "Phil and I's" and blushes. She'll reemerge soon enough. Then maybe we'll be wishing for the dreamy Stevie again."

"Not me," Carole declared. "Barry had to call Stevie's turn three times this morning in class. She was too busy helping Phil untangle his reins!"

Lisa laughed. "Enough! I'm putting my saddle away and then I'm going to check on Major. He had a stone in his shoe today and I want to make sure it's not still tender. See you at lunch." She walked over to the tack room.

Somebody had put a saddle where Major's belonged. Lisa didn't know whose saddle it was, but she had a good idea whose mistake it was, and his name was Fred. There were several empty saddle racks. Lisa moved the saddle to one of them and put Major's in its proper place. She looked around. A lot of the saddles were carelessly balanced on their racks. Lisa shifted them so they all sat straight and, frowning at Fred's carelessness, left the tack room.

Major was in his own stall in the lower section of the barn. She wanted to keep an eye on him until she was sure his foot was all right. Most of the time, when a horse had a stone stuck in his shoe any tenderness disappeared as soon as the stone was removed. Lisa was just being cautious, because every once in a while a stone could cause trouble that continued after it was removed.

Lisa clipped a lead to Major's halter and led him out into the open area. She walked him the length of the barn. He seemed fine, just as she'd expected. She returned him to the stall and closed the gate.

Basil, Carole's horse, had the stall next to Major's. Lisa checked on him as well. He was fine. But there was something wrong with the horse next to Basil. It was Alamo, Nora's horse. Lisa knew that Nora had finished class over an hour earlier, but the horse still had his saddle and bridle on. Nora wouldn't be riding him for at least another hour, so there was no need for him to be tacked up while he was supposed to be resting in the stall.

Fred again.

Lisa considered the possibility that Alamo was going out again so soon that leaving the tack on was intentional. However, the last time she'd seen Nora, the girl was dismounting and handing the reins to Fred, and Lisa remembered distinctly that Nora had said she was going to take a swim before lunch. No, there was nothing intentional about this—it was just laziness. Lisa did what had to be done. She brought Alamo out of the stall, removed his saddle and bridle, put him back in, and took the tack up to the tack room.

When she'd finished putting Alamo's tack away, she found Betty in her office. Lisa didn't like tattling, but the horses' welfare was at stake here. It mattered.

She told Betty about the mess in the tack room and about Alamo's tack being left on him. Betty didn't say much besides "Hmmm," but her lips set into a thin angry line and she glared.

"Thanks," Betty said, dismissing Lisa.

Lisa didn't know what that meant. Probably Betty didn't like tattling any more than she did. It was a rotten thing to do, but at any stable, horses came first.

BY THE FOURTH day of camp, the girls were so well settled in that they felt like they'd been there forever. Stevie and Carole were getting good at being bad, Lisa was getting better at being good, and they were all having a wonderful time. While Lisa and Carole's favorite class was jumping and Stevie's favorite was whichever one she had with Phil, they all agreed that they liked their early-morning trail rides the best. Anybody who wanted to could join in. Others were expected to use the time to work on specific skills in the ring. The trail ride came before breakfast, when the sun was just up and the fields were still dewy. It was an informal ride, one without constant reminders about keeping heels down and toes in, shoulders back or chin up. It was just for fun, and it was *lots* of fun.

"Sitting trot and then canter!" Eleanor called from her lead position. At the sound of her words, the horses came to life, ready to do what their riders wanted, ready to follow Eleanor's instruction.

Max always told his riders that horses couldn't speak English, so they had to use their hands, legs, and seat to communicate. Lisa suspected that wasn't entirely correct. Most horses she'd ridden seemed to know the words for the gaits. As soon as Eleanor called out the word "trot," Major was trotting. It didn't take much longer until he was cantering.

Cantering was wonderful. It was sort of a rocking gait, and Lisa slid forward and back slightly in the saddle with Major's strides. Although it was much faster than the trot, it was smoother and Lisa felt more secure. Major seemed to feel her excitement and responded with both greater power and smoothness. Lisa couldn't help herself. She grinned with the pleasure of the experience.

Eleanor's hand went up and the riders slowed their horses to a trot and then, quickly, to a walk. Carole pulled up beside Lisa.

"It's wonderful, isn't it?" Carole asked.

Lisa nodded.

"It's what riding is about, you know. I don't mean

just cantering. A horse shouldn't be asked to canter too much. What I mean is—"

"I know," Lisa said. "Riding is about having fun, and this is as much fun as there is, right?"

Carole smiled at her friend. Sometimes she couldn't believe how much Lisa had learned about riding in just a few short months. Lisa was good already, and she was going to get a lot better as time went on.

"That's one of the things I was going to say, but there's something else, too. The thing about riding is both learning enough to have fun, like we are right now, and then having enough fun to learn, like we do in class. The more you know, the better you ride, and the more fun it is."

The trail was narrowing, so Lisa dropped back behind Carole in line. "You mean that one day I'll enjoy this even more?" she asked.

"Absolutely!" Carole called over her shoulder.

Lisa sighed contentedly. There was a *lot* to look forward to!

AT LUNCH THAT DAY, Lisa found that there was even more to look forward to.

"Girls and boys, may I have your attention, please," Barry said, standing up in front of the group as they began eating their tuna fish sandwiches.

"Oh, this is going to be our surprise event," Phil

said, leaning toward Stevie and her friends to explain. "Barry does something special at the end of the first week of every session. Last year, we went to see Combined Training at a nearby stable. That would be great—"

"And this year, I have planned something entirely different," Barry was saying. "Tomorrow morning after breakfast, we are leaving on an overnight camping trip. We will return the following afternoon. Please make sure that all your horses are in shape for the trip and that you have—"

Barry went on. He had a nearly endless list of things they had to do before they could go. The girls remembered their last overnight, right after Lisa had come to Pine Hollow and started riding. It had been fantastic, and they were sure this one would be, too.

"Give me a break!" somebody growled. It was Debbie.

"What's the matter with an overnight trip?" Carole wanted to know.

Debbie made an unbelievably rude face. "Overnight? When we've got a show to train for? The next thing you know, he'll have us doing—"

"Mounted games!" Barry announced. "Tomorrow after dinner when it's still light, we'll set up teams and have a sort of mini-gymkhana!"

Many campers clapped with delight. Debbie didn't.

Neither did Elsa. The Saddle Club girls didn't care what those two sourpusses thought. They'd been working hard on their skills and it would be fun to put them to the test with some games.

Lisa remembered what Carole had said to her on the morning trail ride. It seemed that her prediction was already coming true!

CAROLE TIGHTENED BASIL'S girth and checked the stirrup length. In general, stirrups were the right length for a rider if they were about the length of the rider's arm. Nobody but Carole should have used Basil's saddle, but she could tell at a glance that somebody had fiddled with her stirrups. *Fred again,* she told herself, shortening the leather by two buckle holes.

Carole actually wasn't sorry she had to fuss with saddle adjustments, because right on Basil's other side, a drama was unfolding. As long as she had an excuse to be where she was, she could get an earful.

"I'm just not feeling very well, Barry," Debbie whined. Carole, reaching under Basil to needlessly straighten the girth, saw a phony pained look on Debbie's face.

"Well, *where* aren't you feeling well?" Barry asked impatiently.

"Oh, sort of here," she said, gesturing vaguely toward her entire body. Carole thought that was even more fake than her last statement.

"Have you seen the nurse?" Barry asked.

"No, but I've had this happen before," Debbie said. "It'll be all better in a day or so."

Carole didn't think there was anything Barry could do about Debbie's mysterious stomachache and apparently he agreed. He told Debbie to take her gear back to the cabin. She could stay in the camp until they got back from the trip. Carole could see the pleased look on Debbie's face as she returned to Cabin Three. She'd bet a stirrup to a saddle that Debbie's vague ailment would be cleared up within the hour and she'd be on her horse, in the ring, practicing for the horse show all alone, all day.

Or would Debbie be all alone?

"Barry, can I talk to you?" It was Elsa. It turned out that she had a strange pain in her right ear. Elsa said she didn't think it was serious, but she could remember one time when she'd had an ache very much like this one and within a few hours, she'd been horribly sick, so she thought maybe it wouldn't be a good idea to go on the camping trip, and didn't Barry agree?

Barry didn't agree. The tone of his voice made it

clear to Carole that he'd had about enough games from Elsa and Debbie. On the other hand, Carole suspected that Barry would decide to let Elsa stay in camp because she and Debbie deserved one another and the rest of the campers deserved a vacation from them.

As Carole figured, Barry told Elsa she could stay at camp. Like Debbie, Elsa was grinning victoriously as she returned to the cabin. Carole would have loved to see their faces when each discovered that the other had wangled her way out of the camping trip.

Finally satisfied with her stirrup length, Carole lowered the flap of her saddle, secured her pack, and mounted up. It was time to hit the trail.

She turned around in her saddle, looking for her friends. She couldn't wait to share the wonderful news about Debbie and Elsa.

"MORE THAN TWENTY-FOUR hours of trail riding—isn't it fabulous!" Lisa said to Carole as they proceeded through a woody area.

"Especially without the Miss Uncongeniality Award winners," Carole agreed.

"Only trouble is that I'm missing a jump class," Lisa remarked.

Carole's eyes lit up. That meant she had an idea. One of her favorite things to do was to share her riding

65

knowledge with her friends, and most of the time, they welcomed it. If this was going to be a way to learn jumping on a trail ride, Lisa was willing to listen.

"Try this," Carole told her friend. "I think Barry's about to start us trotting. You can do it in jump position. It's not the same as working with cavaletti, but it's important."

Of course, Lisa thought. Eleanor, the jump instructor, kept stressing the necessity of a good jump position. In jump position, the rider's seat was slightly raised, and you leaned forward with your back parallel to the horse's neck. It was the position a rider needed to go over a jump, remain balanced, and absorb the impact of landing with the knees. It was critical to have a good jump position, so it was important to practice as much as possible. Lisa rose slightly, leaned forward, and kept her hands still at the horse's neck.

"Good job," Carole said. "Remember to keep your toes up and your hands steady."

At the front, Barry raised his hand to signal a change of pace. In seconds, they were all trotting. Much to Lisa's surprise, the other campers were following her lead and trotting in jump position. It seemed that even without the presence of Debbie and Elsa, the riders were competitive. Nobody wanted anybody to practice anything more than anybody else. Lisa didn't know whether to laugh or be sad. Since Carole was right there, they exchanged looks and laughed. It was better than being sad.

When they finished the trot and were walking again, Carole continued instructing Lisa. Carole was a natural teacher. She knew a lot about horses and riding and she liked to share it. Sometimes her friends got a little tired of it, but this time, two things kept Lisa from stopping her. The first was that everything Carole was telling her was absolutely right. The second was that every rider within earshot was hanging on to Carole's every word. It was not just funny, it was hilarious.

Stevie, who was riding next to Phil, was close enough to see what was going on. Lisa spotted the familiar mischievous grin on her friend's face and knew something good was coming.

"Hey, Carole!" Stevie called, spurring the horse toward her best friends. "Is Lisa having trouble with her form again? Let *me* help!"

When Stevie arrived, the fun began. She told Carole to ride on the other side so they could both watch Lisa, but she really meant so they could watch the other riders. Then Stevie started barking instructions, and they were all wrong. The eavesdroppers followed every word she said. Within a few minutes, Stevie had them all riding sitting on the back edges of their saddles, arms fully extended at shoulder height, legs straight and stretched forward.

Barry turned to check on his riders. He was completely astonished to see all of them, except The Saddle Club, posed like zombies on horseback!

"Halloween requires costumes and your horses require proper riders!" he snapped. "All of you! Back in position! We're going to canter!"

Lisa hoped that the sound of his horse's hooves covered the burst of giggles from The Saddle Club.

"What was that all about?" Phil asked Stevie when she returned to his side.

"Just a little joke," she said, embarrassed. After all, Phil had followed her silly instructions, too.

"What kind of joke?" he persisted.

"It's all this dumb competition," she began. "Even without Elsa and Debbie, it's like everybody's spying. I just thought I'd give them something for their trouble. It was pretty funny, you know."

"To you, maybe," Phil said.

That was all he said for a while. Stevie didn't like the idea that she'd made him feel foolish, but, she reasoned, he'd been acting stupid by following her directions.

After what seemed a long time, but was really no more than five minutes, he made a peace offering. "I brought some marshmallows," he said. "Want to sneak out of camp after lights out and have a little picnic of our own?"

Stevie grinned and nodded. "Yeah, I'd like that," she said, glad that his feelings weren't still hurt.

WHEN THEY REACHED the campsite, The Saddle Club girls knew just what to do. The rule on the Pine Hollow trip was horses first, riders second. They dismounted and untacked their horses and led them to the nearby stream, where they could get a drink of water. Then the horses would need grooming and fresh hay, followed by more water and, finally, a full meal of grain, which had been delivered to the campsite's paddock. After that, the girls would check their tack and stow it for the night. Then it would be time to set up the campsite.

It was that simple—and it was that complicated.

"I can't lift the saddle."

"*I've* got to have something to eat first."

"I don't know how to do this stuff."

"Why can't Fred do it?"

"I thought we were supposed to learn to ride, not work!"

And so on. The Saddle Club couldn't believe the way some of the campers were acting. Some of them made honest attempts to complete the obvious chores like untacking, but a lot of them seemed to think that everything except the actual riding was beneath them.

Stevie, Carole, and Lisa were too well trained by

Max. Nothing having to do with stable management and horse care was beneath a good rider. Patiently, the girls pitched in to help other campers complete the work. It didn't earn them many thanks. Mostly what they got were surprised looks.

Carole helped the others with untacking, Lisa managed the watering and feeding, and Stevie supervised grooming. Stevie, it turned out, was the all-time champion hoof-picker.

"Three stones!" she announced proudly as the third pebble in one horse's hoof hit the ground. Her friends applauded. The other campers remained mystified.

When Fred delivered the first bale of hay to the paddock area, Lisa snapped the wire that held it and began breaking it into one-horse flakes. But something was wrong, and she knew what it was right away. The hay had that same odd, almost sickly sweet smell that she'd noticed in the moldy bale back at camp.

"Fred, this stuff doesn't smell right to me," she said.

Fred shrugged and walked away.

Lisa couldn't feed that hay to the horses. It would almost certainly make them sick. One horse with colic was bad news, but a whole paddock full of them would be a disaster. She got one of the boys to give her a hand. Together they carried the moldy bale into an open area of the woods and spread it around on the forest floor, where it would eventually dry out and where no horses could reach it. Then they found a fresh bale, which they opened and fed to the horses in the makeshift paddock.

Barry and Betty were busy overseeing the mixing of the horse's grain. Lisa didn't want to bother them about Fred's most recent mistake. Besides, she wasn't too sure it was her place to tell them. After all, no harm had been done. She told herself she'd think about it later. Her thoughts were interrupted by more squabbling campers.

"I'll tell you one thing. I don't care *what* Barry said. I'm not picking up kindling for every single fireplace in the whole campsite. I'm not sitting at every fire, so I'm not building every fire!"

"Me, neither!" said the girl's companion.

Well, at least there were two campers who agreed on something!

Lisa returned to the campsite and helped pitch tents. Carole, being a Marine Corps brat, was of course the champion at that. Finally, the campers finished their chores. At last they could enjoy the campsite.

It was a nice campsite, with tents pitched among tall pine trees. Carole like camping in piny woods, because the pine needles cushioned the ground and that was good for sleeping. The area was open enough so that there was no danger from the camp fires. Leaning against neighboring tree trunks, Carole and her friends could see the clear sky above. It was still light. They were having an early dinner, so there would still be plenty of light for their mounted games.

"This sort of reminds me of the story of The Little Red Hen," Carole remarked to her friends, taking her first bite of Trail Stew and washing it down with fruit punch. "Nobody wants to share the work, but everybody wants to share the cake."

Stevie and Lisa agreed totally.

"Even Phil seems to catch the disease sometimes," Stevie remarked, surprising Lisa and Carole with her frankness.

The girls ate the rest of their meal in silence. For one thing, they were really tired, too tired to do their usual chatting. For another, right then, there didn't seem to be anything to say. It had all been said and it was trouble and they all knew it.

THE FIRST GAME Barry chose for them to play was Follow-the-Leader. He very wisely chose Stevie as a leader. Nobody was more able to do so many ridiculous things on horseback. The only problem was that the first thing Stevie did as leader was to imitate the silly position she'd gotten everybody into on the afternoon ride. Both Carole and Lisa were laughing so hard that they couldn't do it.

"You two, you're out!" Barry yelled.

They pulled over to the side and watched the rest. Stevie had the riders sit both cross-legged and backwards on their saddles—horses standing still, of course. She tried a sidesaddle seat, but it was difficult without a genuine sidesaddle, and she almost fell off herself. When Phil and another rider did, they joined Carole and Lisa on the sidelines.

At the end of the game, Barry took over and started them on Simon-Says. Lisa and Carole thought Stevie had done more amusing things, but it didn't matter. It was all fun.

Next, they played a game called Touch Wood. It was sort of like tag, but anybody touching wood—for example, a tree, a fence post, or a gate—was safe. But every time the whistle blew, everybody had to change trees or whatever wood they were touching.

"This is wild!" Lisa gasped, swapping trees with Carole at a canter while Nora chased both of them.

"And a good learning experience, too!" Carole said, reaching as long and hard as she could for her new tree, but she wasn't fast enough.

"You're It!" Nora declared.

Watching Carole, Lisa thought about what she'd said about learning. It was true. The game was great practice in horse control, particularly direction changes. Fortunately for Carole, she was a good enough rider that she wasn't It for long. Within a very short time, Lisa was It.

I'm learning, I'm learning, she told herself as she dashed after the riders who scattered across the field. *I'm learning. And most of all, I'm having fun!*

After Touch Wood, they played another variation,

Freeze Tag, which involved even more horse control than Touch Wood, since anybody who had been tagged had to remain completely still—as did the horse.

The riders concentrated so hard on their games that they barely noticed when the sun set and night came on.

"Time to quit," Barry announced. "All of you walk your horses until he's cooled down, untack him, and give him water and fresh hay. We'll meet at the camp fire in half an hour for ghost stories. Anybody who wants to can tell a ghost story, but the principle character in the story *must* be a horse!"

Contented and tired and looking forward to a quiet camp-fire time, Carole quickly took care of Basil and then helped Lisa finish putting away Major's tack.

"Wait until Barry hears the one about the werehorse!" Carole said to Lisa.

"That sounds like a Stevie kind of story," Lisa remarked.

"Yes, it does," Carole said. "And speaking of Stevie, I haven't seen her for a while, have you?"

Lisa hung Major's bridle over his saddle. "Yes, actually, I did see her—or at least the back of her. I think she and Phil are going to miss your story about the werehorse. I also think we may have to cover for her."

"What are friends for?" Carole asked. She gave

Basil a final pat on his nose. Then she turned to Lisa and slung her arm across her friend's shoulder. "Okay, so now this werehorse makes friends with a vamp-mare . . ."

STEVIE WONDERED IF she would ever get used to the feeling of Phil holding her hand when they walked. It wasn't a very efficient way to walk through a wooded area—single file was much better—but it was more fun.

"Did you bring the marshmallows?" Phil asked.

"Oh, no, I forgot. How dumb of me!"

"That's okay. After that dinner, I'm not very hungry."

"Me, neither," Stevie said. "Maybe that's why I forgot the marshmallows. You know, I really didn't want them, but I didn't know it."

Phil smiled. It was that smile that made Stevie's knees melt. "Why don't we sit down someplace?" she suggested, hoping she could sit down before she fell down. Not that his smile could really make her faint, but a full day of riding hadn't helped her knees, either.

"Here's a clearing, I think," Phil said. It was awfully hard to see. The night sky was overcast and they were deep in a forest, but there appeared to be a small open space. Carefully, Stevie lowered herself onto the crunchy leaves, sitting cross-legged. Phil sat facing her and took her hand. She no longer shivered when he did that, but she did tingle.

"Tired?" he asked.

"A little," she conceded. "I like riding and I like doing a lot of it, but Barry's schedule for us is really rugged."

"Too much for the famed Saddle Club?" Phil teased.

Stevie wasn't crazy about his tone. Phil was very special to her, but so was The Saddle Club, and she didn't like him making fun of it.

"The Saddle Club is made up of me and my two best friends," Stevie said, knowing she sounded defensive. "We've accomplished some pretty good things together in the past, and I think you'll have a chance to see us do impressive things in the future, too."

"I will?" Phil said, obviously curious.

"Yes, you will," Stevie assured him. "In fact, in case you didn't know it, we're working on several projects at this very minute!"

"Here, with me?"

"No, I don't mean here. I just mean we're in the process. It has to do with riding and it has to do with the show next weekend and it has to do with some of the campers who think they are going to win absolutely everything at the show."

"You mean like me?"

"Huh?" Stevie responded in surprise. "You mean *you* think you're going to take all the prizes?"

"Is there anybody here good enough to beat me?" Phil asked.

Stevie thought about it for a minute. It was too dark to see Phil's face, but it certainly sounded to her as if he were completely serious. It had never really occurred to her that Phil might feel that way. He was a good enough rider—experienced, secure—but a champion? No, she was better than he was.

"I'm asking," Phil repeated. "Do you think you and your friends can beat me?"

One of Stevie's biggest faults was that she often spoke before she thought.

"Of course we can beat you," she said, absolutely certain that she was one hundred percent right.

"That's what you think." He spoke sharply. Stevie was angry. How could he possibly think that he was as good a rider as she was? He was *almost* as good as she was, but not better, and certainly not better than Carole.

"You're crazy," she snapped. "The Saddle Club is going to outride, outrun, and outribbon every single rider in this camp. You included."

Stevie stood up. Phil stood up, too.

"I—" he began. Stevie didn't let him finish. She didn't want to hear whatever it was that he had to say. If he thought he was better than she was, well then he

78

could just spend some time alone with that wonderful thought.

"I'll see you in the morning," she announced. She spun on her heel and marched through the woods. Branches snapped in her face, but she didn't feel them. She nearly tripped over a root, and didn't notice. A briar ripped at her sweater. She didn't care. For a second, she thought that she heard Phil call her name.

"Better than I am? No way!" she said to herself. "Better than Carole? Out of the question!" She continued talking as she stormed through the forest.

The woods were unfamiliar, but she remembered that the campsite was in a valley and that she and Phil had been walking uphill all the way. In just a few minutes, she came upon the flickering flames of the campsite. Unnoticed, she slipped into the tent she shared with Carole and Lisa. She put on her pajamas and climbed into her sleeping bag. She was still too angry to sleep, though.

Outside, beyond the canvas walls of her tent, she could hear her friends talking.

". . . And then the werehorse said to the vampmare, 'Don't worry, my bark is worse than my bite.' And the vampmare replied, 'That's funny—mine isn't!'" There were giggles and laughter. Stevie didn't laugh. Right then, nothing was funny, except maybe the idea that Phil-the-super-duper-rider who thought he could take all the prizes might, just might, get lost in the woods.

And *that* was a comforting notion to go to sleep by, Stevie thought, drifting off at last.

9

"Do I DETECT trouble in paradise?" Lisa asked Stevie as casually as she could manage. She was riding next to Stevie as the campers returned to Moose Hill and for the first time in days, Phil was not in sight.

"Why would you say that?" Stevie retorted.

"Maybe it has something to do with the stony look on your face," Carole said. "Which, I might add, perfectly matches the one on a certain guy's, although you might not know it, since you haven't looked at him all day."

"Who?" Stevie asked innocently. Her friends got the message.

"Well, well!" Lisa said lightly. "Looks like the old Stevie is back!"

Stevie just glared. It was clear that she wasn't up for

any teasing. Lisa and Carole decided to leave her alone.

For Lisa, it was a little sad to be returning to Moose Hill. She'd had a wonderful time on the trip, enjoying every minute of it and learning every minute of it, too, thanks to Carole.

"Since we missed jump class again today," Lisa said, "would you be able to work with me on the cavalettis and low jumps during free time this evening?"

"Oh, sure," Carole replied enthusiastically. She was as glad for an opportunity to teach as Lisa was eager for one to learn. "You know, I think you'll have a good shot at earning a ribbon in the Beginning Jumper category at the show. Don't you agree, Stevie?" Carole asked.

"I don't want to talk about the show," Stevie grumbled.

Carole and Lisa were surprised. Whatever it was that was wrong with Stevie, it wasn't just Phil. And it was clear that until Stevie got into a talking mood, they weren't going to learn a thing. In the meantime, the best thing to do was to stay out of her way.

LISA HAD HAD a vague hope that the enjoyable time the campers had shared at the campsite, with the mounted games and the silly ghost stories, might improve the general attitude around camp and make a change in the way campers took care of their horses when they returned to camp. She was wrong.

The horses had no sooner reached the barn than the campers were nearly shoving one another aside to find the best untacking position, which was nearest the tack room and required the shortest walk carrying tack. Everybody seemed grumpy and selfish. Nobody wanted to do their own work, much less help others. It wasn't the way riding should be, Lisa thought angrily. Friends helped one another and had fun working together. At least that was what she had found in The Saddle Club. So why couldn't everybody see that? Why couldn't everybody cooperate?

The whole operation was complicated by the fact that the farrier was coming in the morning. Barry had made an announcement about it. Most horses needed new shoes about once a month. A couple of the camp horses needed shoes and Barry wanted to make sure everybody who needed them would get them. All of the campers were to make a special check of their horses' hooves and shoes, and any horse who needed new shoes would be kept in a stall in the barn overnight. The farrier would arrive at dawn and most of the horses would have their shoes by noon.

Lisa finished untacking Major, got him a bucket of fresh water, and led him out by the paddock, where she could groom him in the sunlight.

Every grooming began with a check of the horse's hooves. Lisa began with Major's left front foot. There was a lot of dirt lodged in there, but it all came out with a simple picking. She tapped the shoe. It was secure. One down, three to go. His left hind foot wasn't so easy. The mud came out, but as soon as she tapped the shoe with the pick, it dropped off. That meant that Major would have to spend the night in the barn, waiting for the farrier. Worse still, he might not have his new shoes in time for her jump class. Lisa sighed. If riding horses meant having a wonderful time, it also meant learning patience.

Major's right front shoe was missing and had to be replaced. If one was gone, all four had to go, because it meant the other three might go as well. There was no getting away from it: Major needed new shoes. And in the meantime, Lisa really shouldn't ride him. She hoped Carole would let her ride Basil when they practiced this evening.

Lisa finished grooming Major, packed up his grooming gear, and took him into the stable area beneath the main barn. As she was giving him fresh hay in his stall, she suddenly remembered that she'd wanted to tell Barry about the moldy hay Fred had brought on the trip. She finished her work with Major and returned to the main level of the barn.

Barry was there, all right, but he was very busy.

Debbie, it seemed, was now completely recovered from whatever it was that she'd been sick with yesterday and was having a heated argument with Barry.

"You said the judging at the show would be fair!" Debbie said hotly.

"And it will be," Barry replied, trying to sound calm.

"How can it be fair if one of the other rider's *mother* is a judge?" Debbie challenged.

"She's a good judge," Barry said. "She's judged all kinds of competitions, including American Horse Show Association shows."

The more Lisa listened, the more she learned. It turned out that one of the judges was Elsa's mother. No wonder Debbie was so upset! It might even make her *really* sick! It occurred to Lisa that if Elsa's mother was going to judge the show, it might not be too wonderful for The Saddle Club's latest project, either, but she quickly dismissed the thought. She would love it if The Saddle Club could take all the ribbons at the show and teach some people lessons, but as she'd learned from Carole, the most important part about riding was learning enough to have fun.

In any case, it was clear that this was no time to talk to Barry, and Eleanor was nowhere in sight. That meant it was time for her to unpack her own overnight sack, put on a bathing suit, and test the waters in the pond. Without regret, she left the barn.

"STEVIE?"

Stevie didn't look up. She was working on Topside's coat, grooming it to a wonderful sheen. She knew who was talking to her. She didn't want to talk to him.

"You there?" Phil asked.

"Hmmm."

"Teddy's favoring one of his legs. He won't let me touch it. Can you help him?"

That put Stevie in a quandary. She was still steaming mad at Phil and she didn't want to lift a finger to help him. But helping Teddy was another matter. It was unfair to make Teddy suffer just because she was mad at his owner. Besides, since Phil had put it in terms of helping Teddy, she decided she could do it.

"You're the best there is at picking out stones. That's what I think it is. I hope—"

"Let's see," Stevie said abruptly. She put down the tools and looked up for the first time. Phil had crosstied Teddy right across the barn from Topside. It was almost true that she hadn't noticed Phil until he had spoken.

She rummaged through her tool bucket, took out her own hoof pick, and walked over to the horse.

Stevie could see right away that Teddy's left front foot was bothering him. A horse at rest might lift a rear foot and casually shift his weight or just point the toe, holding the heel of the rear foot off the ground. But, when a front foot was held that way for a long time, there was probably something wrong.

Stevie approached Teddy. She patted him and spoke to him reassuringly. The last thing she wanted to do was to startle a horse with a sore foot.

"He was okay when I was riding him. I'm sure I would have noticed. So he must have just picked up a stone on the way into the barn. Isn't that strange?"

Stevie just grunted. She spoke gently to the horse. "It's okay, boy. I'm not going to hurt you. No trouble; here, boy. Just let me have a look."

She slid her hand down his leg, put her shoulder against his, and reached for the hoof. Teddy lifted it for her.

"How do you *do* that?" Phil asked. Stevie didn't bother to answer. After all, if Phil thought he was such a hotshot on horseback, why should he need any horse-care tips from her?

Gently, she probed the tissue of the hoof, removing dirt with her pick. She didn't see anything wrong right away, but as she tapped the shoe, she knew there was something in there, because Teddy flinched at the touch.

She kept talking to him. It was the best way she knew to calm a horse, and this one needed calming. So did his owner, but Stevie didn't speak to Phil.

"You picked something up here, didn't you, boy?" She felt under the shoe with the pick. "I feel something there. We'll get it out." Whatever it was, it wouldn't budge with the pick. Stevie tried the next best thing—her finger. She probed until she could reach the stone and then, slowly and carefully, began moving it. Every time it moved, Teddy reacted. Although she didn't like hurting him, it would hurt him a lot worse if she didn't get it out.

"It's coming now, boy. It'll just be a little bit longer. Hold on there, okay?"

With a final tug, Stevie got the stone out. It clattered to the barn floor. Stevie picked it up to examine it.

"That's a nasty one, boy," she told Teddy, looking at the sharply pointed stone that had been giving him so much trouble. "I don't know how you stood it at all. Now let me have another look at that hoof."

There was a bucket of water nearby. Stevie took her water brush, dipped it in the bucket, and began washing the sole of the horse's foot. When the area was clean, she could see some discoloration. "Looks like you've got a bruise here, boy," she said to Teddy. "It may be nothing, but if I were you, I'd tell my owner that I should stay in the barn tonight and be checked by the farrier in the morning. Besides, you don't want to go running all over the paddock competing with those other horses when you've got a sore foot now, do you?"

She put the horse's hoof down and stood up. "That's a good boy," she said, patting him.

"Thank you, Stevie," Phil said. "You're the best at that."

"I'm glad to know you think I'm the best at something!" Stevie retorted and, without another word, returned to grooming Topside.

She thought Phil Marston had a lot of nerve trying to make her feel better by saying she was good at getting stones out. She *was* good at it, but it wasn't what she wanted to hear him say.

When she finished with Topside, she turned him out into the paddock with the other horses and she returned to the cabin. Lisa had said something about a swim before supper. That would be good—especially if there were no boys there.

10

LISA WAS HAVING a wonderful dream. It was all about the camp-out—the trail ride, the games, the ghost stories around the camp fire. She was listening to more ghost stories around the camp fire. She could almost smell the pungent smoke. It tickled her nostrils and irritated her eyes. She was roasting marshmallows. But there was no smell of marshmallows. There was just the smell of smoke.

Lisa sat upright in bed. There was *still* a smell of smoke. "Fire!" she whispered, almost too frightened to say it out loud.

"Hmph," rumbled one of her sleeping cabin mates.

She sniffed again. There was no doubt about it. Something was burning and Lisa had the awful feeling it wasn't a camp fire. She hopped out of her bed and ran to the window. She could see the barn at the top of the hill. A flicker of orange was coming from the hay-loft.

"*FIRE!*" Lisa yelled. Everybody was awake at once.

The girls didn't wait to dress. They ran out of their cabin, screaming out the frightening word *fire* as they rushed through the cabin area. Other campers quickly joined them.

Lisa raced up the hill, Carole and Stevie beside her.

"It's the hay," Lisa said. "I know it's the hay! All that moldy hay, and Fred left it in the barn. It started a fire!"

"Come on," Carole urged. "Right now, that's not important. Someone's told Barry. He'll call the Fire Department and they'll take care of the barn. We've got to help the horses!"

The Saddle Club knew they only had a few minutes and every second could mean a horse's life! Barns were filled with things that burned well. Hay, grain, straw, dry wood—all of it would fuel the fire, and within a short time the whole thing could just about explode.

Carole pointed to the upper paddock on the far side of the barn, where the horses were beginning to panic. The horses clustered near the barn, as if they were looking for the safety of a familiar shelter. They shifted and pranced, nudging and frightening one another. Their ears were pinned back in fear and tension, their eyes were opened wide, showing white all around. The horses were in terrible danger and every instinct they had was putting them at greater risk.

"Get them away from the barn!" Carole cried. "It could collapse on them!"

Lisa saw at once that she was right. If the animals could be moved to the other end of the large paddock and kept there, they'd be safe no matter what happened to the barn. Cooped in the paddock next to the barn, they only terrified one another, endangering themselves even more. But what could the girls do?

"The hilltop!" Lisa cried to Carole. "If we can get them on the other side of the hill, they won't see the fire, and maybe they'll stay away."

Carole nodded. There wasn't a second to spare on conversation. She barked orders at everybody nearby, and everybody began following them.

"Lisa, Debbie! Climb the fence on our side—don't go inside, the horses could crush you—and try shooing them away from the barn. Jack, Nora, Elsa, go get cavalettis, jumps, barrels, anything you can think of to create a makeshift fence to restrain the horses in the far end of the paddock. You four, bring water, hay, grain, anything you can lay your hands on, to give the horses when they get there. We'll need a big welcoming committee to make them feel at home. Seth, you help Lisa and Debbie. Use your shirt to wave at them if you want. Anything to get them to move, because I've got the feeling that wall's going to collapse. And when it does, the horses aren't the only ones who will have to be out of its way!"

Lisa looked over her shoulder at the barn. The long upright slats of wood were glowing red with the heat and licking flames were visible behind them. The hay in the loft was burning so fast that the entire barn could be gone in just a few minutes. She began waving her arms at the frightened horses, just as Carole had told her. It was hard to imagine that this frantic herd of horses, prancing, jumping, and whinnying with fear, were the same horses who had been so obedient just a few hours ago when they'd been ridden. Her eyes searched among them for her own horse. But she didn't see him. Maybe he was smarter than the others. Maybe he was already safe at the far end of the field.

Then the realization hit her. Major wasn't safe in the field. He wasn't safe at all. *Major was in the barn!*

STEVIE RAN TO the lower entrance of the barn where the horses were stabled. The fire had started in the loft, at the top of the barn. "Hot air rises," she told herself. "It'll burn, the whole thing will burn, but it goes up faster than it comes down. I've got time. I've got time."

But when she got to the barn, she wasn't so certain.

The air was filled with the sound of crackling fire and it was close, too close. She could barely breathe, but the only thought she had was for the horses. Especially one horse—Teddy. She had put him in the barn, and she would get him out. There wasn't time to get Barry or Eleanor to help. All she had to do, she told herself, was to open the door. The horses would run.

She could hear their loud whinnies and cries above the terrifying crackling of the consuming fire. The horses stomped on the wood floor in complete panic, drumming their hooves irregularly.

The she heard one cry, louder than the rest. She couldn't wait. She had to free the horses. It didn't matter where they went. It just mattered that they didn't stay.

Without another thought, Stevie grabbed the handle to the door and pulled.

NEARLY FIFTY HORSES pressed forward in the upper paddock toward the barn. The fence was strong, but it wasn't designed to withstand pressure like that. Lisa could feel the wood wobbling under the crush of the horses' power. She waved frantically at the animals, but it was as if they didn't see her at all. They pushed her hands away with their noses. Debbie, next to Lisa, wasn't having any more luck. Eleanor and Betty joined them, as did six other campers. Finally, with so many people trying to get them to move away, the horses stepped back, but the horses in the rear hadn't gotten the message. They pushed the whole herd forward again, surging against the weakened fence.

Lisa looked around, thinking furiously. They needed something really visible, something that would be impossible for the horses not to notice. She spotted a small stack of rags by the spigot that were used to dry the horses after their baths.

In a flash, she hopped down from the fence, retrieved the rags, and handed them out to all the people standing by the fence. A few campers looked at them, momentarily puzzled.

"Wave them!" Lisa yelled. "Anything to get the horses' attention and frighten them away from the barn instead of toward it!"

The campers followed her instructions. It seemed to help, but Lisa didn't think that it would be enough.

Then came two sounds that she had been expecting to hear—one bad, one good. The first was the collapse of the loft floor. There was a loud crash as it landed on the main floor of the barn, spreading the fire further and faster. The horses jumped back in surprise, but then quickly resumed their press toward the building.

The second sound was one of sirens. The Fire Department had arrived. The barn was burning too fast to be saved, especially since the loft had collapsed, but maybe the firemen could keep the fire from spreading.

Lisa returned to her work.

NEARBY, CAROLE WAS thinking as hard and as fast as she could. She'd never seen anything like the horses' frantic press to return to the barn, and she'd never seen horses less interested in nine people waving rags. If only just one horse would start to retreat, Carole was sure others would follow him to safety. Normally, waving a single rag would be enough to send a herd of horses on the run. She'd even witnessed Topside completely miss a jump in a horse show because a thoughtless spectator had waved her cloak.

Topside—where is Topside? Carole asked herself. Although Stevie was riding Topside at camp, Carole had ridden him at Pine Hollow a couple of times and she knew what a wonderfully obedient horse he was. Then it occurred to her that if she could get on Topside's back, she'd have a chance to convince him to run for safety—and maybe convince the rest of the herd as well.

Swiftly, she boosted herself up onto the fence. She just *had* to find Topside. Unfortunately, Topside was a bay horse, which meant he was brown with a black mane and tail—like almost every other horse in the paddock! Carole anxiously scanned the herd.

And there he was. Like the others, he was clearly

terrified. He was frightened by the sound and garish light of the fire, but he was also alarmed by what the other horses were doing.

"Here, boy," Carole said as calmly as she could. Horses, she knew, couldn't understand most words, but they were experts at tone of voice. She tried to keep her voice even and soothing. Topside's ears flicked toward her in response. She was just able to reach out and pat his neck. Then the throng of horses moved to one side, carrying Topside with them. His ears flattened again. Carole followed them, shifting her position on the fence.

She could do it, she was sure. She *had* to do it, but she sure needed help. The best help in the world with Topside was Stevie. *Where was she?*

THERE WERE EIGHT horses in the stable area of the barn's lower level. Stevie looked around. She was alone. She didn't have time to go for help. She was going to have to do this herself.

Common sense told her to release the horses farthest from the door first. She dashed in, ran for the most distant stall, opened the door, and tugged at the horse's halter. He whinnied a sound somewhere between angry and scared.

"I know just how you feel, boy," she said. Firmly, steadily, she led him to the door and walked him through it. As soon as she released his halter, she gave him a slap on the flank. He neighed loudly and took off in the direction of the pond. Stevie hoped the horses she released wouldn't run too far, but she hoped they'd run far enough. There would be plenty of time to find them, as long as they were alive.

Wasting no time, she went on to the next horse. In the eerie, orangish light, she thought she recognized him. Major! Lisa would be glad she'd saved him. Major followed the first horse off into the darkness.

In the split second before she returned to the barn, she heard the sound of the loft falling—and the Fire Department arriving. Maybe, maybe, she'd get some help from them. Maybe they'd be able to save some of the barn.

As Stevie rapidly led the horses out one by one, she thought about the camp's nice old barn—the cool feeling of the stable area on a hot summer day, the old-fashioned drive-through design, the tack room, and the other storage rooms with the wagons and the sled. She hoped some of those things would be saved. But horses came first.

Stevie kept looking for Teddy. She hadn't found him yet, but it was very hard to see in the stable area at all. She knew he was there. She wanted more than anything to get him out, but she couldn't waste time looking for just one horse. They all needed freedom.

And she needed time!

FOR ONCE, CAROLE was glad about Fred's carelessness. He'd left a lead rope slung over the fence instead of putting it away as he should have. It was just the thing Carole needed.

The next time the horses surged toward her, she slipped her hands between the slats of the fence and clipped the lead rope onto Topside's halter. It wasn't exactly a snaffle-bitted bridle, but it would have to do because it was all there was.

Then she reached one hand over the top of the fence, took the lead rope in that hand, and climbed up. She knew she wouldn't get a better opportunity than this.

Talking constantly, softly, surely, using his name, patting his neck, Carole slowly lowered herself onto Topside's back. She was in pajamas and barefoot. She had no saddle, no boots, no spurs, nothing to tell Topside she meant business, except her calves and her voice.

She gripped him with her legs to let him know she was on board and she was in charge now. She wanted him to feel that he didn't have to make any more decisions in this very frightening experience—Carole would do it for him.

"Okay, Topside," she said. She clucked her tongue.

His ears straightened right up. It was a good sign. It meant he heard her and was alert for other signals. "This is going to test your skills as a roundup horse and mine as a cowboy. We don't have any time to waste, so let's get down to business. Let's go."

She nudged his belly with her bare feet. He tensed under her. She felt his uncertainty. She didn't want him to be uncertain. She wanted him to follow her instructions without question. She kicked him. At that, Topside seemed ready to take orders from her, but by then Carole was in the middle of a sea of horses, with no place to go!

At that instant, the first gigantic arc of water reached upward from the other side of the barn, suddenly visible to the horses. As one, the animals stepped back in fear, opening up their ranks ever so slightly. Carole held her hands low and pulled on the lead rope and prayed that Topside would recognize the signal as if it were from a bridle with a bit. For a moment, he stood still. Then, slowly, carefully, he began to walk backwards.

"Good boy!" Carole said, and she meant it!

"OUCH!" STEVIE SAID. One skittish mare had just kicked her. She rubbed her shin. It was swelling already, but it wasn't bleeding. She'd be okay. The mare would be all right as well. Her skittishness was actually helping her, because it meant she was anxious to escape. As soon as Stevie unbolted the door to her stall, the mare hightailed it out of the barn to safety.

"Teddy, Teddy! Where are you?" she called, coughing. The smoke was beginning to billow down into the lower level. It was much harder to see than it had been just a few minutes before.

Stevie found a gray horse cowering in the corner of a stall. She reached in over the half-door, hooked her fingers through his halter, and pulled gently.

But there was nothing gentle about the horse's reaction. The horse reared on its hind legs, terrified, shrieking loudly. His movement was so sudden that he pulled Stevie right up off the ground and halfway over the edge of the door. She managed to release her fingers from the halter and backed out of the stall before the horse could land on her.

"Swell—I'm trying to give you a hand and you think this is the right time to get on your own two feet!"

It wasn't much of a joke, but it was the best Stevie could do. In fact, she was quite proud of the fact that she could still make a joke, even a feeble one, at a dreadful time like this.

"Listen, let's save the fun and games for tomorrow. Then you can do your Hi-ho-Silver imitation. I might even clap. For now, let's stick to routine. I tell you what to do, you do it."

The gray eyed her warily, but didn't protest when she snapped a lead on his halter. He also didn't move when she tugged at it. She tugged it harder. Then she yanked it. He yanked back. This horse wasn't going to budge.

One of the very first things a horse is taught to do, is to obey a halter lead rope. This horse was so upset and frightened that he had obviously forgotten everything he'd ever been taught. Stevie was trying to save his life, but he was acting as if she were trying to make him do something unpleasant, like lead him onto a van—

That was it! There were lots of tricks to putting horses on vans, and the first was a blindfold. Within a few seconds Stevie had torn off one of the legs of her pajamas. It was the only thing she had that would work, and besides, she'd never liked the little flowers on them. For a moment she imagined explaining to her mother what had happened to the pajamas. "See, we had this barn fire, Mom . . ." Stevie smiled to herself as she worked. Talking reassuringly to the gray horse, she slipped the homemade blindfold over his eyes. If he couldn't see anything, he'd have to rely on her. At least that was the idea.

It worked. Stevie tugged at the lead rope. One foot came forward. Before the horse knew what he was doing, he had followed Stevie out of the stall and was letting her lead him to the door. She took him all the way out of the barn before she took off his blindfold. She was afraid that once he could see, he might make his escape back into the barn. That would be awful.

"Get out of here!" Stevie yelled at the gray. She released the lead rope and slapped him hard on the rump. He looked over his shoulder at her with what she was sure was a dirty look. She whacked him again, harder. He bolted for freedom at full speed.

Now seven horses had been freed. *But where was Teddy?*

11

ONCE CAROLE WAS on Topside and Topside was paying attention to her, it began to seem as if everything were easy—especially when she had so much help from the other campers and the staff.

She got Topside to canter toward the herd, which made the horses shift over toward one side, even though they were still terrified of the fire. On Carole's signal, the campers at the fences began waving their towels. Eventually they got the horses' attention. Topside, whose bloodlines were one hundred percent Thoroughbred, now worked the horse herd like an experienced quarter horse. Quarter horses were the breed preferred by cowboys for their strength, stamina, speed, and intelligence. Topside was showing all these qualities. It was as if he understood the task before him, not just from command to command, but as a whole job. Topside began charging the herd and getting it to go in the right direction.

Not all the horses were cooperative. There were several who just wouldn't join the ranks as the herd began to back away from the barn.

Debbie saw the problem and found the solution. Her own horse, Bellevue, was one of those at the fence. Debbie found a way to climb up near him and, before he could object, she mounted him bareback. Holding his mane like reins, she began to ride him.

It was what Bellevue had needed, just like Topside. Debbie circled the herd, moving around to the side opposite Carole. When Carole approached the herd from one side, Debbie did the same from the other. Lisa and the other campers at the fence continued to wave.

Just three horses remained at the fence. One of them was Basil, whom Lisa had been riding just a few hours earlier. It seemed impossible that so much had happened in such a short period of time. Lisa glanced at the barn. This was no time to get philosophical. She hopped into the paddock and when she could get Basil's attention, she gave him a firm smack on his rear. It was just what he needed. Basil and the other three horses ran after the herd.

"Yahoo!" Nora called, running back to the fence. "You were fabulous."

"You did exactly the right thing!" Elsa said. The other campers standing by the fence applauded.

"It was teamwork," Lisa reminded them. "We were great. All of us."

"We're not done, though," Elsa said. "We brought everything we could find to make a fence, but now we've got to set it up. If we don't look out, we'll have every one of those horses back here in no time."

Lisa smiled to see that everybody who had been working with the herd was now joining Elsa in building a temporary fence. It had always been her experience that when people worked together, things got done. She was pretty sure this team could contain a mere herd of horses!

"Where are the horses?" someone asked. Lisa spun around. It was Phil.

"They're over on the other side of the hill," Lisa answered. "We got them away from the barn. They're safe now."

"All of them?" he asked.

"Sure, all of them," Lisa said. "You don't see any here now, do you?"

"Did you see Teddy? Was he there?" Phil asked.

"It's hard to tell them apart in the dark, Phil," Lisa said, with more patience than she felt. "But the horses that were in the paddock are safe. They're over the hill."

"But Teddy wasn't in the paddock," Phil said, almost stumbling over his words. "Stevie told me to put him in the barn—for the farrier."

Lisa had been concentrating so hard on the horses in the paddock that she'd completely forgotten about the horses in the barn. Phil's words reminded her that Major was in the barn, too. Major and Teddy were both in the barn—and where was Stevie?

"Oh, no!" Phil gasped. He ran. Lisa followed him. They couldn't get within thirty feet of the side entrance to the barn, though. The firemen wouldn't let them.

"Too dangerous," one said. "The whole side's about to go."

"But there's someone in there!" Phil said urgently.

"And it's my best friend!" Lisa added.

"Nobody's in there," the fireman said. "That would be crazy! Stand back now. And stay clear."

"TEDDY?"

The horse answered with a nicker. Stevie kept calling his name and followed the sound of his nicker to find him.

He was there all right, but Stevie knew as soon as

she found him that the fire might not be his worst problem.

Teddy was in a box stall, larger than the others. He was lying down, completely immobilized with terror. Experience had taught Stevie that every horse had his own distinct personality. At that moment, Teddy's wasn't helping him at all.

Stevie remembered how Phil had had trouble with Teddy when his foot hurt. She also remembered how she'd calmed him with her voice and gotten him to lift his foot. Now she had to do something similiar, only it was going to be very hard to sound reassuring with the fire crackling above her and the heat increasing every second. She didn't feel calm at all.

She started talking to the horse. She didn't think Teddy cared what she said, but he listened. She babbled on, not really aware of what she was saying, but as she spoke, she hooked on a lead rope and began matter-of-factly getting the frightened horse to his feet. She was surprised to find that she'd been telling him the story of Goldilocks and the Three Bears— Teddy Bears, of course.

At first, Teddy seemed to like it. Slowly but steadily, he rose to his feet. Then he stopped. He wouldn't move an inch. Stevie tried the makeshift blindfold. It didn't work. She tried tugging, then she tried yanking.

He wouldn't budge. Teddy felt secure in his box stall, and no matter how treacherous it really was, he didn't want to leave it.

But Teddy was also a trained riding horse, and there were some things which were always true about a riding horse. Stevie decided it might be the one way left that would work with Teddy. She entered the box stall, gave herself a boost on an overturned water bucket, and mounted Teddy. She was right about one thing. Once he had a rider on board, he wasn't going to stand still. Before Stevie even got a good grip on his mane, he was off!

The horse seemed to smell the fresh air and, having made up his mind that that was where he was going, wasted no time about it. He flew out of the barn, up the small incline of the entry path, and along the trail toward the pond. Stevie held on for dear life! This horse hadn't been named after the Rough Riders for nothing!

Most of the horses had headed for the pond. Stevie was certain Teddy would do the same. Teddy did, but he didn't stop at the beach the way the other seven horses from the barn had done. He kept on going at full gallop! The last voice Stevie heard as she and Teddy flew past the cabins was Phil's. It was faint but distinct.

"Stevie!"

Stevie was a good rider. She knew a lot about how to control a horse, how to make it do what she wanted, and how to keep it from doing what *it* wanted to do. But all of these things were difficult riding bareback without a bridle. On a still-terrified Teddy, they were impossible. There was only one thing she could do, and that was to hold on. The horse raced through the woods, snorting and sweating up a lather. He stumbled on rocks and roots, brushing up against branches, trees, and briars. Stevie's legs got scratched a dozen times and she could feel blood trickling down them. It didn't matter, though. The only thing that mattered was saving Teddy. As long as she was with him, there was a chance she could keep him from killing himself. Until he was ready to stop running, there wasn't much she could do, but she could be with him to calm him when he wore out. She clutched his thick mane with both hands, gripped his sleek belly with her cut legs, and leaned forward, making herself as small a target as possible for the branches that lashed at her body.

All the time she talked soothingly to the horse. "And then Goldilocks sat in the great big chair. 'Oh, no,' she said. 'This is much too big for me.'" She couldn't believe she was telling a fairy tale to a horse. It probably wasn't doing Teddy much good, but she knew she needed to talk. It was a way of keeping herself from being terrified, and it was a way of reminding him she was there—not that it was working very well for either of them.

Teddy was a big strong horse. Stevie was afraid he could keep on running for hours. She was more worried for his safety than for herself. Every time he stumbled on something, he risked seriously hurting himself. If the brambles and prickles were hurting her, she hated to think what they were doing to his beautiful and delicate legs. She'd once seen a horse hurt so badly that he'd been put down. She didn't want the same thing to happen to Teddy—especially not after she'd saved him from a fire!

Stevie clung tightly to his neck. She couldn't let Teddy get hurt. She just couldn't!

She kept on talking to him, and finally he began to slow down. His gallop wound down to a canter. It should have been an easy rocking gait, comfortable even bareback, but Teddy was lame. He stumbled with almost every step, now feeling the pain of wounds that had been numbed for a while by his terror.

The canter became a trot.

"Whoa there, boy," Stevie said. She tried shifting her weight, as she would have in a saddle, to signal him to stop. He slowed to a walk and then stopped.

Stevie made him walk until he cooled down and then she didn't move from his back until she was certain he wasn't going to take off again. They were in a clearing. She had no idea how far they were from camp or how they'd get back, but she could see that there was nothing for Teddy to fear in the clearing. The fire was a nightmare that was well out of sight, and, she hoped, out of mind.

She patted his neck soothingly, reassuringly. Teddy nodded his head in a familiar gesture. He was telling her that he was okay. She hoped he was right.

Slowly, Stevie slid down off his back. Moving carefully so as not to startle him, she checked him out. He had some nasty cuts on his legs, and the bruise on his hoof where she'd removed the stone was obviously bothering him a lot. Carrying her over all that rough terrain probably hadn't helped, either.

Stevie looked around and found that she and Teddy were right next to a stream. She tested the water. It was cool and seemed fresh. She led Teddy over to it and let him have a sip. Then she scooped up the cool water in her hands and began cleansing his wounds. He pulled back from her, so she began talking again.

"Once upon a time . . ."

Teddy stood still while Stevie finished washing his cuts, talking the whole time. She could see just well enough in the moonlight to be fairly certain the bleeding was slowing down in most of the cuts. One of the cuts, though, was more serious. Stevie looked around for something to use as a bandage. The obvious answer was her other pajama leg—after all, she'd already sacrificed the first as a blindfold.

It did the trick. She wrapped it carefully around Teddy's leg and tied it securely. Within a few minutes, the bleeding stopped.

"Don't get into any more trouble, okay?" Stevie told Teddy. "Unlike you, I've only got two legs. I'm completely out of spare pajama parts!" She sighed. As long as she could joke, she was fine.

Stevie knew she ought to try to go back to camp. She knew people would be worried about her and Teddy, but she also knew she and Teddy were tired, very tired. The last thing they needed now was to wander through the woods and get even more lost than they already were. She secured Teddy's lead rope on a branch near some wild grass that he could snack on, and sat down, leaning against a pine tree. She'd rest for just a minute.

The next thing Stevie knew, it was broad daylight. She was startled awake by the sound of her own name.

"Stevie! You're all right!" Phil said, kneeling beside her.

She smiled weakly. "Yes, I am, and so is Teddy, though he's got some cuts. I tried to bandage one of them—" she tried to explain. She wanted to assure Phil that everything was okay, but he didn't give her a chance.

"Shut up," he said, nearly whispering. "Because I can't apologize to you if you're doing all the talking."

Stevie didn't say a word.

"You're good at taking care of horses. You're also good at riding them. You're a true friend, Stevie Lake, and I'll be honored to be in the same horse show with you when the time comes and I won't be surprised if you win every ribbon there is because you've got more guts than anybody I've ever known. What I'm trying to say is I think you're terrific. I think you're the greatest girl I ever met, and I don't want you to be mad at me anymore."

"I don't care about the horse show," Stevie said wearily. "All I care about is the horses. And I'm not mad at you," she promised. "Boy, I'm tired. I hope I'm not dreaming you're here. How did you find us anyway?"

"We knew about what direction you'd taken off in, so Barry and I drove this way. You weren't hard to spot. You're only about ten feet from the road. We brought a van, so we can take you and Teddy back to camp right now."

Stevie stood up and looked around, seeing the locale for the first time. If she'd known about the road in the dark, she might have been tempted to try to return on her own. She was glad she hadn't. She couldn't have walked another step. Neither could Teddy.

"Now about my horse," Phil said. "I hope he hasn't gotten too used to flowered bandages. Do you think the other horses will make fun of him?"

Stevie smiled. It felt very good to know that Phil could still joke, too.

STEVIE REALLY WANTED to see Lisa and Carole. There was so much to say, so much to tell them.

As Barry drove the van into camp, Stevie got her first look at the burned barn. Like many fires, it had done some unpredictable damage. The loft was completely gone and a lot of the main floor had been destroyed. Some parts had hardly been touched, though. The tack room, for instance, was dusty, smoky, and soaked from the firemen's hoses, but the tack would be fine after a good cleaning.

"Oh, that's great!" Stevie said. "That means we can still have our classes today!"

Barry looked at her sternly. "I think that today any rider who spent the night saving the lives of eight horses and tending to another in the pitch-black forest, ripping up her pajamas—to say nothing of her legs—just to protect a horse's, should definitely take the day off. Besides, there's something else you should see."

Phil had brought along a pair of Stevie's sneakers. She was glad to have them as she walked around the charred beams that lay scattered on the ground. She was even more glad to have them when Phil took her hand and led her to the barn's lower entrance.

It was the same place she'd been just a few hours earlier. She remembered what had happened so clearly that she could almost feel the presence of the terrified horses and her own fear. She could hear their anxious cries, the nervous stomping of their feet in the dim light of the lower stable. It was the same place, but it didn't look like it at all. It had been transformed into a yawning, pitch-black hole. Nothing was left of it except a few metal pieces that had survived the fire. Stevie picked up a charred bucket handle.

"Right after you and Teddy made your exit, the main floor collapsed in this section. The whole area was totally destroyed, and if you hadn't been here to save the horses, they would have been destroyed as well," Barry told her.

"And if you hadn't done such a fast job of it—" Phil began.

"I get the picture," Stevie interrupted. She didn't

want him to say the words. She began shivering, and the full weight of the work she'd done and the danger she'd barely escaped came crashing down on her. "Um, maybe I should go lie down," she said a little unsteadily.

"Here, I'll help you." And Phil leaned over and picked her up, just like that!

Stevie sighed contentedly. This was definitely the most romantic thing that had ever happened to her. She rested her head on Phil's shoulder and was nearly asleep by the time she reached Cabin Three.

THE SADDLE CLUB Meeting that afternoon lasted a long time. This Saddle Club Meeting was very different, though, because every single camper at Moose Hill was included. They each brought a pile of tack, a tin of saddle soap, water, and extra sponges. They found a shady spot near the mess hall and began to work, talking as they cleaned tack.

Stevie told everybody all about her adventures in the lower barn.

"You were a hero!" Lisa declared.

Stevie shook her head. "No way. I wasn't waving towels at a frightened herd of horses who could have trampled you in a second. And I didn't mount one of those horses in the paddock. Now *that* was heroic."

"You should have seen the fence builders, Stevie,"

Carole put in. "While some of us herded the horses, the rest put up a fence, instantly. They could have been trampled, too."

Stevie smiled a little to herself.

"What's so funny, Stevie?" Nora asked her.

Stevie shrugged. "Carole and Lisa and I decided long ago that what makes us friends is that we're all horse crazy. I think it may be true of all of us—this whole group. Being horse crazy made us do the things we did last night, and look at us now." There were smiles and nods of agreement. "On the other hand," Stevie continued, "if you *really* think about what we did last night, you'd have to conclude that we're all actually just *plain* crazy!" Everybody laughed. It was a wonderful sound.

Barry joined the group then. He sat down, picked up a bridle, and began soaping it.

"There are a couple of things you should know," he informed the campers. "The firemen pinpointed the start of the fire, and there's no doubt about it—it began in the moldy hay in the loft. What happens with moldy hay is that the process of rotting creates heat and oxygen. I don't want to get too technical, but at some point, there's enough heat and enough oxygen so that the whole thing begins to smolder. It doesn't take much to start hay burning. Every stable manager knows it. And now you've seen the consequences. I'd given instructions to have the moldy hay removed from the loft, but apparently those instructions weren't followed. The person responsible for that has left camp."

Lisa had figured as much when she'd seen Fred earlier that day, angrily dumping his duffel bags into a station wagon and leaving camp.

"There is a bright side to all of this, though. First, and most important, all the horses are safe. There are minor injuries to take care of, but thanks to quick thinking and action on everyone's part, the horses are okay.

"The other bright side is that although I loved that old barn, with its wonderful hayloft and smooth wooden floors, it was a barn, not a stable. I'll be able to rebuild with the insurance money and we'll have a real stable. It'll be better than ever when you all return next year.

"Now, the final thing I want to say is that some of you have been concerned about the horse show and the judges who will be working with me and—"

Debbie interrupted him. "Barry, can I say something before you continue?"

For a second, Barry looked dubious. "Sure," he said.

"I was acting dumb and selfish and I apologize for questioning the judging. Don't make any changes, okay?"

Barry paused before speaking. "I wasn't going to," he said. "But I'm glad you agree."

Lisa smiled. Debbie had come a long way from the girl who had had an argument with Barry just the day before. Actually, everybody had. It hadn't taken much, Lisa thought to herself. Just a barn fire, terrified horses, courage, bravery, and the total cooperation of about thirty people who had previously viewed everyone else as a competitor instead of a teammate. No trouble at all.

13

LISA WASN'T CERTAIN whether it was more fun to get ready for a horse show or to be in one. All she knew was that she was having a great time.

"You look like an old pro," Carole said, admiring Lisa's outfit.

"I'm not, but my clothes *are*," she joked. "I had to borrow gloves from Elsa, and I'm carrying a riding crop that Jack needs right after me. It belongs to Phil."

That was the way the show was going. Everybody was pitching in to see that all the riders did the best they could. And all of them *were* doing their best.

"Well, good luck on the jumps," Carole said.

"Thanks," Lisa said. She might need some. After all, she'd only been jumping since camp started. But she didn't really care if she took a ribbon. There were other beginners who were better than she was. She was just glad for the chance to show what she'd learned in ten days.

"Smile," Betty said to her, breaking her train of thought. "You're on!"

As soon as Barry called her name, she nudged Major into the ring. She circled it once, paused to tip her hat to the judges, just as she was supposed to, and then began her exercise.

Major loved it, but Lisa loved it even more. She had four jumps to go over. None of them was high, but her style and form were more important than how high she jumped. Major cantered gracefully toward the first jump. Just as she'd practiced a hundred times before, she rose in the saddle, leaned forward, held her hands by Major's neck, and gave him as much rein as she thought he would need. At precisely the right moment, Major rose in the air and, it seemed to Lisa, flew right over the poles. He landed softly, and she shifted her weight and slid back into the saddle. *Perfect!*

After that, nothing else mattered to Lisa. If she'd fallen off at the next jump she wouldn't have cared. She'd done one jump exactly right and she was proud of herself. Other people seemed to agree. Carole and Stevie and the rest of the campers were clapping for her. They all knew how much work that one jump represented. All that practice, all those hours had been worth it. As it turned out, she didn't have to worry about the other three jumps. They went just fine. Lisa had the feeling, though, that no jump she ever made would feel quite as good as the first perfect one she made in a show.

STEVIE SMOOTHED HER jacket while she and Topside waited their turn.

"Stephanie Lake!" Barry announced. Time to go.

Stevie and Topside had already competed in the Intermediate Jumping and Conformation events. Now, they were in Dressage. This event tested the training of both the horse and the rider. It was an opportunity for both Topside and Stevie to show good balance, concentration, and obedience. It was sometimes hard for casual viewers to see what was happening, especially when it was done well, because in Dressage, the horse had to respond to nearly invisible commands from the rider.

Stevie entered the ring, saluted the judges, and started her prepared ride. Her routine had been designed to show Topside off to best advantage, and as she began, her head was swimming with dozens of terms she'd been studying, like rhythm, cadence, hocks engaged, collection, and, most of all, impulsion. Topside didn't know any of those words, but he did everything perfectly. Together they made circles and curves at walk, trot, and canter. Stevie changed diagonals and leads, and their transitions were smooth as glass. Topside was in top form. Stevie couldn't help grinning triumphantly. By the time she finished her stationary turns, one pivoting on a foreleg, another on a hindleg, Stevie knew she'd been perfect.

She completed her exercise and rode out of the ring to the sound of applause. She didn't waste any time gloating about it, though. There was a lot of work to do. Since Teddy's legs were still healing, Phil was riding Topside, too. They had to adjust the leathers for his lanky frame.

"He's great," Stevie said to Phil, patting Topside lovingly. "You'll be fine. You're better at this stuff than I am, and Topside's better than both of us."

"I don't care about that now, Stevie," Phil said. "Really."

"Me, too," she said, and she meant it. "It was really dumb, that idea we had about taking all the ribbons. It wasn't any better than what Elsa and Debbie were doing. We should have known better. Riding is for having a good time."

"You got that right," he agreed. "By the way, I heard that Elsa and Debbie asked Barry if we could all go out on another camp-out tonight after the show, and he said yes. Still got those marshmallows?"

"Philip Marston!" Barry announced.

"You're up!" Stevie said, nodding in answer to his question. "Go get 'em!"

CAROLE WAS IN all the advanced classes with both Elsa and Debbie. Only two other riders were in those classes, because the advanced riders were so experienced.

Lisa, Stevie, and Phil watched them in awe.

"This is so great!" Lisa said. "I mean, having this chance to see kids who are so good. That big horse show we went to in New York was fantastic, but in a way I think this is even better. Those people at the show were almost professional riders, way better than I'll ever be. But these guys are really good riders and they're my age. It's fabulous."

"You mean *she's* fabulous," Stevie said, watching Debbie go over the jumps. "See how her body sort of folds when she gets ready to jump? It isn't exactly leaning forward. It's just about perfect."

"Wow," Lisa said, admiring Debbie's skill. "She's as good as she said she was."

"You're only ever as good as you are," Stevie pointed out. "Talking doesn't make you better. She learned that."

"We *all* did," Phil said.

Then it was Carole's turn. She was wonderful, too.

Lisa had watched her jump a lot, but she'd never seen her do better. When Carole was finished, there was a lot of applause. And nobody clapped louder than the other riders in the event.

At most shows, Lisa knew, ribbons were awarded immediately after each event. Barry had decided to do it differently. She suspected he wanted to minimize their importance, but he needn't have worried. At the end of the show, many riders almost forgot to come to the awards ceremony. It just wasn't important. What was important to each and every one of them was that they'd all learned and had a chance to show what they'd learned.

There were plenty of ribbons to go around. Lisa, Stevie, and Carole had each done well in their events and had blue and red ribbons to take with them. They were pleased, but they were also pleased when their friends got ribbons as well. They knew their accomplishments couldn't be measured in just ribbons.

One thing that could be measured, though, was how much they all wanted to cool off in the pond before their final night at camp.

"Last one in has to pick up all the kindling tonight!" Jack shouted. It didn't take any of them long to get into the water.

CAROLE TOLD ANOTHER ghost story at the camp

fire. This one was about Frankenstallion. The campers made s'mores as they listened, joining in with suggestions as the story progressed. They all laughed as Frankenstallion ended up marrying Marezilla and they had a baby named Dracufoal.

After a while, the campers began singing songs, starting, naturally, with the theme song from the Munsters. Stevie sat next to Lisa and Carole. Phil was nearby.

He tapped Stevie's shoulder. "Want to go for a walk?" he asked. Quietly, they sneaked away from the camp fire. They didn't do such a good job of sneaking, though, because as soon as they were standing, all the other campers turned and began waving good-bye to them.

Stevie blushed. "I've had enough of fires," she began to explain. "See, I had this frightening experience—"

"Let's just go, Stevie," Phil said. He smiled and took her hand and they left, hearing the teasing laughter behind them.

"I can't believe it's almost over," Stevie said. "Two weeks seemed like such a long time, but now, *poof!* It's done. But so much has happened in two weeks. All those classes, the first camp-out, the fire, the show, and now our last camp-out."

"Last camp-out? No way," Phil said. "I think we'll be back next summer for more of them, and I think we'll be seeing each other in between."

Stevie certainly hoped so.

She and Phil walked to the edge of the temporary paddock where the horses were housed for the night. A stream flowed along one side of it. They sat at the edge of the stream, took off their shoes, and dangled their feet in the cool water.

Stevie and Phil were silent for a long time. The field ran uphill and several of the horses stood on the top of the hill, silhouetted against the cool, deep blue sky by the moon beyond them. One rose his head and nickered. Another responded, nuzzling at his shoulder. Stevie could hear the horses nearby munch on fresh hay and grass contentedly. There were other night sounds—the brook, crickets, even an owl.

Stevie thought that this was maybe the most beautiful place in the world. She looked at Phil. There was just one more thing that could make it more beautiful. And at that moment, he leaned toward her and kissed her for the first time.

"HE KISSED YOU!" Lisa almost shrieked. The girls were back in Willow Creek, gathered at the edge of Stevie's swimming pool, sharing secrets. Camp was over, but they had all acquired enough memories to last a lifetime!

Stevie nodded excitedly. Telling her friends about her first kiss was *almost* as much fun as doing it.

"Like, on the lips?" Carole said.

Stevie nodded. "You're not jealous, are you?" she asked a little anxiously, suddenly aware that she was the first of them to be kissed by a boy.

"Jealous?" Lisa repeated. "Of course I'm jealous, but one of us had to be first and Phil's a really neat guy, so I'm glad it was you."

"Me, too," Stevie grinned.

"I don't mind, either," Carole reassured her. "But tell me about it again—you know, the part about the horses on the hill?"

Stevie laughed. For now anyway, horses were still more important to Carole than boys, but Carole was glad her friend was happy, and that was fine with Stevie. Stevie told her again about the horses on the hill.

"It must have been beautiful," Carole sighed.

"It was," Stevie said. "Believe me, it was."

"Uh-oh, here she goes looking all lovesick again," Lisa teased her. "Remember, Stevie, how Carole had to bail you out of making a fool of yourself in class by getting you to have a coughing fit?"

"I remember, I remember," Stevie said. "And I promise I'll never do it again. Well, maybe never."

Carole and Lisa laughed. It was nice having Stevie back to normal again.

Lisa wanted to make sure Stevie didn't leave anything out, so she pumped her some more about her walk with Phil. Carole was a little distracted; she'd been thinking about something else.

"Tired of the four hundredth go-round of Stevie's first kiss?" Lisa asked, noticing that Carole's attention had slipped.

"Oh, no," Carole grinned. "I'm ready for four-oh-one any time, but I was remembering something else, too. Remember how Kate Devine told us she'd quit competitive riding because the competitiveness was keeping her from having any fun? I think we had more than a taste of that our first week at camp, and she's right. That's no way to ride!"

Lisa began combing her hair. "No, the best part about riding is doing what The Saddle Club does. We help one another."

"Right," Stevie said. "Just the way all of the campers were doing by the time of the show. It was great. It was like having twenty-seven more members of The Saddle Club."

Carole looked surprised. "Would you really want twenty-seven more members?" she asked.

"No way!" Lisa said. "I like us just the way we are. At least that's my vote."

"Maybe not *twenty-seven* more members," Stevie said thoughtfully. "But how about one more?"

Lisa and Carole didn't have to ask her who she meant. Friends just knew those things.

THE SADDLE CLUB

HORSE WISE

BONNIE BRYANT

For Judy Boehler and Gwen Schmitt

CAROLE HANSON HUMMED to herself as she removed her horse's bridle and hung it on the hook by the stall door. Then she began unbuckling the saddle. The horse, Barq, stood patiently while she worked, as if he knew what was coming. Carole patted him affectionately. She liked what she was doing, as she liked everything there was to do with horses.

Suddenly she heard a grumbling noise. Was it Barq? Carole stopped humming and looked at him with concern. If he'd made that sound, then something was very wrong. She might even have to call the vet. She heard the grumbling sound again.

Carefully, Carole put her ear against the horse's belly. She didn't have a stethoscope, and if the horse was really having a stomach problem, she would be able to hear it better this way. There was no sound, except . . .

"Hey, Carole, I've heard of getting close to your horse, but aren't you carrying it a little too far?" A familiar voice snickered.

Carole straightened up and glared at Veronica diAngelo. Veronica rode at Pine Hollow Stables with Carole and Carole's two best friends, Stevie Lake and Lisa Atwood. But Veronica was definitely not one of her best friends. She was a spoiled little rich girl who cared more about her expensive riding clothes than the health of her horse.

"I thought I heard his stomach grumble," Carole explained. Veronica didn't deserve an explanation, but Carole couldn't help herself. She was a natural-born teacher when it came to horses and riding and was always eager to share her knowledge with others—even lost causes like Veronica. "See, if his belly's grumbling, it could be the start of a colic attack, and that's serious, because—"

"What you heard grumbling was your friend Stevie," Veronica rudely informed her before disappearing toward the locker area.

Carole peered over the stall door to see what Veronica was talking about. Stevie was standing in the hallway with her horse, patiently cleaning Topside's hooves. But the noises she made as she was working weren't patient at all.

"Grrrr," Stevie grumbled, unaware that Carole

was watching. "I hate it, I hate it, I hate it." She swept her dark blond hair back from her face and concentrated on her work.

"You hate cleaning hooves?" Carole asked.

Stevie looked up at her friend. "No, I hate school," she said. "It's only three days into the new semester and I already have seven impossible things to do, including one especially horrible science project. If I don't keep up with school, Max won't let me ride, and if I can't ride, what's the point of school? I just wish they'd teach us about horses in school instead of all this other garbage. Then I'd be a straight-A student."

"Did somebody mention me?" Lisa asked, joining her two best friends. Stevie and Carole laughed. It was accepted among them that Lisa was the best student, just as Carole was the horse expert and Stevie was the best at jokes, practical and otherwise. But when it came to loving horses, they were all equal.

"Yeah, I did," Stevie said. She bent her head and resumed cleaning Topside's hoof. The stone that was wedged under the horse's shoe came loose and dropped to the wooden floor of the stable with a satisfying thunk. Stevie grinned triumphantly at the sound and looked up at her friends. "It's this horrible science project. What do you know about osmosis?"

Lisa looked thoughtful. "Well, it's the tendency

of a substance to pass through a semipermeable membrane from an area of higher concentration to an area of lower concentration."

Stevie sighed. "Does that mean if I put my science textbook under my pillow, all the knowledge will transfer into my brain overnight?"

"Only if your skull is semipermeable," Lisa informed her.

"Wait a minute. I'm the one who tells the jokes," Stevie said, laughing. She unhooked Topside's cross-ties and led him toward his stall. Her voice turned serious. "But jokes won't get me out of this one."

It sounded to Carole like trouble was brewing. She considered the situation as she returned to Barq's stall to finish grooming him. Max Regnery, who owned the stable, had a strict rule that all the young riders had to maintain a good school average. Stevie had always found a way of just getting by, skirting disaster throughout the school year, but Carole was afraid that sooner or later her friend's grades would drop just a bit more than Max liked. Then Stevie wouldn't be allowed to ride until she brought her grades up.

As far as Carole and her friends were concerned, not being able to ride was the worst possible punishment. The three girls loved horses so much that they'd formed The Saddle Club. So far they were the only full-time members, though they had some friends who lived out of town who were honorary members. The club had only two requirements for membership: the members had to be horse crazy and they had to be willing to help one another out. Since they'd started the club, they'd shared many wonderful riding experiences—and they'd had a lot of opportunities to help each other.

Carole thought that Stevie's problem might be the beginning of another Saddle Club project. She peered into the stall next door, where Stevie was beginning to groom Topside. "I think we ought to have a Saddle Club meeting after we're finished," Carole said.

"Great idea," Stevie agreed. "But I don't know about Lisa. Is this piano-lesson day?"

Carole couldn't see Lisa, but she knew where she was. Pepper's stall was three down from Barq's, on the other side of the walkway. "Hey, Lisa, is this piano-lesson day?" she called.

"No, that's Thursday," Lisa called back from the stall.

"Then I think we need to have a Saddle Club meeting after we're done with the grooming."

"Super," Lisa said. "Let's meet at TD's in about half an hour." TD's was their favorite, and most fattening, hangout. It was an ice cream shop, officially named Tastee Delight. The Saddle Club always abbreviated that to TD's. "Now," Lisa continued, talking to herself, "if only I could get this darn saddle off fast so I could *start* the grooming!"

"Saddle Club to the rescue! I'll be there in a minute," Carole told her friend. She quickly finished the last of Barq's grooming and left the stall to help Lisa. Before she could get to Pepper's stall, however, she found herself once again face-to-face with Veronica diAngelo.

"Saddle Club?" Veronica asked. "What's a Saddle Club?"

Carole was speechless. It occurred to her for the first time that she didn't know if The Saddle Club was supposed to be a secret. She hadn't been thinking about secrecy when she'd yelled to Lisa. She'd only been thinking about Stevie's science project and Lisa's saddle.

"I mean, is this some sort of thing the three of you cooked up while you were at that riding camp?"

That was just like Veronica. The little rich girl didn't know what to do when other people had things she didn't. Veronica was actually jealous that the three other girls had gone to riding camp. She envied their adventures there. *If only she knew,* Carole thought to herself.

Veronica stood squarely in Carole's path, hands on her hips. She made it impossible for Carole to evade either her or her question.

Carole put her hands on her own hips, stared Veronica straight in the eyes, and spoke. "Your lipstick is smeared."

Involuntarily, Veronica's hand went to her mouth, and in that instant Veronica lost the standoff. She ducked and slithered past Carole, heading, no doubt, for a mirror. Carole continued on her way to Pepper's stall.

"Nice work!" Stevie called after her.

"Piece of cake," Carole acknowledged breezily. Then she walked into Pepper's stall. There was a lot she wanted to tell Lisa about untacking.

AS IT TURNED out, by the time the girls got to TD's, there was a lot more than a science project to talk about. They had to consider the meaning of what they'd already come to think of as The Letter. Within a minute and a half of their arrival, they'd ordered their sundaes and solved the problem of Stevie's science project.

"Of course I'll help you," Lisa said. "Now let's get to the other thing."

"So what do you think this is about?" Stevie said, holding The Letter in her hand. It was a note Max had given to every young rider as she or he had left Pine Hollow after class, announcing a meeting for all riders and their parents the following Tuesday.

"I hope there isn't going to be some horrible change at Pine Hollow," Stevie said.

Lisa looked upset. "Oh, I hope not," she said. "I like Pine Hollow just the way it is. I don't want Max to change anything."

"It might be something really great," Carole said. She was always optimistic when it came to riding.

"What could be great that has to do with our parents?" Stevie asked. That was a good question.

"Maybe it's something simple, like a new schedule," Lisa suggested.

"We wouldn't have to have a meeting for that," Stevie told her. "But we would *have* to have a meeting if something drastic was about to happen."

"What do you mean by drastic?" Carole asked.

"Oh, you know, like Max moving to Alaska, or going into the insurance business, or like he's decided not to teach young riders anymore. Things like that."

"That's not just drastic, that's *drastic*," Carole said.

The girls sat glumly, pondering all the awful possibilities.

"Who's got the peanut-butter crunch with blueberry sauce?" the waitress asked. Carole and Lisa pointed to Stevie. She was always ordering the most outrageous combinations. When people suggested she did it to keep others from nibbling at her sundae, she flatly denied it. But it was a fact that no one ever asked for a taste of her sundaes. Even the waitress made a face as she put the order in front of Stevie. She gave Carole and Lisa their orders and the girls began eating their ice cream in gloomy silence. Just when they thought things couldn't get any gloomier, Veronica diAngelo and her friends arrived at TD's. Veronica sauntered over to their table.

"Well, hello," she cooed sweetly. "You three together again? It seems like you're always together. Is this some sort of club or something?"

Stevie gave her a withering look. It didn't have any effect. Subtlety was lost on Veronica.

"What do you want?" Carole asked her, hoping a more direct approach would get her to go away.

"Oh, I thought you'd want to know my good news," Veronica said.

"I'm positively dripping with curiosity," Stevie drawled sarcastically.

"Well, you can switch your curiosity to envy because on Monday, my new horse is arriving."

Carole couldn't help it. The envy overwhelmed her. It was all she could do to keep from showing her feelings. "That's nice," she said with the utmost control. "What kind of horse is it?"

"It's an Arabian. She's a dark chestnut mare and I'm going to call her Garnet. I'm sure you'll all have lots of fun watching me ride her." With those words, Veronica tilted her chin up in her I'm-bettter-than-you—in-fact-I'm-better-than-everybody way and walked off, followed by her cadre of admirers.

"And I'm sure we'll enjoy watching you *not* take care of your horse, too," Stevie hissed at the departing girl.

"This is horrible!" Lisa said. "She rode her last horse

carelessly and he got killed because of it. How can she be getting another?"

"Easy," Stevie said. "All she has to do is to ask Daddy!"

Carole grabbed her spoon and dug into her sundae, trying to hide her hurt and anger. She thought about Veronica's earlier horse, a Thoroughbred stallion named Cobalt. Carole had loved and cared for him more than Veronica had. She'd ridden him better, too. He'd been a beautiful and expensive horse, but he wasn't suitable for Veronica at all, and that had cost him his life. The only good thing that had come out of Cobalt's life with Veronica was his foal—a coal-black colt named Samson who belonged to Max.

"Remember after Cobalt died, Veronica decided she wasn't ready for another horse—actually had to stop her father from buying one for her?"

Stevie and Lisa nodded.

"Well, she's still not ready!"

"Do you think The Letter could have anything to do with Veronica's horse?" Lisa asked.

"I hope not," Carole said. "We'll all be better off if we can ignore this whole thing. So, let's think some more about The Letter. Any other ideas?"

"Yeah—how about Max has sold Pine Hollow to some developers who are going to make a shopping mall," Stevie suggested.

"You're going from bad to worse," Carole said.

"Well, now, wait a minute," Lisa said. "Do you think the mall would have a Gap?"

Carole's jaw dropped.

"I was joking—I was joking!" Lisa said hastily.

Carole liked a joke as well as the next person, but she couldn't find any humor in the idea that something awful was about to happen to Pine Hollow.

"You know, I just remembered something," Lisa said. "When Max handed me The Letter, he had this kind of funny grin on his face. Whatever it is, I think he's happy about it. Maybe we're going about this all wrong. Maybe it's really good news. Remember the time we thought the stable was in trouble?"

"Boy, were we ever wrong!" Stevie grinned at the memory. "We did get a lot of new riders for Max, though, didn't we? Hey, maybe Max has decided to have more riding classes," she added thoughtfully.

"Or maybe more horses!" Carole suggested, brightening.

"Or maybe he's decided to expel Veronica!" Stevie said mischievously.

"Now, that would be more than good news," Carole said. "That would be—" She tried to think how to describe it. "Christmas and birthday all rolled into one!"

"YES, OF COURSE we'll be there, dear," Mrs. Atwood told Lisa at dinner that evening. "The library committee can do without me for one meeting."

"You *will?*" Lisa said, sounding more surprised than she thought she ought to sound. "I mean, this is some sort of meeting Max wants us to be at. It has to do with riding," she added, just to be sure her parents understood. After all, they had never been very enthusiastic about her horseback riding. She couldn't think of a reason why that could be changing so suddenly. "Horses, I mean," she said, to further emphasize her point.

"Is there any other kind of riding?" Her father smiled.

Lisa thought maybe she'd done some unnecessary explaining. "No—it's just that, well, you sort of surprised me. I mean, usually you aren't so—oh, I don't know."

"We'll be there, Lisa," her father said. "Seven-thirty on Tuesday." Her parents exchanged glances.

Lisa began eating her salad. Something was up. She had a perfectly nice set of parents who were usually very predictable. Their eagerness to come to Max's meeting puzzled her.

"I saw Veronica diAngelo's mother the other day," Mrs. Atwood said. "Did you know Veronica is getting a new horse?"

"I heard," Lisa said.

"She told me how wonderful it will be for Veronica to have a horse of her own. You know, owning and caring for a pet like that can be so good for somebody like Veronica . . ."

"To say nothing of the horse," Lisa said sarcastically.

"Oh, yes," Mrs. Atwood agreed, oblivious to her daughter's tone.

Something was definitely up.

THINGS WEREN'T AS quiet or as mysterious down the street at Stevie's house.

"Pass the biscuits," her older brother, Chad, said.

"You've already had three," Stevie's twin brother, Alex, argued, reaching across Stevie to grab the biscuits for himself.

"There's a meeting," Stevie began.

"No, I want the meat first," Chad interrupted.

"What's the meeting?" Mrs. Lake asked.

"At Pine Hollow," Stevie began again. "It's on—"

"Oh, here we go with good old Pine Hollow," Alex teased.

"Sounds like Marsh Mallow to me," Chad added. "Hey—do you think that's Stevie's favorite food because it reminds her of horses?"

"No, I thought she liked to take pills because they remind her of her boyfriend, Phil!" her little brother, Michael, piped in.

Stevie sighed, but she didn't let it show. Phil Marston was her boyfriend from riding camp. He lived about ten miles away and she didn't see him often. She did, however, hear about him a lot from her brothers! It wasn't easy living with three brothers. It was made harder by the fact that she was the only one in her family who cared about horses and horseback riding. Chad had tried it once, but it wasn't because he liked horses. It was because he'd had a crush on Lisa and wanted to get her attention. Now, all three of her brothers seemed to be ganging up on her to keep her from telling her parents about the meeting. As far as Stevie was concerned, that was just the inspiration she needed to persist.

Stevie raised her voice a notch. "I said, there is going to be a meeting next Tuesday at Pine Hollow, after riding class."

"You can go as long as your homework is done," her mother said.

"If that includes her book report on *Silas Marner* from last spring, she'll never make it!"

"Shut up," Stevie said. Only a creep like her twin brother would remind her parents about that book report at a time like this. "I know *I* can go to the meeting. What about you, Mom?"

"Me?" her mother asked, taking the bowl of potatoes out of Chad's hands before he could empty the entire dish onto his plate. "Am I supposed to go?"

"And Dad," Stevie said, looking at her father, who was studying the pattern Michael had made with his squash. Michael often tried to make his food look as though he'd at least tasted it by spreading it around his plate so he wouldn't have to eat any more of it.

"Tuesday, dear, can you make it?" Mrs. Lake asked Stevie's father.

"That's my soccer game," Chad said before his father could answer the question.

"You weren't invited," Stevie said.

"Yeah, but Mom and Dad were invited to the game."

"To watch you warm the bench?" Stevie asked.

"I scored two points last game!"

"Yeah, for which team?" Alex snorted.

"So, I kicked it the wrong way, so? You want to make a federal case out of it?"

There was a second of stunned silence at the table. Then everybody burst into laughter—including Chad, though he had the good grace to blush as well.

"Who are you playing against this time?" Michael asked.

"Same team," Chad said. "Coach said they begged us for a rematch!"

"I'm not surprised," Mr. Lake said.

"Next Tuesday?" Mrs. Lake asked. Stevie nodded. "We'll be there."

Stevie felt a rush of relief. Things had to be much easier for only children.

"NEXT TUESDAY?"

"Yes, Dad, next Tuesday," Carole said.

She and her father, a Marine Corps colonel, were in the kitchen of their house on the outskirts of Willow Creek. It was the home the two of them had shared alone since the death of Carole's mother when Carole was eleven. She and her father both missed her mother terribly, but were glad to have each other to share their sadnesses and their joys. In spite of a few weird habits and hobbies, Carole thought her father was probably the greatest guy in the world.

"That's Navy-Bean Soup Night at the Officers' Club," he said.

Navy-bean soup was one of his weird habits.

"Dad," Carole said with a touch of exasperation in her voice.

"Well, what's this meeting about, hon?" Colonel Hanson asked.

"I don't know, Dad. If I knew, I promise I would tell

you. All I have is this letter that Max gave us. It says we should be there, with our parents."

"Well, I'm not—" He was interrupted by the ringing of the phone. He swept it off the hook and spoke into it smartly. "Colonel Hanson!"

That was another one of his weird habits. He never could seem to remember that when he wasn't in his office on the base, he didn't have to answer the phone that way.

At first, Carole thought the call might be for her, but it was clear that the caller wanted to talk to her father. She turned her attention back to fixing dinner. They were having tacos, and Carole was in charge of making the beef filling. Her father was in charge of preparing the toppings. Carole checked the beef, which was done and staying warm in the electric frying pan. It was time to set the table.

Without thinking about it, Carole took three place mats out of a drawer and put them on the table. When she saw what she'd done, she moved the third mat into the center of the table to use as a hot pad. It was a mistake she made often. The sight of the third mat at the table somehow made her feel as if her mother were still with them.

"Oh, I know that one!" she heard her father say into the phone. "It's an elephant with wrinkled panty hose!"

"Is it Stevie?" Carole asked. The colonel nodded. Carole shook her head. Stevie was *her* best friend, but you'd never know it by the way Stevie and her father chatted on the phone. Both of them loved old corny jokes, and once they got started, there was no stopping them. Carole lowered the heat on the beef filling and began chopping lettuce.

"All right. So what's green and goes slam! slam! slam! slam!" There was a brief silence. "Give up? It's a four-door pickle!" Colonel Hanson chortled.

That was as much as Carole could take. Besides, she nearly sliced her finger as well as the lettuce. "My turn," she announced, wresting the phone from her father. He relinquished it gracefully and took over the chopping. "What's up?" Carole asked. She wrapped a paper towel around a small cut.

"I can't believe it, but both my parents are coming! I could just about kill my brothers—in fact I may still do it—but at least my parents will be at the meeting. They can sit with your dad."

"I don't know about that," Carole said. "I still haven't convinced him to come."

"Listen," Stevie said, "if I could talk my parents into it, you can *definitely* talk your dad into it."

"I just wish I knew what 'it' was," Carole said.

"Whatever 'it' is, it's important," Stevie said. "So go for it!"

"You have the most amazing way of seeing everything as a contest," Carole observed. "Like everything can be solved by winning one for the Gipper."

"Not everything," Stevie conceded.

"Such as?"

"Well, not science projects," she reminded Carole.

"True. Listen, I have to finish getting dinner together," Carole said. "Talk to you tomorrow."

Stevie wished her good luck and they hung up.

"What was that about?" Colonel Hanson asked.

Carole decided to let Stevie be an inspiration to her. "Oh, she was mostly calling to tell me how excited her parents are about going to the Pine Hollow meeting next Tuesday, and how glad they are to take time out of their busy lives to do something with their daughter, since it's something that matters a lot to her. Sure, it's a sacrifice. I mean, her father has to skip the annual Lawyer of the Year dinner, and he was supposed to receive the award, and her mother was scheduled to present a case to the Supreme Court the same day, but she told the justices they'll have to reschedule. It's a good thing they've got such flexible schedules, and nothing as critical as Navy-Bean Soup Night at the O-Club. Dinner's ready."

Carole filled the taco shells, served the rice and beans, and handed her father a dish.

"Pretty important, huh?" Colonel Hanson asked Carole while he sprinkled his tacos with cheese and olives.

"To me it is, Dad," Carole said. "I mean I really don't know what it's about, but it has to do with riding, and anything that has to do with riding is important. Can you come? Please?"

"Tell you what," he said. "I'll come to your meeting and then you and I can have dinner afterward at the Officers' Club."

"Gee, what an interesting idea," Carole said, pleased with his solution. It meant she'd have to wear a skirt to the meeting to be dressed properly for the O-Club dining room, but more importantly, it meant her father would be there. She felt giddy. "Do you suppose they'll be serving anything special that night?"

Her father grinned. Carole wondered if he'd known from the beginning that he would come. It didn't matter. He'd be there.

3

Lisa was working on algebra in the study hall when the door to the room opened. She didn't even notice.

X squared times X cubed equals X to the fifth, plus Y cubed times 7 times Y to the eighth power equals—she chomped on her eraser. It tasted terrible and didn't help at all.

"Lisa Atwood?" the study-hall monitor called. Lisa looked up. "There's a message for you." The monitor brought her the note. She didn't think she'd ever gotten a message in the middle of a study hall before—or in the middle of anything, for that matter. It made her a little nervous.

"Please meet your parents in front of the school at the end of the day," the note read. It was signed by the vice-principal of her school.

Lisa stared at the note, reading it again several times. The message didn't become any clearer on rereading. Why on earth would her parents come to the school to pick her up? Their house was only a few blocks from school, a short walk that Lisa did by herself two times a day.

She remembered when one of her classmates had gotten a note like this. Her mother had been very ill. Perhaps one of Lisa's grandparents was ill? They'd all been very healthy when the family had visited them over the recent holiday weekend. But even if something had happened to one of them, why would her parents pick her up at school? It didn't make sense.

Lisa was a very logical person. It was one of the characteristics that helped her be an A-student. She applied all her logic to the situation, but nothing suggested itself as the answer. Logic wasn't going to work, she realized. She decided to return to algebra.

Y^3 *times* $7Y^8$ . . .

"Why would anybody want to multiply Y times itself three times, then multiply that by 7 and *that* times Y times itself eight times?" she asked herself. It was clear logic wasn't going to help her on that one either.

The bell rang. Lisa folded the note, put it into her algebra book, and headed for her history class.

"Hey, Lisa, is something wrong?" It was Carole. Although the two girls went to the same school, Carole was in the grade below Lisa and they rarely saw each other. If ever there had been a time when Lisa wanted to talk to Carole, this was it, but she had only three minutes between classes.

"Something's up with my parents," she explained quickly as they walked toward their next classes. "They're picking me up after school, but I don't know why. I'll call you tonight, if I can."

The look of concern on Carole's face was unmistakable. Lisa realized Carole probably had gotten notes at school about her mother.

"It's probably nothing to worry about," Lisa said. "After all, the note said they'd both be here."

"Oh, yeah, right," Carole said. "Well, call me tonight." She waved and headed for her English class.

Lisa was glad she'd been able to make Carole feel better. She just wished she could do the same for herself. Who could concentrate on the Wars of the Roses when she had gotten a note from the vice-principal? She felt in her pocket. It was still there. It was real.

The rest of the day was almost a total loss for her. She got three wrong answers on her history quiz and ended up telling her algebra teacher she didn't care what Y^3 times $7Y^8$ was, surprising both of them with that announcement. Usually Lisa cared very much about Y cubed.

At last the final bell rang. Lisa didn't even stop to think about what books she needed to take home. She grabbed all of them out of her locker and dashed for the front door of the school.

Both of her parents were standing at the curb, looking healthy and happy. What was going on?

"Oh, darling, we have such a wonderful surprise for you!" Mrs. Atwood announced, barely glancing at the colossal stack of books Lisa was carrying. Her father opened the trunk and Lisa dumped her lockerful of books into it. Then he opened the rear door of the car for her. Lisa slid into the backseat.

"Wonderful?" Lisa asked. "Tell me. I've been worried sick ever since I got your note!"

"We thought you might be," Mrs. Atwood said. "It was sort of a little joke."

What kind of a little joke was that? Suddenly Lisa didn't care what their wonderful news was. She was annoyed with their sense of humor.

"Well, aren't you going to ask?" her mother demanded as they pulled the doors shut on the car. "Don't bother, I can't wait to tell you. Your father and I have decided to buy you a horse! When I learned that the diAngelos were buying a new horse for Veronica, it just made sense that you should have one, too. So I spoke with Veronica's mother and she mentioned a horse she'd heard about."

Lisa wondered if she'd heard the words right. A horse? Her parents were going to buy *her* a horse of her own?

Her father started the car and drove them away from the school. Lisa hardly noticed. She was thinking about a horse—*her* horse. She could see it in her mind's eye. He was a sleek gray, tall, with slender but strong legs. His name was Silver. She'd whistle for him in the mornings and he'd come galloping across the paddock, nuzzle her shoulder, and stand still while she slid onto him, bareback.

She could almost feel the dewy grass tickle the bottoms of her bare feet and brush against her legs, the wind on her face, and the strength of the animal beneath her. Her horse—her very own horse.

Lisa sighed.

"Is something wrong, dear?" her mother asked.

"Oh, no. Everything's great. Really great. Tell me again about the horse we're seeing."

Mrs. Atwood fished a slip of paper out of her purse and read from it. "It's a gray mare named Streamline. She's belonged to this farm all her life and she's supposed to be very gentle. That's what the lady kept telling me on the phone."

Lisa had learned a few things about horses in the time she'd been riding. A horse that one person found gentle, another might find uncontrollable. She decided to reserve judgment about the animal until she was actually on her back. Still, she had a feeling that a horse named Streamline had to be wonderful.

Mr. Atwood turned into a drive marked by a hand-painted sign that read Horse for Sale. Lisa could feel her pulse quicken. As soon as the car pulled to a stop, she was out of the door. She waited impatiently while her mother knocked on the farmhouse door, and barely noticed as her parents introduced themselves and chatted with the owner. When the owner, Mrs.

Brandon, led them to the paddock, Lisa could hardly speak. She stared excitedly, waiting for Streamline to appear when Mrs. Brandon called her.

Nothing. There was no sign of Streamline.

"She usually likes to graze on the other side of the hill, where there's a little stream. Want to walk down there?"

Mrs. Atwood looked dubiously at the muddy ground and her suede pumps. She and Mr. Atwood decided to wait by the barn. Lisa and Mrs. Brandon would walk across the paddock.

Mrs. Brandon gave Lisa some carrots for the horse, and they started across the field. Mrs. Brandon led the way.

"She's a real sweet horse," Mrs. Brandon said, repeating her earlier statements. Lisa felt a little uneasy. Of course she wanted a sweet horse; she didn't want a wild, uncontrollable animal. But it seemed that all anybody could say about this horse was how sweet and gentle it was. There was a limit to sweetness, even in a horse.

Mrs. Brandon whistled. "Streamline!" she called. "We've got some juicy carrots for you!"

Nothing.

At last, Lisa and Mrs. Brandon reached the top of the hill and there, just as Mrs. Brandon had predicted, was Streamline. She was a big, tall gray horse whose coat had whitened with age. Lisa stopped and watched her while Mrs. Brandon approached. The horse didn't move. She continued munching contentedly on the sparse grass in the muddy paddock. When Mrs. Brandon clipped a lead rope on her, she obediently stopped munching and followed her owner.

"She's a good horse for a young rider, you know," Mrs. Brandon said when she and the horse reached Lisa. "Very gentle and sweet."

"Can I ride her?" Lisa asked.

"Of course. Her saddle's in the barn. Would you like to lead her?"

"Yes, but can I ride her now, I mean bareback?" Perhaps it was silly of her, but Lisa still had that picture in her mind of riding her own horse bareback in the early morning. It was something she'd done when she'd been at a dude ranch belonging to Kate Devine, an out-of-state Saddle Club member. They had all gone for a bareback ride at sunrise with their new friend, Christine Lonetree. To Lisa, it was part of what having her own horse would be like.

Mrs. Brandon shrugged. "Suit yourself," she said. "The horse is gentle enough."

Mrs. Brandon gave Lisa a lift onto the horse. Lisa thought it might not have been necessary. She was beginning to suspect that Streamline was so gentle that she could have hauled herself up by the horse's tail and Streamline wouldn't have protested. And that was a problem. This horse seemed to have no spirit to speak of.

Lisa nudged Streamline with her heels and the horse

began walking on signal. It was a smooth gait, but most walks were.

"Can I take her to a trot?" Lisa asked.

"If you can stay on," Mrs. Brandon said, handing Lisa the lead rope.

Lisa kicked again. Streamline kept on walking placidly. It took another half dozen kicks before Streamline was trotting, and that lasted only a few steps before the horse resumed walking again. Lisa tried clicking her tongue and slapping the mare's flanks with her hand, but it didn't inspire Streamline. Lisa began to wonder how a horse whose best gait— perhaps only gait—was a walk, got the name Streamline. She didn't want a wild horse she'd be worrying about all the time, but she did want a horse with some independence.

"We've been using her for rides with the children around here," Mrs. Brandon said. "Wouldn't hurt a fly, you know."

"I can tell," Lisa said.

"Anybody's real safe on this horse," Mrs. Brandon said.

"I'm sure they would be," Lisa told her. Mrs. Brandon looked pleased. Streamline must have been a wonderful horse for the Brandons—just what they'd needed. Mrs. Brandon appeared to be glad that Lisa could appreciate the horse's strong points.

"Everybody likes Streamline. You do, too, don't you?" Mrs. Brandon asked.

Lisa nodded. Of course she liked Streamline. How could anybody not like her? The problem was that Lisa didn't want to *own* Streamline. She didn't know how to explain this to her parents without hurting Mrs. Brandon's feelings.

Lisa's parents were waiting for them expectantly at the paddock gate. "Do you love her?" her mother asked.

Lisa felt uncomfortable with the question, but she knew what her answer was going to be. "She's a really sweet horse," Lisa began tactfully.

Mrs. Brandon interrupted before Lisa could continue. "Sure your daughter loves Streamline," she said. "Everybody loves Streamline, but she's not the right horse for Lisa and I'm not going to sell her to you."

Mr. Atwood was astonished. "What are you talking about? You said the horse was for sale. We can pay your price. Don't you want the money?"

Mrs. Brandon tied Streamline's lead rope to the fence and helped Lisa dismount. "Money isn't the issue here. Your daughter and my horse are the issues. Your daughter's a good rider and she's going to be a better rider. Streamline's a good horse for bad riders, but a bad horse for good riders. She's safe and gentle, but Lisa's already outgrown Streamline's temperament and she'll want a different horse within a year. That's not fair to either of them. Streamline belongs with a family with a lot of little kids who will use her as a first horse, where she'll get loads of love. And Lisa deserves a horse she can grow with."

Lisa patted Streamline and gave her a carrot.

"How do you feel about this, dear?" Mrs. Atwood asked.

"I couldn't have said it better myself." She climbed over the paddock fence and, while her mother scraped the mud off her shoes, Lisa got the names of a couple of other places where she might find a horse for herself.

"Good luck!" Mrs. Brandon called. Lisa and her parents waved good-bye. Streamline just munched contentedly on the sparse grass.

IT TOOK LISA two trips to get all of her books out of the trunk of the car. She wondered, as she carried the second load up to her room, how she'd managed to get them all out there in one trip in the first place. It must have been adrenaline, she decided.

She was still full of adrenaline, too. She had some absolutely wonderful news to share with her friends. Even though Streamline wasn't the horse for her, her parents weren't giving up. They were serious about buying her a horse, her very own horse. She could hardly wait to tell Carole and Stevie. She raced up the stairs with her second load of books and headed for the phone on her bedside table.

Stevie's line was busy. Stevie's line was always busy. Even when Stevie's parents had given up and gotten a separate line for Stevie and her brothers, the problem hadn't been solved. In fact, Stevie and her brothers seemed to spend *more* time on the phone. Lisa thought about pretending that she'd forgotten Stevie's number and calling on the parents' line, but she didn't think the Lakes would believe her.

She decided to call Carole instead. The phone rang three times before Carole answered it, out of breath.

"Hi, Carole, it's me, Lisa. Did you have to run for the phone?"

"No, I mean, yes. Well, sort of. See, I just got home from Pine Hollow and I was in front of the house, so I heard the phone ringing and I had to run a bit. No trouble. Let me just get my book bag off." There was a pause and Lisa heard a loud thunk. "I had to call you anyway, so I'm glad you called."

Carole's tone of voice made Lisa realize that her own good news was going to have to wait until her friend had told her what was bothering her.

"What's up?" Lisa asked.

"Oh, it's Veronica. You won't believe it. She's got her new horse *already*!" Carole had been there when the van had arrived, and she told Lisa all about it.

"That horse just about prances instead of walking. And what a face!"

Arabians were famous for having pretty heads and faces, and Garnet, it seemed, was no exception. Garnet was being stabled in the stall that had belonged to Cobalt. Cobalt's death had hurt Carole deeply, and the more Carole talked, the more Lisa realized that her friend was afraid that Veronica's carelessness was going to hurt her new horse as well.

". . . and she just yanked at the lead rope when the horse was coming out of the van! That's no way to unload a horse. You *lead* them, you don't yank them. You know that. I know that. Everybody but Veronica knows that! So why is it that Veronica's the one with the new horse?"

"You know as well as I do," Lisa said, but Carole didn't respond to her comment.

"Then, the horse hadn't even been out of the van and on hard ground for thirty seconds when Veronica was looking around for somebody to help her! That girl doesn't know the first thing about horses! Owning a horse is really a lot more responsibility than it is fun—though I'd gladly take on the responsibility. Anyway, for me, *anything* to do with horses is fun. I'd even enjoy mucking out the stall for my own horse. But nobody who isn't willing to do the work should take on the job. And Veronica thinks cleaning a *water bucket* is beneath her. Believe me, she shouldn't take on the job of owning a horse. She's just not fit to own one. You should have seen the business of the blanket!"

Lisa listened while Carole described Veronica's unwillingness to put a blanket on Garnet, even though there was a chill in the stable. Mrs. Reg, Max's mother, who helped her son run the stables, had loaned Veronica a blanket for the horse, but Veronica was upset because she didn't like the color of the blanket. Lisa knew that everything Carole was saying was true, and that Veronica was really very unfit to own Garnet, just as she'd been unfit to own Cobalt. She hadn't learned a thing from Cobalt's tragic death. But Lisa felt there was more to what Carole was saying than that.

Lisa knew Carole well enough to know that horses were her life, not just a fashionable hobby, as they were for Veronica. What Carole wanted more than anything was to own a horse. It was something she dreamed about every single night, and Lisa thought that underneath all the anger, her friend was very jealous.

It would not have crossed Carole's mind to be envious of Veronica's designer clothes, her big house, her own VCR, her gigantic swimming pool, or her vacations in Europe. None of that meant anything to Carole. What meant something to Carole was horses. Veronica had one, Carole did not. And that was something to envy.

It suddenly occurred to Lisa that Carole might be jealous of her, too, if she had a horse. The thought upset her, and she couldn't quite bring herself to tell Carole about her parents' decision. She didn't even want to tell her about Streamline and the wise owner who didn't want Lisa to buy her.

"So, guess who got to groom Garnet?" Carole continued, not noticing her friend's silence. "You got it. I groomed her. You won't believe how silky her coat is. It's very soft and it gleams when you groom it just right. After I was all done, Veronica's parents came in and admired the horse—not the job I'd done, of course—the *horse*. They are just as awful as *she* is! By the way, speaking of parents, what was up with yours this afternoon?"

Carole could talk about horses by the hour, but eventually, she would remember other things, too. Lisa had been hoping that Carole would forget about the note and how upset she'd been in school. But Carole was a good friend. She cared too much to let those things slip for long.

"My parents?" Lisa said, stalling for time.

"Yeah, the note they sent you—that they were picking you up. What was that all about?"

"Oh, that. It turned out to be nothing at all. They were together and knew they'd be near school when it let out, so they just picked me up and drove me home." The explanation sounded lame, but Lisa hoped it would work.

"Oh," Carole said. "I'm glad everything's okay. I've got to go now. I'm going to make a list of gear that Veronica will have to get for Garnet. She'll never do it without my help, you know, and a horse really ought to have its own grooming gear—especially a horse as good as Garnet. Bye. See you in riding class tomorrow, and then at Max's big meeting! Any more ideas what it's about?"

35

"No brainstorm yet. Bye-bye."

Lisa hung up the phone. She felt terrible about keeping the truth from Carole. What was the right thing to do? She was too confused to figure it out herself; she needed help.

One thing she'd learned over the last few months was that she could always get help from The Saddle Club. Obviously she couldn't talk to Carole, but she could discuss the problem with Stevie and possibly come up with a solution.

Lisa reached for the phone again, but then she had a better idea. Stevie was expecting her to come over and help with the science project this evening anyway, so it could wait until after dinner. She'd go to Stevie's house and tell her about it, in person. Stevie would know what to do. Stevie always had the answer.

"WAIT A MINUTE," Lisa told Stevie as she stared at the confused array of seeds, pots, and dirt better known as Stevie's science project. "You have to be logical. Now, let's think this through. Your project is to show how important water and light are to seed germination. So you set up one pot with seeds that get both light and water, one that gets light but not water, and one that gets water but not light. Oh, yes, and one that doesn't get either. That's very important. That's your control."

"That's it?" Stevie asked.

"Yeah, that's it," Lisa said. "And it turns out that you need both light and water—big surprise—to get the seeds to grow. It'll take about ten days to get conclusive results. Don't forget which pots need water, okay?"

Stevie nodded sheepishly. It always seemed simple once somebody helped her sort out what was important from what wasn't. She was very glad Lisa had come to help her. As she began putting soil in the pots, she told her so.

"Thanks a lot. I probably would have figured it out eventually, but you saved me a whole lot of trouble. When I couldn't reach you this afternoon, I was going to call Carole, but she was so upset about Garnet—did she tell you?"

"Yeah, she did," Lisa said. "And that reminds me of what I wanted to tell you about—"

"You should have seen Veronica this afternoon," Stevie interrupted. She really wanted to tell Lisa what it had been like. "She out-Veronica-ed Veronica! That horse wasn't out of the van two seconds before she was looking around for somebody else to do her work for her! Of course, Carole pitched right in. When there's a job to be done and it has to do with horses, it's Carole to the rescue. Veronica's unbelievable! And the really insane part was that her parents were right there and they didn't even seem to notice that Veronica was totally useless!"

Each of the four pots in front of Stevie was now two-thirds filled with soil. Stevie opened the seed pouch. She'd chosen radishes because they grew so fast. She dumped one quarter of the packet in each of the four pots.

"Stevie! You don't need to put so many seeds in!" Lisa said.

"This way at least something will grow," Stevie reasoned.

"And you may have to change your experiment to whether plants need any room in the pot to grow!"

Reluctantly, Stevie fished the extra seeds out of each pot and then covered the remaining ones with another half inch of soil. She patted the soil down gently, dusted off her hands, and began to write the labels. When she finished, she noticed the labels were smeared with dirt. She stuck them on the pots regardless. Stevie figured it didn't matter much. The pots were dirty anyway. Growing things was a dirty business.

"So anyway," Stevie continued, anxious to finish telling Lisa about Veronica, "Carole groomed Garnet and I got her feed ready. Veronica stood there with her hands on her hips, like a queen overseeing her servants. Honestly, that girl has no business owning a horse! The worst of it is, she's got one, and I don't!" It didn't seem fair to Stevie. A horse was something to be earned!

She poured water into two of the pots and then realized that Lisa was being strangely silent.

"Is something wrong?" she asked Lisa. "I mean,

other than the obvious fact that Veronica doesn't deserve Garnet?"

"Oh, no," Lisa said. "It's just that—uh, well, I'm sorry I missed seeing Garnet today. I guess she's a real beauty."

"She is," Stevie assured Lisa. "But don't worry. You'll have plenty of opportunities to see Garnet, and groom Garnet, and feed Garnet, and clean Garnet's tack. You just won't have a chance to ride Garnet. That privilege will be saved for the queen herself. Now help me find a space in my closet for the pots that don't get any light, will you?"

THAT NIGHT, LISA lay in her bed, her head swimming with confused thoughts. Something was terribly wrong, and she needed to understand it. As she had done with Stevie's science project, she tried to sort the facts into logical order.

She had some good news, really good news, but if she told the two people she most wanted to tell, she might hurt them. It wasn't as if it were good news that she could hide. After all, a horse was too big to hide for very long. Then her friends would be angry at her for not telling, *and* jealous of her as well.

Because it was jealousy that made them so angry at Veronica, wasn't it?

CAROLE WAS HAVING a difficult time concentrating on her riding class. She found herself looking at the door almost every minute. She was waiting for her father. He'd said he would be there and she knew she could count on him. She wasn't worried that he wouldn't show up, she was just anxious that he was coming. She was also more than a little anxious to know what the meeting after class was all about.

"Now I want you all to canter without stirrups," Max announced. "This is a balance exercise for you. Cross your stirrups up over your saddle and . . . begin!"

Carole followed his instructions, as she always did, but her eyes remained on the doorway. It confused her horse. One of the first things a rider learns is to look in the direction she wants her horse to go. Horses seem to sense that, perhaps from a shift in balance. Not looking in the right direction is one of the easiest ways to lose points in a competition.

"Eyes forward!" Max warned her. He didn't have to say it again, though, because just then Colonel Hanson arrived. Carole grinned at him and then completely turned her attention to her riding.

Soon after her father sat down on one of the benches around the ring, other parents started arriving. Within a short time, parents were waving at riders, riders were waving at parents, and Max was totally frustrated.

"Okay, I guess it's time to call it quits," he told his students. "I want you to dismount and walk your horses until they've cooled down. Then untack them, water and feed them, and our meeting will begin."

Carole slid down out of the saddle. Her father walked over to her and tentatively patted her horse, Barq.

"Why do you have to walk him?" he asked.

Carole explained that if you put a horse in his stall before he had a chance to walk and cool down, he could stiffen up and have some bad muscle problems, and sometimes complicated digestive problems.

"Oh," the colonel said, holding the reins while Carole loosened Barq's girth for his cooling walk.

Carole was surprised, during the next half hour, at how much she had to tell her father. She had been around horses and loved them all her life. He had always supported her love of horses, and she had always assumed that he knew as much as she did. But, she realized, he really didn't know much about them. He didn't even know how to lead a horse!

Finally, the work was finished. Barq and the other horses were cooled, groomed, bedded, and fed. The riders had changed into their street clothes. It was time for the meeting to begin. All the young riders and their parents gathered in the spacious living room of Max's house, which adjoined Pine Hollow Stables.

"I've asked you all to come," Max began, "because I want to talk to you about an exciting new opportunity for my young riders and their parents. I have just received a letter from the U.S. Pony Clubs, approving my application to begin our own club at Pine Hollow."

Carole couldn't contain her gasp. Their own Pony Club! Max smiled while the others looked at her in surprise. Carole could tell that she and Max were the only ones who really knew what that would mean. She listened excitedly while Max explained it to the others. Pony Clubs were local groups, part of a national organization that sponsored instruction and activities for young riders.

There were usually weekly meetings for each local club and then monthly or seasonal "rallies" where several nearby clubs could get together and have competition and instruction periods.

Pony Clubs also had their own rating systems for members, based on the completion of specific tasks and goals. They weren't just things you could learn from books, either. Every Pony Club member was expected to learn not only about riding, but also about horse care, stable management, and even veterinary care. Pony Clubs really covered just about everything having to do with horses.

"One of the most important factors in having our own Pony Club," Max continued, "actually, the one essential thing, is parent support. Unless we have a minimum of parents from five families, we won't be able to have our club. It would be a big time commitment, I know, but I can promise you that if your son or daughter cares about horses, the time you invest in our Pony Club will be well worth it. Has anybody here ever been in a Pony Club before?" Max asked.

Carole raised her hand. Once, when her father was stationed at a large base in California, there was a Pony Club on the base. At that time, Carole's father had been doing a lot of traveling, so he hadn't been able to be involved at all. Now that she knew how little he knew about horses, Carole didn't think that was so bad.

She told the other riders how much she'd liked the Pony Club and how much she'd learned. "One of the neatest things about it was that you learn so much about everything—and you're tested on it, too. You may be the best rider in the stables, but if you don't know how to mix bran mash for your horse, you're a D-1 with the eight-year-olds." Carole couldn't help smiling to herself. She had the funniest feeling that the arrival of Garnet might have had something to do with Max's interest in a Pony Club for Pine Hollow. Something good was going to come out of Veronica's incompetence after all!

During the next forty-five minutes, Max gave everybody booklets from the USPC, handed out copies of *The Manual of Horsemanship*, explaining that it was the Pony Clubbers' bible, and answered what seemed like hundreds of questions.

One of the parents asked if everybody had to have his own horse to join the Pony Club.

"Not at all," Max said. "The fact is that most Pony Clubbers do have their own horses, but it's not a requirement. Very few of the riders here own their own horses, but they're all eligible for membership. Pine Hollow will permit the use of its horses for approved Pony Club activities. Pony Clubs are good for riders, but they're good for riding, too."

"Will you do all the instruction?" another parent asked.

"No, though I'll usually be part of the meetings. Instruction will come from other experts. Judy Baker, my vet, has agreed to help. Also, the children will learn from other local professionals, the farrier, the saddlery, the grain-and-feed place. But mostly, the riders will learn from you, their parents, and from themselves. Which brings me back to where I began. You parents are a critical part of this. The club needs your help. Do I have any volunteers?"

There was silence in the room. Carole, who was sitting on the floor near Max between Stevie and Lisa, turned to look. All they needed were five hands to go up, five family volunteers who would make the difference between Pony Club and no Pony Club.

Nobody moved. Carole crossed her fingers.

Meg Durham's mother raised her hand.

"Thank you," Max said.

Carole crossed her legs.

Betsy Cavanaugh's father and mother both raised their hands.

"Thank you," Max said.

Carole crossed her arms across her crossed legs.

A pair of parents she didn't even know raised their hands. Another mother raised her hand.

"Thank you," Max said.

Carole crossed her eyes.

Colonel Hanson raised his hand.

"That's it, that's five!" Max announced. "We can have a Pony Club!"

Dad? What is he doing raising his hand? He doesn't know the first thing about horses. He doesn't even know how to lead them! Carole could hardly keep from staring at her father. He beamed back at her proudly. Carole shrugged to herself. What did it matter, anyway? Most of the other parents knew a lot about horses. The only reason her father needed to raise his hand was to keep Max and the USPC happy.

"Now our next order of business is to come up with a name for our club," Max said. "A lot of times, the clubs are named after the towns or the stables they're in. We could call this Willow Creek Pony Club or Pine Hollow, if you like. As far as I know, though, there's no limitation. This is our club and we can call it anything we like, but I do have to put a name on the final application. Any suggestions?" Max paused, but no one spoke. "I'll tell you what," Max continued. "We'll take a little break now. My mother has set out some cold drinks and we can talk about a name when we reconvene in about ten minutes."

"I have a suggestion," came Veronica's unmistakable voice.

"Yes?" Max said.

"Why don't we call it The Saddle Club?"

There were three gasps in the room at once. Carole knew just where the other two had come from. This was Veronica's revenge for being excluded from their club.

"Not bad," Max said. Carole realized he'd seen the

looks of concern on the girls' faces and was stalling for them. "Let's have our break now," he said. "We'll take other suggestions and then vote."

Carole, Lisa, and Stevie looked at one another and nodded. They knew what had to be done. It was time for an emergency Saddle Club meeting. They gathered in an isolated corner of the room, far away from the apple cider and homemade cookies.

"We've just got to vote it down, that's all," Lisa said. "I mean, The Saddle Club is *our* name. It's special and it's not something I want to share with Veronica. She just wants to steal our name."

"I don't think so," Stevie said. "I think she just wants to know what The Saddle Club is. She's forcing our hand so we'll have to tell everybody. Frankly, I don't mind telling anybody about The Saddle Club, but I do mind being forced into it by Veronica."

"Same here," Carole said. "But it's a terrific name. How do we get it voted down?"

"Simple," Stevie replied. "We come up with something better!"

"But what could be better?" Lisa asked. "The Saddle Club is a just about perfect name!"

"For us it is," Carole said. "But when you think about it, it's not really what Pony Clubs are about. Pony Clubs are about learning about horses, not just riding. It wises you up on subjects like stable management and horse care, safety, training. The whole idea is to teach everything. The qualifications aren't just to be horse crazy, like our club, but to learn all the whys and wherefores of horses."

"That's it!" Stevie interrupted her. Carole and Lisa looked at her in surprise. "You said it," she told Carole.

"Me? What did I say?"

"You said it twice, in fact. You said this club will wise us up and teach us all the whys of horses. The proper name of the club, therefore, is Horse Wise." Stevie smiled beatifically, and folded her hands on her lap.

Lisa and Carole, laughing, had to agree. The Saddle Club meeting was over. It was time to return to Max's meeting. They took the last three glasses of cider and returned to their places near Max.

When Max asked for other suggestions, Carole raised her hand. She stood up and explained what she knew about Pony Clubs, stressing the idea of how they made riders *wise* and didn't just teach them about riding, as the name Saddle Club might suggest. She tried to sound very polite to Veronica, but she knew Veronica knew she wasn't being polite. She used every bit of debating skill she had to convince people to vote on their name. Only four people in the room really knew what was going on. It didn't matter, though. The fact was, Carole was winning and she knew it.

". . . so, my friends and I would like to suggest that we name our club Horse Wise."

"Hey, great idea!" Max said, publicly casting his

vote. That was what they'd needed. By voice vote, their Pony Club got its own, unusual name.

Carole felt so good at the end of the meeting that she didn't even care when Veronica make a nasty remark on her way out. "Nice job, Carole," she snapped, "but it means that the first time you ride Garnet will be when it snows in July."

6

WHENEVER THE SUBJECT was horses, Carole was happy. This evening, she was especially happy. Even Veronica diAngelo hadn't been able to ruin it. Pine Hollow was going to have its own Pony Club!

"We're having our first meeting next week," she told her father as they headed for the car.

"I heard," he said. Carole thought maybe he was teasing her a little bit, but she didn't mind.

"It's a mounted meeting, you know," she said as she took her place in the front seat of the car, next to her father.

"I heard, but what does that mean?" he asked.

"It means we'll be mounted—you know, on horseback."

"Oh." Colonel Hanson started the car. "With your saddles, right?"

"Sure we'll have saddles. If there weren't going to be saddles, we'd call it *bare*back."

"That makes sense," he said, pulling the car out of Pine Hollow's driveway. He turned the car toward the base, where the Officers' Club and navy-bean soup awaited them.

Carole couldn't stop talking about the Pony Club. "Then, at other times, we'll have unmounted meetings. I can't wait until the farrier talks to us. That should be neat."

"What's a farrier?" Colonel Hanson asked. "Someone who makes fair coats?"

"Very funny, but no," Carole said patiently. "A farrier is a blacksmith. He makes horseshoes and fits them properly to the horse's hooves and nails them on."

"Nails them? Doesn't that hurt?"

"No, the horse's hoof is like a toenail. As long as the nail just goes into the toenail part, the horse can't even feel it."

"You mean there are other parts to the foot?" her father asked.

"Oh, sure, there's the frog and the bulbs and the sole and that's just the beginning. Horses' feet are very complicated."

"I guess they are," the colonel said. He was quiet for a while and seemed to be thinking. It gave Carole some time to think as well. Carole knew a lot about horses. She'd read a lot of books, but mostly she'd learned because she spent time with people who knew a lot about horses and who had taught her about them. That was one of the best things about a Pony Club. All the members were there to learn and all the volunteers were there to teach them.

But what about a volunteer who didn't know anything? One who didn't know the difference between horseback and bareback? What good was he going to be? There was something else bothering her, too, but she couldn't quite put her finger on it.

Her father began singing. He loved music from the fifties and sixties. He started in on an Elvis Presley medley, beginning with his favorite, "Big Boots."

Carole looked at him from the corner of her eye. Usually, she liked it when he sang or told his silly old jokes. Usually, she liked almost everything he did. But was she going to like it when he became part of her riding and showed everybody that he didn't know anything?

Carole was very proud of her skill in riding and her knowledge. She loved it when people asked her questions and she knew the answer. She knew she had a tendency to give them more answer than they might want. It was something her friends liked to tease her about, but she didn't mind. She still liked just plain knowing.

So now, how were people going to feel about her when they saw that her father, her wonderful father who could do so many other things, was a total ignoramus when it came to horses? And how was that going to make Carole feel?

"Dad?" she said, interrupting "Heartbreak Hotel."

"What, honey?"

"I have a couple of books you might want to look at about horses," she said.

"That's okay, sweetheart," he said. "I'm sure that whatever I need to know, you can tell me."

Carole sighed. That was what she was afraid of.

AFTER THE MEETING, Lisa's parents were more enthusiastic than ever about buying a horse for her. Lisa suspected it was because they had seen how few of the riders there actually did own their horses. She didn't think that was a very good reason for buying a horse, certainly no better than buying one because Veronica diAngelo had one. Still, she herself wanted to own one very much, and as long as her parents wanted to buy a horse, she didn't really care why.

The very next day, they picked her up after school again. The secretary from the vice-principal's office had given Lisa a strange look when she'd given her the second note about meeting her parents after school in less than a week, but that was another thing Lisa decided not to worry about.

This time, the farm was really a horse farm, not just a farm with a horse for sale. Lisa liked the place immediately. It had big, airy, light stalls for its horses. They all opened onto individual outdoor paddock areas.

Those areas, in turn, opened to a large field. The horses had plenty of room to move, but their movements were controlled. The place seemed like a good combination of stabling and pasturing.

The owner, Mr. Jenrette, greeted the Atwoods. He explained that he'd just acquired a horse, Brinker, as part of a package deal, but he wasn't a breeding horse so Mr. Jenrette wanted to sell him right away.

"He's a real beauty," Mr. Jenrette said. "I know you'll love him. I've already had three other phone calls about him. You're lucky that you called first." Mr. Jenrette led them over to the paddock. Brinker was a bay, which meant he was brown with a black mane and tail. Brinker's nose and ankles were black as well— that was called having black points—and he had a white blaze on his forehead.

Brinker was in his paddock. Lisa approached him slowly. He looked up and walked over toward her. It was as if they were already friends. The horse gazed at her curiously, and she patted his forehead. He seemed to like it, so she did it some more. Then she patted his neck.

"Here are some carrots," Mr. Jenrette said, offering her a handful. Lisa took one and gave it to Brinker. She loved the sound of a horse crunching on carrots. Brinker loved the carrot.

"He's not a purebred or anything," Mr. Jenrette said. "But he's got good lines. You'll love riding him for a long time to come."

"What does that mean?" Mrs. Atwood asked. Lisa explained that calling a horse purebred meant that it was registered as part of a breed, such as Thoroughbred, Arabian, or Quarter Horse. Both of its parents had to be registered and had to have the papers to prove it. It was a guarantee of quality breeding, though not necessarily of a good horse, and it was a guarantee of cost.

"You know something about horses, don't you?" Mr. Jenrette asked.

"A bit," Lisa said. "And I read a lot, too."

"I can tell," he said. Then he turned to her parents. "So, do you want him?" he asked.

"Oh, I think so," Mr. Atwood said, and he turned to Lisa for confirmation. "Is this the right one?" he asked.

"He certainly looks good," she said. "And I think I like his disposition—at least his stable manners. But there are lots of things we have to check first."

"Like what?" her mother asked. "The horse is pretty, you like him, he's for sale. What else is there?" Mrs. Atwood turned to Mr. Jenrette for an answer. The answer he gave was to look at his watch, as if he were waiting for the next buyer to show up and make him a better offer. It was a small gesture, but it told Lisa a lot. Lisa had a few doubts, and that little gesture gave her the confidence to follow up on them. Mr. Jenrette seemed to be very anxious to sell his horse.

"I need to check a few things," she said, climbing over the fence into the paddock. It made her even more suspicious that Mr. Jenrette didn't join her and help her. She wanted to check the horse's conformation, to make sure he had no obvious physical defects. She was no expert, so she could have used some expert advice. Why didn't Mr. Jenrette want to give it to her?

An expert could determine a lot of things by looking at a horse. There were many small things that could be wrong that might not mean much at the time of a purchase, but could cost thousands of dollars in veterinary bills over time. There were also lots of things that could seem odd, but not mean anything at all. So why didn't Mr. Jenrette want to show Lisa how good Brinker's conformation was?

Her parents watched, confused, while she checked the points she could. Mr. Jenrette just kept looking at his watch whenever he thought somebody was looking at him. Lisa definitely smelled a rat. Now, instead of being doubtful, she was sure there was something significantly wrong with the horse, and it became a challenge to her. Would she find it before Mr. Jenrette sprained his wrist looking at his watch?

It was almost like a game of Hot and Cold. When Lisa was looking at Brinker's head and neck, his body and his flanks, Mr. Jenrette had his hands on his hips. As soon as she picked up a hoof to examine Brinker's foot, Mr. Jenrette began looking at his watch. She let go of the hoof and the man's hand went into his pocket. When she knelt to study the foot as it sat on the ground, he spoke.

"Did you hear a car come in the drive?" he asked. He wasn't being subtle at all.

The problem had to be in Brinker's feet and legs. Lisa thought she spotted it. There was a complex set of bones at what might be called the horse's ankle, leading up to the main lower-leg bone, the cannon. Lisa didn't know the names of all the parts, but she knew that the lowest portion of the leg was supposed to be at approximately the same angle as the hoof, almost as if it were a continuation of the hoof. That wasn't the case on Brinker. His leg went straight up right above the hoof.

"Hmmm," she said.

"Next people are coming in about five minutes," Mr. Jenrette said.

"I'd like to try riding him, and then we'll have our vet check him out tomorrow," Lisa told him.

"He'll be sold by then," Mr. Jenrette said.

That was when Lisa decided it didn't matter whether she was right or wrong about where the problem was. If Mr. Jenrette expected to sell the horse to somebody who would not have it checked by a vet, he was definitely hiding something a vet would find. Brinker was a pretty horse, and he seemed to have a sweet disposition. But Brinker was not a horse she was going to own.

"No, thank you," Lisa said.

Mr. Jenrette shrugged. "Your loss."

"What's going on here?" Mr. Atwood demanded, suddenly realizing he'd been missing out on an entire drama.

As confident as she was that something was wrong, Lisa didn't want to make a scene. She'd explain to her parents on the way home. She tried to think of a reason that would satisfy them.

"It's just that the color doesn't seem right to me, Dad. You know I've got my heart set on a chestnut," Lisa said. It was about the dumbest reason she could think of for deciding not to buy a horse, but maybe it would work.

"Oh," her father said.

"Sure," her mother said. "Those are the sort of auburn-colored ones, aren't they? I love that color. I'm sure we can find a horse like that for you, dear. I just didn't know—"

"It's okay, Mom, and thanks, Mr. Jenrette," Lisa said, shaking his hand vigorously. She had the wild idea of trying to give his right wrist as much exercise as his left wrist had been getting. It was all she could do to keep from laughing as she did it.

Once the Atwoods were on the road, Lisa's father looked at her in the rearview mirror. "A chestnut?" he asked. "What was that all about?" She'd fooled her mother, but not her father. She doubted that she'd fooled Mr. Jenrette, either.

"Well," Lisa began.

"It was the vet part, wasn't it?" Mr. Atwood asked.

"Yeah," Lisa said, smiling. "As soon as he didn't want a vet looking at the horse, I knew something was wrong—really wrong. I think Brinker has a problem with his hooves and legs, but a vet would know for sure."

"This horse-buying business is a complicated one, isn't it?" Mr. Atwood asked.

"Yes," Lisa agreed. "It is." They had found one horse that was sound, but not right for her. Another was right for her, but not sound. It was a complicated business, and it was even more complicated than her father realized, because he had no way of knowing how much Lisa wanted to tell her friends and how afraid she was of doing it.

"I'm going to be away on business for a couple of days," Mr. Atwood said. "We'll look at more horses when I get back, okay?"

Lisa nodded.

"Don't worry. We'll find you the right horse," he assured her.

Lisa nodded again. After all, that was what she wanted, wasn't it?

"HORSE WISE, COME to order!"

Stevie tugged ever so slightly on Topside's reins. The horse stood still, seeming to sense that something exciting was about to happen. And something exciting *was* about to happen. The first Horse Wise mounted meeting was about to begin. All of the riders were about to become full-fledged members of the Pony Club.

It took a few minutes for all the horses to line up, especially since Veronica was riding Garnet in a group for the first time. It wasn't that Veronica couldn't control Garnet; it was that she didn't want to control her. As long as Garnet was acting up, Veronica was the center of attention and almost everybody had to look at her and her beautiful horse. Stevie stared straight ahead, and so did Lisa and Carole. Finally, Garnet was in line with everybody else. Max gave Veronica a warning look that told her to keep it that way.

"Our agenda for today is as follows," Max began. "First, each of you will receive your official Pony Club pins. You are entitled to wear them as long as you are a member in good standing of Horse Wise."

Stevie decided she intended to be a member in good standing for a very long time.

"Next, we will discuss the schedule for future meetings as well as ratings, and then we will play a learning game. This will be followed by a short trail ride and then the meeting will adjourn one half hour before scheduled to allow you all ample time for grooming and horse care. Remember, stable management and horse care are an important part of Horse Wise and will be required of all members."

That was when all three of The Saddle Club girls looked at Veronica. She didn't look back.

Max asked the sponsors to distribute the pins. Colonel Hanson was the first one to help. He took the pins from Max and began handing them out, walking behind the Pony Clubbers' horses as he went. Everyone at the meeting, except Colonel Hanson, knew that whenever it is practical, it makes sense to walk in front of horses, rather than behind them. Horses like to know what is going on and can get skittish if somebody passes too close to them.

"Colonel," Max said. "It's better to walk in front of the horses than in back of them."

"Oh," the colonel said sheepishly, coming quickly to the front of the group.

"Can anybody tell the colonel the reason for this?" Max asked. Several hands went up. Max called on Stevie, who quickly explained it. She thought she'd done a pretty good job, but after she finished, she noticed that Carole was scowling a little bit. Stevie thought about it for a few seconds and realized that Carole probably wasn't scowling at her. Maybe she was scowling because her father didn't know such a simple thing about horses. Carole was usually so patient when people didn't know things, but of course it was different when it was your own father. Stevie suspected that Colonel Hanson would never make that mistake again.

Once all the riders had their pins on, Max announced his schedule for the next few weeks. As long as the weather was good, they would alternate mounted meetings one Saturday and unmounted meetings the next. The following week, Judy, the vet, would talk to them about horse care, and at the meeting after that, the members would be tested and rated.

Stevie had been reading up on Pony Clubs. And when Phil Marston had called her the other night, she'd asked him about them since he already belonged. In fact, their clubs were in the same district and they'd be seeing each other at rallies. Stevie could hardly wait. In the meantime, though, she'd have to be "rated." Each member would receive a rating according to his own skill level. The ratings started at D-1 through 3, which was for beginners, then progressed to C-1 through 3, B, H-A, and A. Very few riders ever achieved H-A and A and only very good riders, with years of experience, got to B. Stevie hoped that one day she'd be able to be a C, but for now, she figured that she and Lisa were both D's. Carole might make it to C. Stevie wondered what sort of rating they would come up with for Veronica. The important thing about the ratings, and about Pony Clubs in general, was that they weren't just about riding. Horse care was just as important. Stevie grinned. Veronica wouldn't be able to find a stableboy to take the horse-care section of the test for her!

"All right, now, our first activity will be a game called Giant Steps."

Max described the rules. Each rider would be asked a question about horses. If the rider answered correctly, his or her horse could take one step toward a line that Max had Colonel Hanson draw in the dirt. If the rider made a mistake, the horse would have to take a step backward toward another line. Whoever crossed the front line first, won. Whoever crossed the back line was out.

Max began shooting out questions. How many beats were in a walk? Trot? Canter?

Stevie thought they were very easy questions until she noticed that the riders he was giving them to were beginners. They weren't easy questions for them.

"Stevie, name the parts of a horse's neck."

Stevie made a face. Veronica diAngelo laughed. That was the inspiration Stevie needed.

"Poll, crest, and withers," she answered. She was awarded one giant step.

Carole named ten grooming aids, and Lisa told him five registered breeds of horses.

"Veronica, name three parts of the horse's foot."

Veronica shifted uncomfortably in her saddle. Stevie suddenly got the feeling she was going to like this a lot.

"Well, there's the hoof—"

"One step backward," Max announced. "Anybody else?"

Stevie raised her hand. Max called on her. "Wall, sole, and frog," she said. She stepped forward.

"Veronica, I told you to step backward," Max said.

Veronica glared at him. "Isn't it time to stop this game now and go for a trail ride?" she said.

"Not yet." That closed the subject for everybody except Veronica, who was never one to enjoy public humiliation.

Garnet started acting up a little, as if she didn't want to step backward any more than Veronica did. Stepping backward was an easy command and something every horse learned early in training. The command for it was to simply pull straight back on the reins—not hard, just steadily. Stevie watched closely.

Garnet was doing exactly what Veronica was telling her to do, which was to turn around.

In the next moment, Garnet and Veronica had taken off on a trail ride. The Saddle Club had never seen anything like it. She just plain rode out of the ring in the middle of the meeting! Even Max, usually completely composed when he was in a riding ring, gaped. Then, becoming aware that he was staring, he returned his attention to the riders in the ring. "Polly," he said. "Tell me three reasons why a horse might need new shoes."

As it turned out, Max, as usual, had planned everything to be fair. All the riders got some questions they could answer, and by listening carefully, they could learn from the other riders as well. One of the youngest members, Lucy Johnson, was the first over the line when she told Max that a rider always mounted from the left-hand side. Everybody clapped for her because she deserved to win and they had all had fun playing the game.

After that, Max took them on a brief trail ride, across a meadow and into the woods behind Pine Hollow. They met up with Veronica in the meadow, where she had been cantering on Garnet. Max called her over to him and everybody heard what he said.

"Veronica, I understand you were excited about riding your new horse for the first time, but leaving the meeting was childish and wrong. Don't do it again."

Then he dismissed her, directing her to the end of the line of riders. As she passed by The Saddle Club, Veronica smiled triumphantly. Stevie shook her head. Veronica actually thought she'd gotten away with something!

CAROLE FINISHED GROOMING Barq and gave him his feed. She was almost ready to find her father and leave for the day. First, though, out of habit, she walked along the hallway between the stalls, looking to see if anyone needed help with his horse. She didn't have to go far before she found somebody who needed a *lot* of help. It was her own father.

Colonel Hanson was standing in Garnet's stall, holding the horse's reins in one hand and examining the bridle as if it were an interesting specimen under a microscope.

"What are you doing?" Carole asked somewhat impatiently. He did look a little stupid standing there.

"I'm trying to figure out how to take this thing off," he cheerfully replied. "Veronica told me she was tired after her ride and asked if I'd take care of her horse for her. I don't mind, but how do you get this thing off?"

"I'll do it," Carole said, speaking more sharply than she meant to. Her father handed her the reins and stood back, watching her.

Carole was upset. Everything seemed wrong to her. How could it be that her very own father, who always knew everything, didn't even know how to remove a bridle? How could he be a good sponsor for Horse Wise—Horse Dumb seemed more apt to her. Even worse, how could it be that somebody who didn't deserve a horse could have one as beautiful and gentle as Garnet?

"Can I help you out there?" Colonel Hanson asked.

"No," Carole said.

"Then maybe I should see if I can help somebody else."

"Sure," she said, although it occurred to her that if she didn't want everybody to know how ignorant he was, it probably wasn't a great idea to send him out as a helper. What was foremost in her mind, though, was Veronica's carelessness. Her carelessness had cost the life of her last horse. What would it do this time?

"NEED SOME HELP?"

Stevie looked up and saw Colonel Hanson standing at the stall door. "Sure, come on in. Help me get Topside untacked."

"Oh, good," he said. "You can show me how to undo this bridle gadget. It's sure got a lot of buckles, doesn't it?"

Stevie laughed. "It's easy. I'll show you. First, you put on a halter—"

"Why do you do that?" he asked.

"Well, you just do," Stevie said, without thinking. She put on the halter first because she always put on a halter first.

67

"There must be a reason," Colonel Hanson said mildly.

"I suppose," Stevie agreed, and stopped to think about it. "I got it," she said. "You put on a halter and a lead rope so you always have something to control the horse with. A horse like Topside probably doesn't need it, particularly when you're untacking him in his stall, but the time you forget to do it will be the time he's in an open area and he can be out of reach in a second. That's why you should always do it."

"Good," the colonel said, and smiled at Stevie.

Next, she showed him how to remove the saddle. He tried to do it from the horse's right side. Stevie showed him that it should be done from the left.

"Why?" he asked.

Good question, she thought to herself. Saddles were removed from the left because they were always removed from the left. "Actually, I think it's because the horse is used to being approached from the left. It's also the side where most girth adjustments are made, so the leathers are suppler on that side and easier to buckle and unbuckle."

"Makes sense," Colonel Hanson told her.

"Makes sense to me, too," Stevie said. "I never thought about it before, though. I just always did it."

She showed the colonel where to stow the saddle in the tack room and explained the system in there. Then they returned to Topside's stall and began the grooming. It turned out that he didn't know anything

68

about that, either. Although Stevie had shown many new riders how to groom and care for a horse, she'd never had one who asked "why" as often as Carole's father did.

When the last bit of grooming was finished, and Topside had fresh hay and fresh water, Stevie turned to her "instructor" and asked, "Now may I take twenty-five giant steps for all the right answers I've given?"

"Why?" he asked, and they both laughed.

CAROLE CARRIED GARNET'S saddle and bridle into
the tack room, where they would probably stay until Veronica got somebody else to put them on her
horse. Carole frowned, thinking again about how
upside down the world seemed to be. What she saw
when she walked into the tack room made her feel
the world was even more upside down. There was
her father, the Pony Club sponsor, being instructed
on tack cleaning by her friend Lisa.

"No, you just moisten the sponge, you don't wet
it," Lisa was saying. "Okay, now rub in small circles. That works the best."

"Why?" the colonel asked.

Carole felt her cheeks flush in embarrassment.
Her father didn't know *anything*! She hastily put the
tack away and returned to the stable area because she

could leave the room that way without being seen by her father or by Lisa. She almost wished that she'd never be seen by anybody ever again. How could she look her friends in the eye after they learned what a dolt her father was when it came to horses?

There were still several Pony Clubbers in the stalls, grooming their horses. Carole needed a place to hide and think a bit. The stalls wouldn't do. She was too likely to be interrupted, or to overhear her father asking more dumb questions. She noticed that the door to the grain room was closed. That meant nobody was in it. It would give her the privacy she needed.

The grain room was actually quite large, but felt small because of the large sacks and bins of grains it held. Carole was always interested in the variety of grains horses were fed. Sometimes, she'd come in here to work with Max on the recipes, which often varied for each horse depending on his individual needs. Today, she ignored the sacks, except to sit on one in a far corner.

The door flew open. One of the younger riders—Carole couldn't remember her name—entered, followed by Carole's father.

"See," the little girl said. "This is the grain room. We give the horses grain as well as hay."

"Well, now. Tell me, why is that?" Carole's father asked.

"I think the grain has more good stuff in it for the horses—like oats, you know. The hay is good, but it's not enough by itself."

71

"That's a good answer. Thanks, Melanie," the colonel said. Then, for the first time, the two intruders noticed Carole.

"Hi, there, daughter dear," said the colonel. He grinned at Carole.

"Are you *her* dad?" the young rider asked in surprise. Carole cringed.

"Yup!" he answered. Then the two of them left. Her father waved before the door closed. She didn't wave back. Carole put her elbows on her knees and her chin in her hands. As she did so, her hand brushed against her new Pony Club pin. She played with it absently as she thought. The Pony Club was something she wanted to be part of. It was something she cared about. She also cared about her father. He was a terrific dad, but a lousy horseman. These were two very important parts of her life, but they were separate parts, meant to stay that way.

She had to do something. Her father couldn't go on like this. He wasn't any use to the club, and it was embarrassing. Maybe, if her father could take lessons someplace else—not Pine Hollow—and read about a hundred books, then, *maybe* he'd be almost ready to think about being a Horse Wise sponsor. But not now. Not until he was ready to stop asking questions and begin answering them.

Carole realized she might not be the best person to tell her father this. He might not take her seriously, or she might even hurt his feelings. But he would take

Max seriously, and since Max was a professional, her father wouldn't take his criticism personally. That was where she would go. Max would understand and help her. Satisfied that she had the right answer to her problem, Carole stood up from the sack that had served as her seat and left the grain room.

"Hi, Carole," Meg Durham greeted her in the stall hallway. "I was just talking to your dad. I showed him how to pick a horse's hooves."

"Was he a good student?" Carole asked drily.

Meg giggled.

Carole was sorry she'd asked. She didn't like the idea of somebody giggling at her dad. She felt as if Meg were giggling at her!

Max was in the hallway, supervising something in one of the stalls. Carole needed to talk to him alone. She walked over to him and waited to get his attention. As soon as she saw what was going on, her heart sank. Betsy Cavanaugh was showing her father how to put a leg wrap on a horse.

"Max, can I talk to you—uh, privately?" Carole asked.

"Sure," he said. A questioning look crossed his face. "Let's go to my office."

When the door closed on his office, they both sat down and Carole began. "It's about—"

"I know. Veronica. What she did at the meeting was totally wrong and then I saw that she really just abandoned Garnet and you ended up doing all the work. I don't think I'm going to be able to change her, you know—"

"It isn't about Veronica," Carole interrupted. "It's about my father."

Max smiled. "It's just great having him here," he said warmly. "He's so enthusiastic! He's got everybody running in circles today. I love it!"

"You love it?" Carole thought she'd heard wrong.

"Every time I turn around, your father is right there, working with another Pony Clubber, one-on-one. It's the best kind of instruction there is. Too few students get it."

"It depends on who is doing the instructing and who is doing the learning," Carole said.

"Oh, absolutely, but I can tell your father really knows how to teach and the riders love him."

"Of course they love him. He's lovable. He's the greatest dad a girl could have. But, well, Max, don't you think it might help him if he had a few, uh, riding lessons or something—you know, somewhere else?"

"No problem there, Carole. I'm doing a weekly class for all of the sponsors. Do you know, some of them really don't know the first thing about horses?"

Now nothing at all made sense to Carole. There was no point in staying in Max's office any longer. Talking to Max wasn't going to help. No matter what anybody else said to her, she knew that her father didn't know what he was doing. He didn't belong at Pine Hollow, and ultimately, he was going to make her look foolish.

The fact that he was a neat, charming guy wouldn't carry him for very long. Eventually, something would have to be done. Carole just hoped she wouldn't have to be the one to do it.

ON MONDAY AFTERNOON, Lisa's parents picked her up once again after school. It was beginning to feel like a comfortable, familiar, but unproductive routine.

This time, the seller was a trainer. Her father had found an ad in the Sunday paper that sounded promising. The horse was a four-year-old bay. Mrs. Atwood was surprised that Lisa was willing to consider a bay, since she thought Lisa only wanted a chestnut. Lisa and her father decided not to try to explain it to her. Mrs. Atwood wasn't stupid, but horse trading was not something that made much sense to her.

"He's a beautiful horse," the trainer, Mr. Michaels, said. One look at the horse and Lisa had to agree. His rich brown coat glistened in the sunshine. "I've been working with him and he learns fast. You're an experienced rider, aren't you, Mr. Atwood?" he asked.

"Me? Not at all. The rider in the family is Lisa. The horse is for her."

"Oh," Mr. Michaels said. Then he furrowed his brow. "I want to sell this horse, but I want the buyer to be happy. This is a good horse and he could be a great show horse someday, but he's young. He needs an excellent rider—one who can continue training him and who has the time and the patience to do it right. I mean, I believe there's championship material here, but I've only been able to start the work. Another year or two, who knows? That's one of the reasons I'm not asking for what I think he'll be worth someday. He really needs more training."

Lisa looked at the horse again. His name was Pretty Boy and she thought it was the perfect name for him.

"Think you want to try him anyway?" Mr. Michaels asked. "I wouldn't blame you."

Lisa nodded. She couldn't resist.

It took a few minutes to tack up Pretty Boy. He fidgeted when the saddle went on and he fought the bit as Mr. Michaels bridled him. Lisa didn't want to notice these things. All she wanted to do was to be in the saddle of the beautiful horse. And very soon, she was. She took the reins in her left hand and climbed on board from the mounting block.

Pretty Boy was tall, dark, and handsome. From where Lisa sat, she was mostly aware of how tall he was. At Pine Hollow, she was used to riding Pepper, who was at least a full hand shorter than Pretty Boy. Horses are measured in hands, which are four-inch units. Pretty Boy pranced about nervously. Lisa leaned forward and patted him on the neck reassuringly. "Easy, boy," she said. He calmed a bit.

"You know what you're doing, I see," Mr. Michaels said. "Now try walking him in a circle. He and I have been working on that."

Lisa signaled the horse with her legs and he responded. She signaled for a right turn and he ignored her. Instead, he stepped backward.

"Be firm," Mr. Michaels said.

Lisa knew that, but it wasn't always easy to do. She signaled again, and he ignored her again. She tapped Pretty Boy on the left front shoulder with her riding crop. At last he turned right and began walking around the ring.

After the second time around the circle, she decided to try a trot. She nudged his belly to get him going. It worked, and he got going, but at a canter, not a trot. For what it was worth, it was a perfectly wonderful canter. Lisa felt as if she were on a rocking chair, gracefully shifting back and forth. But it wasn't what she'd told the horse she wanted him to do. Lisa gave him a slow-down sign with her reins and seat. He slowed to a walk.

It took four more tries to get Pretty Boy to trot and sustain the gait. A trot was a jogging gait and on most horses it was bumpy. Somehow, Pretty Boy managed to do it smoothly.

"Hey, this is a great gait!" Lisa said. "And I love the canter, too, only I don't like it when he wants to canter and I want to trot." Lisa brought Pretty Boy to a walk and rode him over to where her parents and Mr. Michaels were standing.

"That's the problem, isn't it?" Mr. Michaels said.

"Yes, it is. He's a wonderful horse, but not for me."

"You two seem to be speaking a language I don't

understand," Mrs. Atwood said. "What's going on here?"

Lisa tried to explain. "Mom, he's a great horse—or more accurately, he *will* be a great horse, but he's not fully trained. See, what I need is a horse I can ride. I just have a couple of hours a week to ride, and I'd spend them all training, not riding, if we bought Pretty Boy. Now, if you wanted to think about making a pasture out of our backyard and building a stable there, where I could have the horse right there—and maybe have a trainer come two or three hours a day to work with Pretty Boy so he'd be ready for me to ride when I wanted him—"

Mrs. Atwood looked horrified. "Are you actually suggesting that we change our entire—"

"Hold on, there, ma'am," Mr. Michaels said. "Your daughter's right about what it would take, but I think she's joking. She knows this isn't the right horse for her. Am I right?" he asked Lisa.

"Right," she said. "But if he's still for sale when he's five . . ."

"I'm hoping to find Pretty Boy a home for life right now. But I'll keep you in mind."

Lisa dismounted and helped Mr. Michaels untack the horse. As she did, she thought about the kind of owner Pretty Boy should have. She should be an experienced rider, but one not so set in her ways that she wouldn't have fun with a spirited horse. Pretty Boy should belong to somebody who spent a lot of time with horses, maybe even worked with them for a living. He would need a shot at show riding, jumping, and hunting, all kinds of experiences. Lisa hoped very much that Mr. Michaels would be able to find exactly the right person for Pretty Boy.

"LISA, YOU'D BETTER come over," Stevie said excitedly on the telephone Tuesday evening. "You've got to see what's happening to my radishes!"

"Radishes? What radishes?" Lisa asked. She had been interrupted in the middle of her history homework and she hadn't yet cleared her brain of the Wars of the Roses to shift into radish gear.

"You know, my *radishes*!" Stevie said insistently.

Then Lisa remembered Stevie's science project. "Oh, *those* radishes. What is it? Is there a problem?"

"No, but they're doing things. You have to see!" Stevie didn't wait for an answer. She hung up the phone.

Lisa giggled to herself. When Stevie got excited about something, no matter what it was, it was almost impossible not to get excited with her. So much for the

Wars of the Roses. She couldn't keep the reds and whites straight from one another anyway.

Lisa grabbed a sweat shirt, told her parents where she was going, and was out the door before anybody could object. She wasn't going far anyway. Stevie's house was just at the other end of the block.

Thinking about Stevie made her think about The Saddle Club and the secret she was keeping from her two best friends. Some secrets were nice, but it depended on whom you were keeping them secret from. Lisa also knew that if she didn't tell her friends, they'd find out about it somehow. Lisa's mother would tell Mrs. diAngelo, who would tell somebody else—maybe even Veronica—and Carole and Stevie would be sure to hear about it. And the only thing worse than keeping a secret from her friends would be having her friends learn about it from somebody else—especially Veronica diAngelo! Lisa had to tell them soon.

"I will," she said out loud to the cool evening. "I'll tell Stevie tonight. Right now, in fact. Then it won't be a horrible secret anymore and I can stop worrying about it." Just saying it out loud made her feel better. She was practically skipping by the time she mounted the steps to Stevie's house, and she was definitely skipping when she climbed the stairs to Stevie's room.

"Look at these guys!" Stevie said, proudly showing Lisa one of her radish pots. "I mean look and see what Mother Nature has done here!"

Lisa dropped her sweat shirt on Stevie's bed and

joined Stevie at her desk, where the lamp on it was totally focused on "Pot Number One: Light and Water." At first, Lisa didn't see a thing. Then, when she took a closer look, she detected quite a few little greenish-white sprouts pushing up through the dirt.

"They're growing!" Stevie said. "It's really working. Aren't they just so cute you can't believe it?"

At first, Lisa thought that cute was a strange word to describe the tiny radish shoots, but the more she thought about it and the more she looked, the more she decided Stevie was right. "Definitely cute," she agreed. "And how about the other pots?"

"Nothing."

"Great, that's just the way it's supposed to be," Lisa said. "See, I told you it would be easy."

"I've decided something," Stevie said. "As soon as this crop of radishes is ready to be harvested, I'll call you and you can come over and have your choice of the bounty of my science experiment. I'll even provide the salt—that is, if you like your radishes with salt. All because you're a real friend."

Lisa knew that Stevie said it to be funny and to thank her. Stevie was being so nice that Lisa felt guilty. It was time to be a real friend and tell Stevie her secret.

Stevie didn't seem to notice that Lisa had something on her mind. "I was at the stable today," she said. "I left my backpack in my cubby after Horse Wise on Saturday. So, of course, I had to go get it because I had my homework assignments written on the back of The Letter, which was still in the backpack. Anyway, guess who else was there? It was good old Veronica diAngelo. Was she there to exercise Garnet and take care of her, groom her, and things like that? No, she was not. She was there because she wanted to check the color of Garnet's blanket against samples she had for a new pair of riding pants and jacket. She wanted to match her clothes to the blanket so they'd be color-coordinated when they had their picture taken together. Can you believe her?"

"No, I can't," Lisa said truthfully. "Sometimes it seems like we've seen everything, but when it comes to Veronica, I'm afraid we haven't even begun to scratch the surface. Some people deserve horses. Veronica definitely doesn't."

Stevie took out the chart she'd devised for noting the progress of her seedlings and carefully measured the tallest of the radish plants. It was three eighths of an inch high. She wrote that down and then wrote large zeros in the other columns. "It feels like a real accomplishment," she announced, replacing the pots on the windowsill. "I'm actually going to have all the information I'm going to need to do this science project right. You are such a pal."

"Thanks," Lisa said. She didn't feel like a pal. Stevie's comment about Veronica and Garnet brought back all of her doubts about sharing her secret. Half an hour later, when Lisa returned to her own room and the Wars of the Roses, she still hadn't told Stevie about her parents' decision to buy her a horse.

"AN IMPORTANT PART of being a Pony Clubber is keeping your own horse's health and maintenance book," Max told the members of Horse Wise the following Saturday.

He handed each club member a folder with individual record sheets in it.

"You'll need to fill these out and bring them to every rating and, even more important, you'll need to keep them up to date. As you'll see, the sheets require certain specific information. Judy is here today to help you all learn how to check on your horse's health and fill out these sheets . . ."

As Max continued talking, Carole looked at her booklet. It was designed to be a year-long log of everything from the horse's basic health, like his normal pulse rate and temperature, to the veterinary visits, cost of horse care, and income of the rider. Carole knew about the care book from the last time she'd been in a Pony Club.

"The first thing we need to do is to learn how to check a horse's pulse," Judy said. "Colonel Hanson, can you show us how to do this?"

Carole felt a nervous twinge in her stomach. If her father had read one of the three books she'd left on his bedside table last week, he might, just might, have learned what to do. Otherwise, it was going to be another embarrassing moment for her. She held her breath.

The colonel stepped forward to where Judy held Patch, a black-and-white pinto, by his lead rope. To Carole's dismay, he grinned and reached down and put his hand against Patch's foreleg, as if it were the horse's wrist.

Carole groaned out loud. Nobody heard it, though. Everybody was laughing too loud. Carole hung back in a corner, hoping that nobody could see her, hoping, in fact, that nobody would know she existed.

"Nice try, Colonel," Judy said. "But you flunk." More giggles. "Anybody want to show this man what to do?"

A few hands went up. Judy called on Stevie. Stevie showed Colonel Hanson and everybody else the two easiest places to check a horse's pulse. The first was in between the animal's jawbones, at the curve of the cheek. The second was on the horse's belly, right behind his elbow.

Stevie put her hand under Patch's jaw, checked Judy's watch, which had a sweep-second hand, and counted the beats for fifteen seconds.

"Twelve," she announced. "Multiply it by four and get, uh—" She looked at Lisa, frantically. Lisa just gave her a dirty look. "Oh, yeah, forty-eight," Stevie concluded sheepishly.

Judy and everybody else laughed. Then Judy had everybody come and check Patch's pulse rate. When all the Pony Clubbers had done it, she turned back to Colonel Hanson. "Think you can do it now?" she asked.

"I'll try," he said, and then, to Carole's relief, did it correctly.

Judy then proceeded to demonstrate how to check the horse's respiration or breathing rate. This is important for a rider to know, because the respiration rate, among other things, is an indication of whether a horse is overheated or not. After Judy had completed her instruction, each rider was told to fill in the record book for his own horse.

Carole picked up a pencil and headed for Barq's stall. Barq wasn't her very own horse, of course, but he was the horse she had been riding most recently at Pine Hollow. The horse she had ridden before Barq was Delilah, a palomino mare who was a wonderful horse to ride. But she had just foaled a few months earlier and was spending her days with her colt, Samson. Samson's sire, or father, had been Veronica's stallion, Cobalt. Carole had to pass their little stall and paddock on her way to Barq's. She noticed Samson frolicking around the paddock, obviously in a good and playful mood. Delilah stood serenely nearby, watching him with one eye, and nibbling at grass sprouts. Sometimes horses seemed very human to Carole, and this was one of those times. Samson was like a rambunctious toddler, and Delilah his overtired mother. The sight made Carole smile for the first time since the Horse Wise meeting had been called to order.

She continued to Barq's stall. It took her only a few minutes to check his condition and jot down the figures. Then she had to draw his significant markings. For Carole, that would take a little longer. Barq was a bay with Arabian blood, and he had a white blaze on his face that looked like a streak of lightning. That was how he got his name, because *Barq* meant lightning in Arabic. It was a tricky marking to draw. Carole turned over his water bucket, sat on it, and studied the horse so she could draw it properly. Drawing was not one of Carole's strongest talents. In fact, she doubted that she'd be able to draw it properly no matter how hard she tried.

"Rats," she said, breaking the point of her pencil on the point of the lightning streak. She'd have to go to Mrs. Reg's office to sharpen it. Carefully, she fastened the stall door behind her and walked toward the office.

The whole stable was bustling with activity as all the Horse Wise members were trying to complete the work in their health-and-maintenance books. Judy was helping one young rider take her horse's temperature. Stevie was checking to see if Topside had a tattoo. Even Veronica was working. She was sketching in Garnet's color. Since she was a solid chestnut, it was fairly easy to do, but Carole had to give Veronica some credit. It was work.

While Carole was sharpening her pencil, her father

came into the tack room, which adjoined Mrs. Reg's office.

"Oh, there you are," he said. "Listen, Max wants to have a short sponsors' meeting after Horse Wise is dismissed. Would you mind waiting around for me?"

"No problem," she said. She really didn't mind, and besides, it would give her a chance to talk with Stevie and Lisa alone.

"Thanks," he said. "And one other thing—what's normal temperature for a horse?"

"Ninety-nine and a half to a hundred and a half," Carole answered automatically.

"Oh, good," he said. "I thought that little fellow out there might be coming down with something and I wasn't sure what I should do for him. But it's just a normal temperature."

"What were you going to do if he had been sick?" Carole asked out of curiosity. She was sorry the minute she asked.

"Oh, you know, the usual. Tea and cinnamon toast and he can stay home from school one day, but he'd have to see the doctor to be allowed to stay home any longer than that."

Carole knew, beyond any doubt, that he'd used that line on whatever Pony Clubber he was "helping." It was his rule of thumb whenever Carole got sick at home. It made sense at home and always made her laugh, too. But that was at home. This was at Pine

Hollow. They weren't the same at all. Carole knew that. Why didn't her father?

She didn't know what to say to him, so she decided not to say anything. "See you later," she said, escaping to the privacy of Barq's stall. On her way there, she found Stevie and Lisa and told them they *had* to have a Saddle Club meeting in the tack room after Horse Wise. While her father was busy, she could use the time to apologize to her friends for his dumb behavior. She hoped they would understand.

STEVIE TOOK TOPSIDE's saddle off its storage rack and rested it on the bench in front of her so she could clean it. She'd finished her Horse Wise work before her friends and was able to get a head start on cleaning tack. She was already working on the stirrup leathers by the time Carole and Lisa arrived.

"You know, I think I preferred it this summer when we could ride every day, not just twice a week," Stevie told them.

"Of course you did!" Lisa said, laughing. "Riding five or six times a week is *much* better than going to school."

"For once, that isn't what I mean," Stevie said. "It's that there's so much to learn about horses. I don't think you can learn all you need to know twice a week—even with Horse Wise, which, by the way, I love a lot!"

"Me, too," Lisa agreed. "Everybody does. Even Veronica was doing something for Garnet when I passed her stall."

"Not something really tricky like untacking her, was it?" Stevie asked sarcastically.

"No, she was patting her," Lisa admitted.

"Well, that's a step," Carole said. "I didn't think she knew that much about horse care." Carole shook her head in disbelief. "Why her parents ever bought her another horse—especially a horse like Garnet—is beyond me."

"Well, because they could afford it," Lisa offered tentatively.

"Money isn't the issue," Carole snapped. Lisa and Stevie looked at her in surprise. "Well, I suppose in Veronica's case, it *always* is. But that's not what I mean. You shouldn't get a horse because you can afford it, or because your parents think you're wonderful, or because you can talk them into it. You should get a horse because you can take care of it, because you know the things you need to know, because you can be responsible for it."

Carole picked up Barq's bridle and began polishing it vigorously. She continued talking. "The thing is that I don't envy a lot of stuff Veronica has, like the big house and the designer clothes and all that. But I *do* envy her owning Garnet. It makes me so angry because I don't understand it. She's a pretty good rider, all right, but she doesn't know the first thing about taking care of her."

"You have to deserve a horse," Stevie agreed.

"Anyway, that reminds me of what I wanted to talk to you guys about," Carole said. "My father."

"You deserve him!" Stevie said. "He's just wonderful. We all adore him, you know."

Carole looked at her quizzically. "I guess I do know, but what I don't know is, why? I mean, Horse Wise is about getting wise about horses, not answering his 'whys' all the time. He knows less than Veronica does. It's really embarrassing."

Stevie was surprised by Carole's words. It had never occurred to her that Carole could be embarrassed by Colonel Hanson. Stevie could be embarrassed by her parents all the time. But her parents were *parents*. They did typical things like believing her brothers, or telling Stevie she couldn't ride if she didn't study first, or even telling her teacher that she *hadn't* read the book that she'd written the A report on. *That* was embarrassing. But Colonel Hanson told corny old jokes and sang Elvis Presley by heart. He was just wonderful!

"Of course he doesn't know anything," Stevie said. "He's never had a chance to learn, but he sure is learning now. You know, I only had to show him once how to assemble a bridle and he had it. He even remembered the names of all the parts. You should have seen him showing that little boy in Horse Wise, Liam, how to mount his pony. Your dad was terrific. And he did it right, too. And he made it fun. Your dad—"

Stevie thought she could have gone on for hours about how great Colonel Hanson was. She also had the feeling that if she did, Carole would never speak to her again. Whatever it was that Stevie thought about Carole's dad, Carole didn't seem to agree. Stevie paused to think about it, exploring the possibilities as she finished soaping the saddle's skirt. Their silence was interrupted by Max's arrival. Max didn't look very happy. In fact, he looked a little frantic.

"Oh, good, girls, I thought I would find you here. I need some help. Someone took off on a trail ride across the fields and left the paddock gates open behind them. Samson's on the loose. Can you saddle up and help find him?"

Max didn't have to ask twice. Each girl took her partially cleaned tack and ran back to her horse's stall. Stevie had Topside tacked up in about three minutes. She was still tightening the girth when she met her friends at the door to the stable. A little colt could get into a lot of trouble in a very short time. There wasn't a minute to waste!

"Let's go!" Stevie said.

"Wait a minute, we need to take a few things with us," Carole said rationally.

"A halter for Samson," Lisa suggested. "And a lead rope."

"Not a bad idea," Carole agreed. "Though he's barely used to the halter and it might not work. But you're right. We ought to have them with us."

"The first-aid kit, just in case?" Stevie offered.

"Yeah, good idea," Lisa said. "I'll go get it from the tack room. And some extra ropes, too. You never know."

"And one other thing," Carole said.

"What's that?" Lisa asked.

"Delilah," Carole said.

Of course, Stevie thought. There was one thing that would be more appealing than anything else in the world to a lost or frightened colt, and that was his mother.

Quickly, Carole snapped a long lead rope on Delilah and fastened it to Barq's saddle. Delilah was a well-trained horse. She would follow along willingly.

"One more thing," Lisa said to her friends. Stevie wondered what it was they might have forgotten. "The good-luck horseshoe," Lisa said.

"Once for us and once for Samson," Stevie said, brushing the horseshoe twice as she passed by. The shiny, smooth surface seemed reassuring to her.

Then they were off!

AS ITS NAME implied, Pine Hollow was surrounded by hills. They weren't very steep, but there were a lot of them. While the hills made it easy to look up and inspect the nearby fields, they made it very difficult to see anything farther than a couple of hundred yards in every direction. Also, since Max had made arrangements with many nearby farmers to ride in their fields, as long as fences were opened and closed properly, it was just about impossible to figure out which direction the rider might have taken. There were signs of horse paths everywhere they looked.

"We just have to follow the open fences," Carole said logically. "And we have to hope that the rider didn't leave them *all* open. As soon as we find the closed one, we've got Samson located, more or less. Then, with some luck, Delilah will do the rest of the work for us, right?"

"Sounds good, except for one thing," Stevie said. Carole recognized Stevie's bad-news tone of voice. "There's only one rider at Pine Hollow who would waft out into the fields without thinking about closing fences behind her."

Carole and Lisa supplied the answer at the same time. "Veronica diAngelo," they said.

"Yeah, and she would not only leave one fence open behind her. She'd leave *every* fence open behind her. Let's face it. If she stays in the fields, Samson will probably be okay, because at least he'll be contained in an open area. The worst thing, though, would be if she went into the woods up on the hill, because once she goes through the last fence up there, there are no more fences."

"Oh, no! The highway!" Lisa said. "Those woods run right by the interstate, don't they?"

95

"Yes, they do," Carole said. "And they're very thick woods up there where a little inexperienced colt could get into a lot of trouble! There's no time to waste! Let's go!"

The decision, then, was an easy one. Since the worst possible outcome was that Samson could have made his way into the woods, they had to go there first. If he didn't turn out to be there, but *did* turn out to be in one of the fields, that could be tricky, but at worst, wouldn't really be dangerous to Samson.

Carole had learned that horses seemed to be able to sense urgency, whether it was to win a competition of some kind or to act in an emergency. Most horse books she'd read said they weren't especially smart animals, but they sure did seem to understand certain things at certain times. This was one of those times. If Carole hadn't been able to hear all four of Barq's hooves hitting the ground as they rode up the rise, she would have sworn they were flying. Delilah kept right up with them, and Stevie and Lisa were right behind her.

Ironically, their trip was sped up by the fact that, as they went from field to field, they only had to pause to close the gates behind them. The way was easy for them—and for Samson—courtesy of Miss Veronica diAngelo.

And then they spotted Veronica. She was having a wonderful time. She and Garnet were cantering in a field next to the woods. It was one of the most level fields in the area, a logical choice for somebody who just wanted to canter. Carole pursed her lips in anger. It was so babyish to think that the most fun you could have on a horse was cantering, just because it was fast. In the first place, it wasn't true. Having fun on a horse meant learning to work *with* the horse, not getting the horse to do all the work. A horse wasn't a race car. In the second place, constantly cantering wore a horse out. Garnet would do what Veronica told her to do, but she'd be tired for days, and could stiffen up badly. Carole wanted to give Veronica a good lecture on her behavior. She would have, but Samson was more important. And Samson was nowhere in sight.

Carole looked at Delilah hopefully. The mare would know where her colt was before anybody could see him. Delilah just looked forlorn and confused. She whinnied. Carole knew she was calling for Samson. There was no answer.

"Where could he be?" Carole asked Stevie and Lisa, who drew their horses to a halt where she was standing. "If Veronica's here, then he can't have gone any farther, can he?"

"Not unless Veronica did," Lisa said logically.

Then, all three of them looked at the fence along the edge of the woods. The gate stood wide open.

"I'd like to give that girl a piece of my mind!" Stevie burst out angrily.

"Me, too, but first things first. Let's find Samson!" Carole said.

She gave Barq a signal and once again, he flew into action.

It irked Carole more than she could say to see Veronica wave to them gaily as they went through the open gate into the woods. Veronica had no idea how much trouble she had caused. She probably wouldn't care when she found out, either.

A four-month-old colt is a curious animal. Carole found herself making lists of ways he could get into trouble—everything from eating poisonous plants, to tripping and breaking a fragile young limb. Sometimes people reported seeing bobcats in these woods. Even worse, sometimes there were hunters, looking for deer, in *and* out of season. A colt was about the size of the local deer. There was a dreadful cold feeling in her stomach.

"Whatever you're thinking, stop it," Stevie said sensibly. "We'll find him. He'll be okay."

It didn't surprise Carole that Stevie could read her mind. Stevie was probably feeling the same way, and so was Lisa. Carole took comfort in the fact that the three of them together seemed to have a way of solving some pretty terrible problems. It wasn't just strength in numbers, because three wasn't a very large number. It was the power of their friendship. That was what The Saddle Club was about. But would friendship be enough this time?

Suddenly, Delilah's ears perked up. Her nostrils flared. She halted, bringing Barq to a sudden stop. Carole watched the mare carefully. She was their leader now.

Delilah pawed the ground and whinnied. Her ears flicked around, listening for a return signal. She took two steps up the hill, and the girls followed. Delilah glanced at Carole. On a hunch, Carole unclipped the mare's lead rope. Carole had the feeling that Delilah was so well trained that she wouldn't run away from her human masters as long as she felt close to them. Without the rope, she could follow her instincts and they would surely lead her to her colt.

For a moment Delilah stood frozen. The girls were silent, waiting. Then Delilah whinnied again, calling to her son. She raised her head high, trying to make the sound carry. Then she waited.

A rustling sound came from the leaves down the hill a bit to the left. The girls eagerly turned their heads in that direction. A squirrel emerged from a pile of leaves and skittered up a tree.

Tentatively, Delilah began to walk up the hill, ducking under branches, and squeezing between trees. There was no way anyone riding could follow her. The girls dismounted and led their horses after Delilah, making as little noise as possible so the mare could hear what she was listening for.

Delilah's pace picked up. Her ears flicked to the left and she turned that way, going straight now. She whinnied louder and repeatedly. Her tail twitched excitedly, and her head bobbed, as she tried to see everything in range.

Then she stopped and whinnied loudly. And, for

the first time, the girls could hear Samson's reply. It was little more than a whimper. The girls wrapped their horses' reins around firm branches, and ran over to see where Samson was.

He'd fallen into a gully totally overgrown with briars. His legs were completely tangled in the mass of leaves and sharp green shoots. He was lying down and seemed to be crying. His slender legs had been poked and torn at repeatedly by the vicious weeds. Blood trickled out of his wounds.

They'd found Samson, all right, but were they too late to save him?

11

"WHERE DO WE begin?" Stevie asked, aghast.

"We begin by freeing him," Carole said sensibly. Carole, who could sometimes be flaky when it came to anything else, was all common sense with horses. She could keep a cool head in emergencies.

"Okay," she began, knowing her friends needed some assurance. "We helped bring this little guy into the world and it's our job to keep him here." It sounded good. Somehow knowing that Samson and her friends were relying on her helped. Her mind was sharp, her mission clear. "Stevie, are you carrying your pocketknife?"

"Of course," Stevie said and handed it to Carole.

"Here's how we're going to do this. I'm going to work on cutting the briars. Stevie, you stay by Samson's head and do whatever you can to keep him calm. I don't want him kicking me if we can help it. Lisa, you put the lead rope back on Delilah and tie her up where she can watch, but not interfere. Stay with her for a while until we're sure she'll stay calm. The last thing we need on our hands is a hysterical mother!"

Stevie and Lisa laughed at Carole's joke. It was good for all of the girls. It broke some of the tension. Carole opened Stevie's old Girl Scout knife and surveyed the situation. The briar was the kind that was like a tough philodendron with stickers on the stems. Once you stepped into it, it acted almost like a Chinese finger trap and there was no getting out without some kind of scratch. Carole quickly realized that she wouldn't be able to keep Samson from getting hurt, and began to see her job as trying to keep him from getting hurt badly. She was going to need his cooperation as much as her friends'.

Samson had slid into a gully where the briar was flourishing. The good news was that he hadn't slid very far. He was lying on his side, and all four of his legs and his tail were entangled.

First things first: Carole needed to know if he had any wounds worse than scratches. Slowly and carefully, to minimize her own scratching, she lowered herself into the gully and sat down next to the colt. He looked at her fearfully. His eyes were wide open and white at the edges.

"There, there, boy," Carole said soothingly. "Take it easy, now. I'm just going to check you out and then get you out." His eyes closed a little bit and he seemed to relax.

"He trusts our voices," Stevie said.

"Maybe because they were the first sounds he ever heard when he was born. Do you think that means he thinks we're his mother?" Lisa asked. At that moment, Delilah whinnied and Samson answered with his own small cry.

"No, I think he knows who his mother is. He just thinks we're a team of capable humans who helped him out of one jam and are going to help him make it out of this one," Carole said. She hoped Samson was right. She began her task.

"What's the first step?" Lisa asked.

"I'm feeling his legs to make sure we're not dealing with any broken bones here. I can also see if any of the cuts are deep."

"Why?"

"Well, if he's losing a lot of blood from something, I won't have time to cut away gently. We'll have to slash at the briars and take our chances on giving him fresh wounds in order to get him out as fast as possible."

Carole clipped a few of the briar's tendrils, snagging her hands as she went. She was closest to Samson's left foreleg. As soon as she could, she reached down and ran her hand along the outside of it. It felt moist, but okay. She felt along the inside, coming back up. "No problem there," she reported to her friends. "Yet."

They were in a very shady area of the woods, and the autumn sun was beginning to sink in the sky, casting long shadows through the forest. Along with all of the other problems they had, Carole couldn't see very well. She was going to have to do the entire check on Samson with her hands.

She reached into the briar again, groping for his right foreleg. "Ouch!" she said. Samson flinched at the sound of her voice.

"Problem?" Stevie asked with concern.

"It's me, not him," Carole told her. "I just got scratched. It's not serious. It just hurts."

"Pull your sleeves down," Stevie suggested.

"Now, why didn't I think of that?" Carole said, withdrawing her scratched arm from the tangle of briars. She tugged her shirtsleeves down and hoped they'd stay that way. "I wish I were wearing one of Dad's shirts today. They're so big, they always come down over your hands."

"Wait a minute," Stevie said. "I think I can help with that. I've got my riding gloves—the ones you guys gave me."

"But they'll get ruined. Those are really nice gloves," Carole protested.

"And you are a really good friend," Stevie reminded her. "Your hands are a lot more important than my gloves."

"Okay. I'm not going to argue. I need all the help I can get." Gratefully, Carole pulled the gloves on, noticing that there was blood on her hands. Was it her own blood or Samson's? Probably some of both, she told herself. She reached back in to check the second foreleg. This time, she felt the sticking of the briar, but it only scratched at the leather glove.

"The gloves help a lot," Carole said. "Thanks, Stevie."

"You're very welcome," Stevie said. "And besides, you gave those to me for my birthday. Christmas is just around the corner. You won't have to think for very long to come up with something for that!"

Carole smiled and was about to come up with a retort for Stevie's remark when she found that Samson's right foreleg was lying in a very awkward position. She didn't like that at all. The leg was bent too high, as if he were reaching for something. Did that mean he had a broken bone? The elbow and forearm were fine, although they were stretched out of position. It didn't make sense. Then, as Carole got to the fetlock, she realized that the colt's leg was hooked on a root that protruded from the ground. It was quite possible that that alone was keeping Samson from sliding farther down the steep sides of the gully.

Samson's leg was scratched, but intact, as far as Carole could tell, but the fact that it was hooked onto something was dangerous.

While Carole shifted her position to examine Samson's rear legs, she turned to Lisa. "If Delilah's okay for a while, could you go to my saddle and get the ropes? I'm afraid Samson may shift around and slide much deeper into this place." She spoke calmly so she wouldn't alarm the colt, but the message to her friend was clear. Lisa wasted no time in following Carole's instructions.

While Lisa retrieved the ropes, Carole checked Samson's hind legs. There was at least one fairly deep scratch on one of them, but it didn't seem to be bleeding too badly. Carole proceeded with her original plan. She began cutting at the briars, silently thanking Stevie for the gloves with every painless snip.

Lisa returned with the ropes. "Here they are, but how are we going to manage this?"

Carole thought about it for a minute. She hadn't been sure exactly what she had in mind when she sent Lisa for the ropes. That part just seemed logical. But what was the next logical step? "What I want to do is to get at least one rope, preferably two, around his belly so that we have him in a sort of a sling in case his leg unhooks from this root here. The problem is that he's pretty heavy and maybe just trying to put the ropes under him will dislodge him. But it's a risk we've got to take."

Stevie stayed at her post, keeping Samson quiet. She stroked his neck and sang to him.

"Good job, Stevie. Keeping him calm is more important than ever now," Carole said, though she was sure Stevie knew that without being told.

"And it's a good thing he likes Beatles songs. I thought 'Hey Jude' was a good idea."

Carole laughed. Jude, as she knew, was the saint of impossible causes. She hoped Samson's rescue wasn't an impossible cause! She quickly used Stevie's knife to cut two lengths of rope, each about twelve feet long.

Lisa held one end of each of the lengths of rope. Carole slid the other ends under Samson's hindquarters, bringing one forward to his front legs and leaving the other at his rear. He didn't seem to like it, but he let her do it. Carole sighed with relief as she passed the rope ends to Lisa.

"Very good!" Lisa said. "I don't know how you did that!"

"I'm not sure I do, either," Carole said. "But it worked, didn't it?"

Just then, Samson announced that he'd had enough. He began to flail around wildly, rocking his head, jostling Stevie, and kicking violently.

This was good news and bad news. The bad

news was that, exactly as Carole had predicted, he unhooked his foreleg from the root and began sliding down farther into the gully. The good news was that, because of Carole's foresight, they'd already planned for that. Lisa held both of the rope loops by herself until Carole scrambled up the hill to help her.

The two girls not only held Samson up, keeping him from slipping farther, but they began stepping backward, away from the gully, tugging Samson upward as they went. The colt struggled to get a purchase on the loose dirt, crying out a couple of times as briars scratched at him, but within a few seconds, he was able to scramble his way up the hillside, out of the dangerous briar patch.

"Give him a hand!" Carole cried to Stevie. Stevie jumped to her feet and grabbed Samson's scruffy mane. She pulled as hard as she could, knowing that she wasn't hurting him because a horse doesn't have any nerves in those hair roots. He certainly didn't seem to mind.

When Samson had gotten his front legs up over the top of the gully, Carole handed her rope to Lisa and went to check the progress of his hind legs. One of them, the one with the deep scratch, was still tangled in a briar. Carole reached over the edge and yanked at the weed. She hoped she had made enough slack to allow Samson to free himself. It worked!

By the time Carole turned around, Samson was standing at the top of the gully, free from all briars, panting with fatigue, but safe.

There was nothing Carole wanted to do more right then than hug Samson and her friends with joy and relief, but she knew the work wasn't finished. They couldn't take the chance, however slight, that something might make Samson run back into the gully. While Stevie and Lisa patted him and led him away from the edge of the gully, Carole retrieved Samson's halter and lead.

"Are you going to put those on him?" Lisa asked, a little surprised.

"We have to," Carole said. "We just can't take a chance with him now. Once he's in the field, we can let him loose. Until then, it's halter or bust."

Carole knew from experience with Samson's earliest training that Samson sometimes fought when the halter was put on him. Sometimes, he'd shake his head quite violently. He just wasn't accustomed to it. So Carole was more than a little nervous.

"What can we do to make him not notice the halter, then?" Lisa asked.

Carole thought for a second. "Delilah!" she exclaimed. "Bring his mother here. He's really too tired to put up much of a fight, and I'll bet you anything his stomach is empty and he's starving. Bring on the Nursing Mama!"

Laughing, Stevie unhitched Delilah and reunited

her with her son. The mare checked him thoroughly, sniffing and nuzzling him, apparently trying to be absolutely certain that this dusty, dirty, scratched-up colt was really her little baby. While the two of them got reacquainted, Carole slipped the halter on Samson and clipped on a lead rope. He didn't pay any attention to her. When Delilah was satisfied that the colt was her lost son, she allowed him to nurse.

"Look at his poor legs," Lisa said, watching the procedure. "Are they going to be okay?"

Carole examined them carefully. "Probably," she said. "There's only one deep scratch and it seems to be closing naturally. However, we could have an infection problem, which would be a lot worse than scarring. Let's get the first-aid kit and kill some germs."

While Samson was concentrating on his meal, Stevie sprayed his legs with the disinfectant, Lisa applied scarlet oil, and Carole wrapped his legs in bandages.

"Hey, check this out!" Stevie said softly, trying not to disturb their patient. "We're all nursing. Samson's doing the baby kind of nursing and we're three Clara Bartons out here on the battlefield of horse care!"

Lisa and Carole laughed, both because it was funny, and because they felt good. They'd done something important and they'd done it right.

"Isn't it wonderful that Samson's okay?" Lisa asked. "What a job you did!" she told Carole admiringly.

"In the first place, *we* did it, not just me," Carole corrected her. "In the second place, we're not quite done."

"Oh, sure," Stevie said. "Judy's going to want to rebandage all the cuts, maybe take some stitches . . ."

"No, before that," Carole said. "Look at Samson."

The colt licked the last splash of milk from his lips and then glanced around. The look was unmistakable. He was ready for his nap. He would never make it back to Pine Hollow and there was no way they could carry him safely.

The girls decided to make him walk with Delilah, at least as far as the safety of the first fence in the fields. Then they would wait with him until help arrived. Max was sure to come looking for them with his truck. Until then, no harm would come to any of them.

A few minutes later, The Saddle Club settled into the sweet grass, not far from Samson, and waited, glad for the quiet and the rest.

Samson was asleep before Carole could get the halter off of him.

"STAR LIGHT, STAR bright, first star I've seen to-night," Stevie said, looking up into the early-evening sky. It was still light out, but the evening star was clearly visible above the southern horizon.

"I know what I'm wishing for," Lisa said, staring up into the sky as well. The minute she said it, she knew it was time to tell her friends her secret. They waited for her to continue. "I'm wishing for words to tell you something I haven't been able to tell you."

"Bad news?" Stevie asked, alarmed.

"No, just hard to figure out. Hard to talk about. But I think I've figured it out now, so I can talk about it." There was a long silence. Lisa continued to look at the sky as she spoke. "My parents had this idea about buying me a horse. I think my mother got the idea because she heard the diAngelos were buying Garnet for Veronica. We even looked at three different horses."

"And you didn't tell us?" Stevie asked. She sounded hurt.

Lisa knew she deserved that, if not a lot more. "No, I didn't. And I felt terrible keeping it from you." Lisa took a deep breath. "I want a horse. It's my dream. The problem was that something told me it wasn't right. And the problem with that was I didn't know what the 'something' was. So I developed this wild notion that you two would be jealous."

"Well, we would be, of course," Stevie said. "But we'd understand."

"That's the part I forgot. Of course you'd understand. Now I know that, but I also know that it's still a bad idea. See, I was concentrating so hard on the idea that you were jealous of Veronica that I forgot what the real reason was for Veronica not to have a horse."

"And that is?" Carole asked.

Lisa had the feeling Carole knew the answer and was testing her. "Because she doesn't know enough about horses to care for her own properly," Lisa answered.

"Go to the head of the class," Carole said.

"Thanks. It took me a long time, but the lesson Veronica gave about responsibility by bad example was as clear as a bell."

"But Lisa, you're more responsible than Veronica," Stevie said.

"Thanks, but a lamppost is more responsible than Veronica. I think I do all right on that part. The part that I'm not so good on is just plain horse knowledge. I'm learning. I know I'm learning, but that's not enough yet. One day, I will have learned enough. Until then, I'm going to thank my parents for the wonderful idea and I'll happily continue riding Pepper."

Carole smiled. "I think you're absolutely right, except about one thing. It's not going to be as far in the future as you may think. You're learning at an amazing rate."

"Becoming horse wise, you mean," Stevie contributed. "Speaking of which, Horse Wise should be helpful. I was looking through *The Manual of Horsemanship*—you know, the Pony Club book Max gave us. Being Pony Clubbers is certainly going to speed up that day for all of us."

Carole sighed audibly.

"What's the matter?" Lisa asked. She was relieved that she'd gotten her troubles off her chest. She hated to think that something was bothering Carole so much that she had to sigh like that!

"Horse Wise," Carole said and then sighed again. "If the stars are granting wishes tonight, I know what my wish is."

"What?" Stevie asked.

"You may not believe this, but my wish is to have Dad not be a Horse Wise sponsor anymore."

Stevie propped herself up on her elbow. "I don't get it, Carole. You've got one of the neatest fathers this side of the Mississippi. Why don't you want him to be a sponsor?"

"Sure, he's a neat guy. He's good at being a father and a Marine, but he's not good at horses. Sponsors are supposed to be able to teach. He can't teach anybody anything about horses because he doesn't know anything."

"Now, wait a minute. He's teaching everybody! He's *terrific*," Lisa said.

"Lisa, you're supposed to be the logical one in this group. That's just not logical," Carole responded.

"No, look at it from our standpoint, Carole," Lisa persisted. "We know your father doesn't know anything about horses, but he *does* know about teaching—and learning. See, what your dad does is make us think. Every time he asks why, two things happen. First, we have to think about what we're doing, and that gives us information. Second, we have to tell him and that gives *him* information. Don't worry, Carole, he's not just neat, he's smart. Before too long, he'll stop asking because he doesn't know and begin asking just to make sure we *do*. That is, if he's not doing that already. In the meantime, what difference does it make?"

Carole couldn't think of a reply so she just stared up

at the sky, which was now becoming a deep, rich blue. A few more stars had appeared. There was an autumn chill in the late-afternoon air.

Carole's mind was a jumble. She tried to sort it all out. She wasn't quite satisfied that her friends were right about her father, though she accepted the fact that everybody liked him. But was that enough? Not really. In order for him to be a good sponsor, he had to contribute some skills to Horse Wise. No matter what her friends told her, Carole didn't see what skills her father had contributed.

Nearby, Samson snorted in his sleep. He seemed to be content and worry-free.

"I think he's dreaming about a palomino filly," Lisa joked.

"Either that or the world-famous Saddle Club Rescue Team," Stevie suggested. "A couple more jobs like the one we did this afternoon and we'll have our own TV show. I can see it now. How about *The Saddle Club Files?*"

"Nah, we need something jazzier. *Saddle Club SWAT?*"

"I've got it! *The Saddle Club to the Rescue!*" Stevie suggested.

"It's not punchy enough," Lisa said. "It has to fit on one line in bold type in *TV Guide*. How about . . ."

The conversation went on like that, but Carole dropped out of it. She was thinking about Samson's rescue. She remembered how worried and scared she had felt, lodged onto the edge of the gully with a foal just as worried and just as scared as she was. Every time she hadn't known what to do, Lisa had asked her what came next. Every time she'd thought she'd known what she might do, Lisa had asked why she was doing it. Lisa's questions had had a good effect. They'd made Carole think about what she was doing. She probably would have figured it out on her own, but having Lisa there to ask had made her consider the problem in a new way and think about the answers.

Maybe, just maybe, that was what her father was doing in Horse Wise. Maybe having one sponsor who didn't know about horses, but who did know about thinking and learning, wasn't such a bad idea after all.

Only why couldn't it be someone else's father?

"Well, I'm going to make a prediction. I predict Max will show up before the temperature drops another ten degrees," Stevie was saying.

Lisa sat up and looked out across the fields. "Well, if those headlights are any indication, your prediction has just come true!"

"Impressed?" Stevie asked.

"Yeah," Lisa said. "Very."

"Don't be," Carole said drily. "Remember that Stevie's taller than you are. She could see those headlights before you could."

"And I thought Stevie was clairvoyant!" Lisa joked.

The girls stood up to wave at Max. He spotted them right away and within a very short time, they had loaded the still-sleeping foal into the back of the pickup truck, where Judy was waiting to take care of him. They tied Delilah's lead rope behind the truck. Max would have to drive slowly, but it made more sense than trying to separate mother and son again.

While the truck lumbered off down the dirt road toward the stable, the girls tightened their horses' girths, lowered their stirrups, and mounted their animals. It was time for them to ride back as well—checking every fence gate on the way.

STEVIE COULD HARDLY believe it was just a week since The Saddle Club's dramatic rescue of Samson. Except for one remaining bandage, which covered three stitches in one of his hind legs, there were no signs that anything bad had ever happened to the colt. He was frolicking around his well-closed paddock with his mother, happy as could be.

Stevie wished she could be as calm. She was a nervous wreck. It was Horse Wise Rating Day.

Since this was the first rating, each person had been allowed to choose what rating he or she wanted to be tested for. Stevie had decided, without looking at the test requirements, that she was certainly a D-3. That was what she'd signed up for. *Then* she looked at the requirements. If she failed the test, she'd be unrated until the next rating. That would be pretty embarrassing. The only rider in the stable who was going to be unrated was seven-year-old Liam, who had just started riding the day of the first Horse Wise meeting.

"Stevie Lake." The examiner called her name.

Stevie felt a severe twinge in her stomach. She shook it off and tried to concentrate. She stepped forward into the ring, riding Topside. The riding test was the easy part. She wasn't worried about that, and within fifteen minutes, she'd performed everything the examiner had asked her to do, including mounting and dismounting, adjusting stirrups, walking and trotting in circles, and changing speeds within gaits. The jumps were no problem at all. She knew she'd passed that section.

Then came the unmounted part of the test. The Pony Club called it Horse Management. Stevie called it The Tough Part. Carole and Lisa had been drilling her all week on horse parts, conformation faults, and coat-clipping techniques. Phil had done the same when they talked on the phone. Stevie knew she could name all the major bones of the horse's legs. She just wasn't sure she knew which was which.

She hoped the examiner wouldn't ask her.

"Good, Stevie," he said, after she told him how to cool down her horse after a ride. "Now, show me the major bones of the legs—fore and hind."

They were the very words she'd been dreading. "Okay," Stevie said, thinking it wasn't okay at all.

Then she looked around and saw that both Lisa and Carole were standing at the edge of the ring watching, with their fingers crossed. What more could a girl want than to have friends like that? She *couldn't* let them down.

"Top to bottom or bottom to top?" she asked.

"Whichever," the examiner said.

Stevie squatted and began with Topside's hoof. "Coffin, navicular, short pastern, long pastern, sesamoid, cannon," she began, reeling them off like a pro. When she finished, she could see that the examiner was grinning. Maybe it was because her friends were still standing there, but they weren't standing there quietly. They were clapping like mad.

"Your cheering section seems pleased . . ." the examiner said.

Stevie held her breath for the rest of the sentence.

". . . and so am I."

"Thanks," Stevie said. She stood up and reached for Topside's reins to take him back to his stall.

"Not quite yet," the examiner said. "There are a few more things . . ."

"I CAN'T BELIEVE how much stuff we have to know," Lisa said, watching the rest of Stevie's test from the edge of the ring. Stevie was the only rider trying for D-3. Lisa had been among many who had been tested for D-1. She was pretty sure she'd passed. She'd find out later when Max awarded the ratings to all of the riders. Stevie and Carole had urged her to go for D-2, but that, like earning a horse of her own, would come in time. Lisa was, above all, sensible. She knew it would be a mistake for her to rush herself—even if her parents tried to do it for her!

"Are you nervous?" Lisa asked Carole.

"Of course I am," Carole said. "Anybody with any sense is nervous before a big test and my C-1 rating is a big test. But you guys helped this week—"

"We helped you?" Lisa asked, surprised. "All we did was to get you to drill us on our test material!"

"That helps me. See, everything you're being tested on, I'm already expected to know." It amused Carole to think about how much she actually had learned while teaching her friends. Her father had also drilled her on additional material. She had the feeling he'd picked up a pointer or two along the way.

"Thank you very much, Stevie," the examiner said. "You can take Topside back to his stall now." Stevie walked Topside back into the stable. As she passed her friends, she winked and said "Whew!" They both knew exactly what she meant!

"The C-1 candidate," the examiner announced. "Are you ready?"

"Five minutes!" Carole said. "Just have to tighten my horse's girth and bring him out."

"See that you do," the examiner said. Lisa didn't like his tone of voice at all, but if it bothered Carole, her friend didn't say anything. As Lisa knew, when it came to horses, Carole was all business. Mostly.

As soon as Carole's rating test was over, Max called all of the riders into his office. It was time to find out how they'd done. Some, like Lisa, who had chosen a rating they knew they could pass, were feeling confident. Others, like Stevie and Carole, who thought they might have been reaching beyond their grasp, were more than a little nervous. The look on Max's face told them nothing.

Carole was actually very nervous. Barq had refused a low jump and she was sure that would count against her, even though it was because he'd been startled by a rabbit. It still shouldn't have happened. Then, Carole was sure she'd gotten confused on the veterinary section when the examiner started asking her about parasites. She couldn't, for the life of her, remember where botflies laid their eggs. Her answer, "In their bot-caves?" got an amused response from nearby listeners. She'd also mixed up poultice bandages and cold-water bandages. She was sure she'd failed.

Carole had enough confidence in herself to know that she would certainly pass the test eventually. She'd try again at the next rating, but until then, if she failed, she'd be unrated. Carole looked at the pile of yellow patches on Max's desk, ready to be handed out. D-level Pony Clubbers got to wear yellow patches behind their pins. Carole had been trying for a green. There were no green patches on Max's desk.

"This is going to be fun," Max said, beginning the awards ceremony at last. "It's going to be fun because, I'm pleased to say, all those of you who took D-level tests passed!"

Carole was sitting between her two best friends. She reached a hand out to congratulate each of them. It was no surprise that Lisa had passed. It was a bit of a relief that Stevie had. Her friends each grasped her hand in return.

"I'll be fine," she whispered to them. "I just attempted too much. No problem. I'll try again."

While Carole tried to control the roller-coaster feeling that had just come over her, Max handed out the yellow patches, announcing each Pony Clubber's name and rating as he did. Most of the Horse Wise members took their pins off and installed their patches right away. Stevie and Lisa didn't. Carole was touched by their loyalty.

"Now," Max began again when all the yellow patches had been distributed. "Only one person here felt she was horse wise enough to attempt a C-level rating, and that person, as you know, is Carole Hanson."

Oh, no! Carole thought. Everybody else in the room had passed their tests. She hadn't. And now Max thought he could make it better by giving a talk on noble attempts. She wanted to sink into the floor and reappear in a different county—preferably in a different universe!

". . . the C levels are tough tests. The examiners can't give much leeway. Either the candidate knows her material, or she doesn't."

Even worse, he was dragging it out. Carole couldn't believe Max would do this to her.

"And, in the case of Carole Hanson, I'm pleased to tell you, she *does* know her stuff! Carole, come get your green patch. Congratulations!"

Had she heard right? Her friends nudged her hard. That must mean something, she realized. She stood up and walked toward Max, almost in a trance.

"You mean botflies *do* lay their eggs in botcaves?" Carole asked. Everybody laughed, even Max.

"No, they don't," he said. "They actually lay their eggs on the horse's underside, but you got half credit for creativity on that one!"

He handed her her green patch. Carole accepted it in a happy daze. She wasn't even sure how she got back to her seat. She was too excited to be aware of mundane things like that.

"Now, there's one more award," Max continued. "It's not exactly covered by the U.S. Pony Club regulations, but there are times when exceptions are called for. Besides, this can be a local award. There's one more member of our club who has made an exceptional contribution, over the past few weeks, and who has set an example on how to become horse wise. Can you all guess who is going to get the final yellow patch of the day?"

Carole knew a cue when she heard one. She stood up again and turned to all her friends in Horse Wise. "I think the man is talking about my dad, don't you agree?"

They did. There was a big round of applause, and an embarrassed Colonel Hanson stepped forward.

Max handed Carole the yellow patch. "Will you do the honors?" he asked.

Carole turned to her dad. She'd seen him receive ribbons and pins many times in the Marine Corps. She knew just what to do. As he stood absolutely still, she pinned the patch on his shirt, then saluted him. He returned the salute sharply. Then she hugged him. He returned that, too. That wasn't exactly part of the Marine Corps procedure, but he deserved it.

Once again, Carole returned to her place with her friends. "Saddle Club meeting at TD's right after this?" she whispered. Stevie and Lisa nodded. There was a lot to talk about.

"I'm almost done now," Max said. "There's one more thing I need to talk about, but I don't really like talking about it at all. If this were a stable matter, I wouldn't say anything, but it's a Horse Wise matter and you all deserve to know."

The Saddle Club looked at one another. What was *this* about?

"Last week, one of our members did something very careless—something no Horse Wise person should ever do. She took a horse into the fields and failed to

126

close gates behind her. As a result, Samson, the colt, got into a treacherous situation, saved only by the quick thinking and able attention of three of our members. The Pony Club regulations allow me some latitude on membership requirements. One of them is horse safety. The member who failed to close the gates has been suspended from Horse Wise for a month. The same would happen to anyone who did something so careless, whether it resulted in damage or not."

Carole looked around the room. She could see that everybody was doing the same thing. She heard one Pony Club member ask another, "Who's missing?" Carole grinned. She and her friends didn't have to ask. It was Veronica. For once in her life—in *their* lives—Veronica was getting properly rewarded for her behavior!

Stevie leaned over to whisper to Carole. "This won't be an ordinary Saddle Club meeting," she said. "This will be a Saddle Club quadruple celebration!"

"Quadruple?" Carole asked.

"Sure. One for each of our patches. And one for Veronica!"

14

"NOW, LET ME see if I've got this straight," the waitress at TD's said. Lisa tried to suppress a smile. Eating ice cream with Stevie had its moments.

"You want hot fudge on vanilla," she said to Lisa. Lisa nodded. She turned to Carole. "And you're having a dish of maple walnut?"

"Yes, please," Carole said.

"And yours," she looked at Stevie over her glasses, "is pineapple chunk on bubble-gum-baby ice cream."

"That's right, and could you put some of that marshmallow goo and a cherry on top?"

A look of terror crossed the woman's face. "I don't know," she said, paling. "I'll ask the chef." She fled from their table, but Lisa didn't think she was out of earshot when they all burst into giggles.

"New woman," Carole said.

"But not for long, I fear." Stevie sighed dramatically. They laughed again.

"Oh, I feel so good," Carole said. "It's a kind of all-over wonderful feeling."

"I know just what you mean," Stevie agreed.

"Me, too," Lisa added. "I'm really glad for both of you, passing your advanced ratings. For me and for now, D-1 is enough."

"Actually, although I'm really glad about my D-3, I think I'm really happier about Veronica getting her just desserts."

"Think she'll learn anything from it?" Lisa asked.

"Maybe, maybe not," Carole said. "She's not a fast learner when it comes to her own faults."

"We, on the other hand, are very fast learners, especially when it comes to horses," Lisa said.

"And science projects," Stevie added. "I handed mine in this week, you know, the radish one. I think the teacher liked it, except for the part where I started watering the pots that weren't supposed to get water because I felt so sorry for those poor seeds. They needed water just like I need my—"

"Here you go, girls." The waitress had come back with their orders.

"—sundae," Stevie finished her sentence.

The dishes were on the table and the waitress disappeared before the girls could thank her.

"I think she wanted to get away from Stevie's order," Lisa said.

"She'll learn," Stevie said, taking her first bite. "It's positively delicious."

Her friends didn't believe her, either.

"What were we talking about?" Stevie asked.

"Veronica, of course," Lisa reminded her. "And whether she would ever learn anything."

"The answer to that is probably no," Carole said. "But who cares about her? We're learning and that's the important thing."

"Boy, are we ever!" Stevie said. "I mean, I learned all about horses' leg bones this week. Didn't think I'd ever know that stuff—didn't think I'd ever need to."

"Leg bones are easy," Carole teased. "Wait until you study up on botflies!"

"Oh, yeah, laying their eggs in botcaves. I loved that," Stevie said, giggling. Carole and Lisa laughed as well.

"You're not the only one who's learning," Lisa said, a little bit more seriously. "I learned that I should trust my friends. When I've got trouble, they won't waste time on dumb things like envy. My friends get right down to the important thing—being friends."

The girls looked at one another, feeling the warmth of the moment and the importance of their friendship.

"Looks like there's been a lot of learning going on," Stevie said, scraping the last of the marshmallow goo from the side of her dish. "What I figure it amounts to is that we're all becoming horse wise!"

Lisa laughed. "You can say that again," she said.

Stevie didn't hesitate. "What I figure it amounts to is that—"

Lisa turned to Carole. "Good," she said. "We've found a way to keep her busy, repeating herself. It's the opportunity we've been waiting for to get a taste of her delicious sundae!"

Stevie parried their advances on her sundae with her spoon. "Horse wise, we can do together," she said. "Sundae wise you can do on your own allowances!"

They all laughed together. It felt very good.

ABOUT THE AUTHOR

BONNIE BRYANT is the author of more than fifty books for young readers, including novelizations of movie hits such as *Teenage Mutant Ninja Turtles®* and *Honey, I Blew Up the Kid*, written under her married name, B. B. Hiller.

Ms. Bryant began writing The Saddle Club in 1986. Although she had done some riding before that, she intensified her studies then and found herself learning right along with her characters Stevie, Carole, and Lisa. She claims that they are all much better riders than she is.

Ms. Bryant was born and raised in New York City. She lives in Greenwich Village with her two sons.